A DEADLY CHECK-IN

A FRENCH QUARTER MYSTERY

JEN PITTS

CONTENTS

For Dave
While you won't go to a haunted hotel with me, thanks for
always picking one with room service.

AUTHOR'S NOTE

While many of the places and events in this book are real, many are not. I hope you will enjoy visiting the real places as well as the fictional ones I created. Hurricane Katrina unfortunately was a real storm, but Hurricane Geoffrey, at the time of publication, was not an actual storm.

1

———————

One good thing about New Orleans is that you can walk down the street soaking wet and only a few people give you a second look. And those people are usually tourists, as locals assume there is most likely a reasonable explanation for the state you're in. Or not. In this anything goes kind of town, a waterlogged woman was just another person roaming the streets.

I had an explanation for my condition, but being pushed into a pool by my newfound cousin was not reasonable. But then again, nothing about Scarlett was reasonable.

Charlene St. Martin, my aunt, along with her children, Jasper and Scarlett, decided not to wait any longer to meet me. I had planned to reach out to the members of my birth family, but I wanted to do it on my own terms. Instead, they showed up at my apartment building, Thibodeaux Mansion, waiting for me to arrive. After an awkward evening in the courtyard in which Charlene babbled, Jasper tried to control his mother, and Scarlett stared me down, I persuaded them to continue our re-introduction the next day.

I had agreed to join them by the pool at their hotel in the afternoon, thinking I would be ready to get to know them. But only Jasper seemed interested in me. His sister only had one thing on her mind. I still wasn't sure what Charlene wanted.

"Sammy, what's going on?"

My friend and neighbor, Neal, ruined my hope of getting home unnoticed. He and Rose laughed and held hands outside our favorite bar, The Gas Light. I kept my head down and picked up my pace, trying not to catch their attention. Neal's shouts meant I couldn't pretend I didn't see him. I gave a quick wave and continued walking.

"Hey, you're drenched!" Neal raced across the street and stood in front of me, so I stopped. "Rose demanded I bring you over to her, so I have to."

Neal put his arm around me even though my wet clothes dampened his yellow New Orleans Past & Present Tours t-shirt and his gray cargo shorts. Rose looked tough with her double pierced eyebrows and steely gaze. While she didn't pull any punches, her kind nature and common sense were the qualities that made her a good friend. And someone you didn't say no to.

Neal guided me across the street. I didn't argue, as the comfort of his embrace and words were what I needed. And he was right. Rose would have insisted he follow me until he brought me over to her.

"There must be a story behind the state you're in, but let's get you inside and dry," Rose said. "Neal, grab a stack of towels from the back for me."

We entered the half-empty bar, and Rose sat me down on a stool. I focused on the worn wooden bar, trying not to make eye contact with the other patrons. The French Quarter was a small community, so it wouldn't be long before the story of how I ended up soaking wet made the rounds.

When Neal arrived with a handful of towels, I looked up into the mirror behind the bar and discovered that my face was as red as my hair. My anger, embarrassment, and frustration were undeniable, and it wasn't a pretty sight. I dropped my head onto the bar top. If only the towels Neal draped around my shoulders made me invisible.

"Come on, lift your head and drink this."

As much as I wanted to, I didn't ignore Rose's commanding voice. In front of me was a mug imprinted with the phrase "Get Lit at The Gas Light."

"So what happened?" Neal brushed his brown hair out of his eyes and took a swig of his Abita beer. "I thought you were going to meet your family, not go swimming in your clothes."

"Give her a moment to gather herself." Rose raised her eyebrows at Neal. "Drink your coffee, Sammy, and tell us your story when you're ready."

"Thanks. Oh, this isn't just coffee," I said after taking a gulp. "It's strong, but it tastes good."

"It's my grandmother's recipe for Irish Coffee. She liked all her drinks with a heavy dose of whiskey," Rose said. "Technically, it should have whipped cream, but if I make that, people will start asking for frou-frou cocktails like daiquiris."

"And I'd have to find a new bar if you started serving those highfalutin' concoctions." Terry, one of the bar's most devout regulars, sat down on the other side of me and gave me his toothless smile. "Now cher, tell me how you ended up looking like a beautiful drowned rat. A swim in the Mississippi ain't good for nobody."

Rose added another dollop of whiskey to my mug and

put a beer in front of Terry. I shouldn't have been surprised to see him, as he always seemed to be here whenever I was. But it was only 4 p.m. and I normally came here in the evenings. Rose took a sip of her own coffee and nodded at me. So I shared my pathetic tale.

"My aunt and two cousins showed up yesterday without warning," I began. "I went to their hotel today and let's just say my cousin Scarlett and I don't see eye to eye."

Rose and Neal had been in the courtyard when my family arrived last night, but they listened along with Terry. Watching their faces go from interested to surprised made me feel better. I wasn't the only one who thought this situation was crazy.

"Finally, after an awkward thirty minutes of my aunt babbling about the St. Martin family history, I tried to show my appreciation, and I said, 'You're my family.' But apparently that was the wrong thing to say." I caught my breath and took a sip of my coffee.

"What was wrong with saying that?" Terry asked. "What happened?"

"Scarlett stood up from the table and screeched, 'You are family in name only. I want nothing to do with you. I'm just here for my inheritance!'"

2

———

"Your inheritance?" Terry took a big gulp of his beer. "I like you even more now that you're rich, darling."

"Sammy is already rich with brains and beauty." Neal put his arm around me.

"Who are you dating, her or Rose?" asked Bob, a regular at The Gas Light.

"Hush." Terry pointed his now half-empty bottle at Bob. "Neal's just a good friend to Sammy. We all know who he's sweet on."

The word was out about Neal and Rose. Last night he announced that he and Rose were a couple. I already knew, but no one else was surprised. Their attraction was clear whenever they were together. More proof that news traveled fast around here.

"I'll drop it, but come on, Sammy, tell us if you're a millionaire." Bob stroked his well-groomed goatee with a grease stained hand.

"I'm not a millionaire unless my family tomb is worth that much," I said.

"So it's a tomb fight." Bob sighed. "People can be pretty territorial about mausoleums."

I twisted in my chair to the murmurs of the audience surrounding me. Regulars filled the bar stools and the nearby tables. Everyone around me was familiar with mausoleum disputes. There must be more fights over tombs in New Orleans than I imagined.

"Are tombs worth a lot of money?" I asked. "I didn't think you could sell them."

"You can sell your mausoleum as long as all the heirs agree to it," Bob explained.

"What do you do with the remains?" I asked.

"It's not a package deal." Bob laughed. "The bodies or whatever's left has to be moved to another tomb or cemetery."

I shuddered, imagining the remains being removed and taken somewhere else. While it made sense, it just seemed wrong to rebury a body.

"So if you want to sell it, you've got to find another burial spot and get everyone to sign off on it, but it might be worth it," Bob said. "I've heard of rich folks offering tens of thousands of dollars for a spot in St. Louis No. 1."

I had no idea they were worth that much. Was money the real reason Scarlett wanted the key to the tomb, not family sentimentality?

"You wouldn't believe the fight my momma and aunt had about our tomb about ten years ago," said Alice, a relative newcomer to The Gas Light. "The police came out and everything. They still don't talk to each other."

I'd be happy not to talk to Scarlett for the next ten years.

"Who got the mausoleum, Alice?" Terry asked.

"We're sharing it. My cousin and I put the deed in a safe deposit box." Alice patted me on the back after grabbing a beer from Rose. "I hope it works out for you, Sammy."

"Scarlett isn't much on compromising." I banged my cup on the bar. "She's obsessed with the stupid tomb."

"That explains her behavior last night," Neal said. "She gave you the evil eye the whole time."

"Are you the next person in line for the key?" Rose asked.

"Yes. My birth father was the oldest in the family, so my mother would be responsible for it," I explained. "If she had lived, she would have passed the key to me, but..."

"But they thought you were dead." Neal put his arm around me again, and I leaned into him. I was grateful to have friends who knew my story.

During Hurricane Geoffrey, my parents died while fleeing New Orleans with my brother and me. Their bodies were recovered in Mississippi and although mine wasn't, everyone assumed I died, too. In reality, the storm blew me into Louisiana where I ended up being adopted. My brother always believed I was alive, but when he found me, it was not a happy ending for either of us.

"Yes, that's why Charlene had the key, but my brother took it from her after he discovered I was moving to New Orleans," I said. "Scarlett says I'm not a St. Martin, which legally is probably true."

I didn't want to change my name from Samantha Richardson to Sarah Jane St. Martin, but I wanted some kind of connection to my birth family. I'd been to the family mausoleum several times, hoping I would remember my parents or my brother. Not one memory came. The hurricane had erased those, too. Something held me back from reaching out to my newly discovered relatives. Perhaps subconsciously I had known it wouldn't go well.

"Forget the law. Do you want the key, darling?" Terry asked.

"I might have given it up, if she hadn't been so cruel." I took a big sip of my coffee, letting the drink warm my throat. It didn't warm my heart. "She told me my parents were selfish and got themselves killed, leaving her family to deal with my brother. I wasn't anybody to them and never would be."

"Oh, Sammy, that's ridiculous and wrong," Rose said. "Scarlett doesn't realize how lucky she is to have you in her family."

"What did your aunt say? Or your cousin? What's his name, Jasper?" Neal asked.

I closed my eyes, wishing I could forget the silence that followed Scarlett's rant. Jasper's face paled and his mother fiddled with her chunky earrings, not making eye contact with anyone. Scarlett tapped her ridiculously long nails on the poolside table. It was as if she was waiting for me to fight her. I didn't take the bait.

"After Scarlett ranted, I just got up and told them we should talk tomorrow after everyone cooled down," I said.

When I tried to leave, I wasn't sure I would even talk to them again. They didn't have a clue about what I had gone through. I was the one who lost her parents, had her brother try to kill her, and found out her adoptive parents paid blackmail money to her biological uncle to keep her.

"OK, but how did you end up wet?" Terry said. "Your cousin sounds meaner than a rabid coon hound, but did she try to drown you?"

"When I went to leave, she saw the key around my neck," I replied.

I shouldn't have put it on that day when I recognized the rage in Scarlett's eyes. After my brother tried to murder me in the tomb, I had stopped wearing it. "I tried tucking it back in my shirt, but she grabbed the chain and wouldn't let go."

After taking another drink of my coffee, I explained how I had grasped her wrist that clutched my necklace. She had pulled hard, but I tugged harder in the opposite direction. Out of the corner of my eye, I realized I was close to the edge of the pool. I had struggled to plant myself firmly, but my feet barely touched the ground as I tried to pull away. Scarlett's glossy red lips had curled into a smile, and she let go of the necklace. Instead of catching my balance, I fell backwards into the pool.

"And she insisted you slipped, but really she made you fall in," Rose said.

"Exactly! But no one believed me." My face flushed from anger and the whiskey. "I'm keeping the key over her dead body!"

3

———

The silence in the room was deafening after that spilled out of my mouth. From Terry's raised eyebrows to the stunned faces of the bar regulars, I regretted my words. I wish I could say it was the alcohol talking, but it wasn't.

"I didn't mean it," I stammered. "I'm just upset."

"Of course you are. Everyone understands you're feeling emotional. No one blames you," Rose insisted.

The surrounding crowd returned to their seats and their drinks. The chattering and the clinking of glasses made the room feel like normal, but I was far from it. A wet, tipsy, and angry version of me wasn't attractive.

"Don't do anything stupid, but I'll get the bail money ready," Neal joked. He hugged me after getting up from his bar stool. "But first I have to give a tour, so you'll just have to wait."

"I knew I could count on you." I laughed. "Thanks. See you later."

"I'll make sure she stays out of trouble," Rose said. She rolled her eyes as Neal blew her a kiss from the door, but she smiled. I was happy their romance was going well.

"I'm sorry, Sammy." Rose patted my hand. "That's a terrible way to get to know your family." She topped off my coffee before she rushed to the other end of the bar to tend to a pair of new customers.

"Now, let me get this straight." Terry grabbed the whiskey bottle and poured more in my cup. "You met these relatives of yours yesterday?"

"Yes."

"You learned about them after that whole thing with your own brother, right?"

"Uh huh."

"And you didn't grow up with much family, did you? No brothers or sisters? Cousins?"

I nodded.

"Oh, darling, you've got a lot to learn." Terry chuckled. Normally his raucous laugh made me smile, but it annoyed me now.

"What do you mean?"

"Now, I'm not trying to offend you. Those pretty eyes of yours are all fired up." He took a sip of his beer and sat up straight. "Let me explain myself. Cousins are like siblings. You love each other, you fight with each other. You can't stand them and then you can't stand to be without them."

"So Scarlett's actions are normal, is that what you're saying?"

"Maybe, maybe not, but don't rule her out just yet. People get possessive over important and not so important things. You said she wants the key to your tomb?"

"Yes, but she didn't need to act so rude or cruel." I bit my lip so I wouldn't rant about her anymore. I'd embarrassed myself enough over her.

"She sounds like my cousin Bobby. He's the curmudgeon of the family. Annoying as all get out, but then he can be funny and generous when you least expect it. Our biggest fight was over who got to inherit Grandpappy's old still. We ended up in the bayou, pushing each other under water and hooting and hollering."

I pulled a towel around me tighter, shivering at the thought of being in the bayou, fighting my cousin. The murky water, mossy tree branches, and hidden snakes would make it a dangerous place to swim, never mind having a battle with your relative.

"What happened with Bobby?"

"The fight ended when a gator headed toward us. We rushed out of that water so fast we fell on each other, laughing like the two fools we were."

"Who got the still?" I laughed, imagining Terry collapsing on the bank of the bayou with his cousin. From the gleam in his eyes to the smile lines around his mouth that cut deeply into his tanned face, it was obvious he loved telling that story, but that he loved Bobby even more.

"We told each other to take it, so then we fought about it all that night."

"Are you still fighting?"

"Sure!" He drained his beer. "We fight all the time, but he's family. He was my best man at my first and third weddings. Maybe he'll stand up for me in the next one."

Terry winked and stood up. "Sammy, families are a strange thing. Full of love, full of hate, full of frustration, and full of fun. Give them a chance, but always stick up for yourself."

"Thanks, Terry. I'll stay away from Scarlett and the bayou, though."

"Now, that's smart thinking. You'll have to excuse me.

The guys are waiting for me to play poker. I keep trying to win back my teeth."

Terry made his way through the tables to return to his friends. Instead of poker chips, they used the stale peanuts from the bowl on the table. No one ever ate the peanuts, but the staff always put them out. I guess they were good for gambling, if nothing else.

"How was Terry's therapy session? Did he tell you about wrestling his cousin in the bayou?" Rose refilled my cup with coffee.

"You've heard that story?"

"Yep. When I had a huge fight with my sister before my shift one day, I stormed into work with a chip on my shoulder. Terry wouldn't let up until I told him what happened." She cocked her head toward his table. "He hides under that Cajun accent and folksy charm, but underneath is a man with a kind heart and a wealth of knowledge about human nature."

I looked over at him, in his paint-splattered overalls, shaggy gray hair, and ragged flip flops. I smiled, thinking of all the people who judged him on his looks alone. There was a lot more to Terry, and I considered myself fortunate that he included me among his friends.

Hold it. Did he say his cousin was his best man in his first and third weddings? What happened with wedding two? Was he still married?

One day I would ask him, but for now the warmth of the coffee had worn off, and the whiskey made me tired. I unpeeled the layers of damp towels off my shoulders, stacking them in a neat pile. Rose handed me another stack of fresh towels, but before I could use them, the bar door flew open.

"Oh, Sammy, thank God you're OK! I thought the ghost sisters got you!"

4

———

The entire bar turned to Beau Boudreaux, who rushed through the door and headed straight to me. He draped a large blue and white striped towel around my shoulders and went to kiss me on top of my head, but stopped. "Oh, that pool chlorine is awful. I must change it to salt water."

I touched my head, feeling the crunchy strands of hair. Chlorine wasn't good for my hair, but I hadn't realized I smelled. Beau's crinkled nose said otherwise. "I'm a mess, but it wasn't just the pool."

"Was it the ghost that pushed you in?" Beau took the stool next to me.

"No, it was my real live cousin, Scarlett."

"Oh, dear."

"I hope she's a better guest than she is a cousin." I pulled the towel around me tighter. "You're sweet to bring me a towel."

Beau's arrival with a towel shouldn't have surprised me. Once you're Beau's friend, he would do anything for you. Even though we met at a murder at one of his properties, we became friends quickly. And his budding relationship with one of my best friends and business partner, Andrew, meant we spent a bit of time together.

"My staff should have insisted you take one with you."

"I didn't give them the chance. I rushed out of there as quick as my soggy shoes would let me." My black Converse sneakers were still wet. I sighed, as these were my favorite pair. "But let's talk about you. Fancy tie you have there."

"I thought I should dress up for my first day as the hotel's owner." He wrenched the paisley teal tie from around his neck and put it on the bar. "My employees would rather use the tie to hang me."

Just this week Beau became the official owner of Hotel Jeanne, a boutique hotel. With its large courtyard, relaxing pool, and perfect French Quarter location, it was a fantastic business investment for him. None of that mattered to him; what he cared about was that it was a haunted hotel.

"I'm sure it's just nerves, on both your parts," I said. "Beginnings are always stressful."

"I hope you're right, but if you find me hanging in the courtyard, the managers should all be suspects." He smiled at Rose, who put a martini with two olives in front of him. "I'll become another ghost haunting the hotel."

"You'll be a handsome ghoul." He was an attractive man with his smooth black hair framing his unlined face. From all his stories he told about moving to New Orleans "eons and eons ago," he must be older than he appeared. "Have you seen any of the ghosts yet?"

"No." He sighed. "When I first heard about you in the pool, I worried that the Abernathy sisters were responsible."

"The Abernathy Sisters?"

"They're the courtyard spirits. The hotel has ghosts inside and out." Beau's love of the paranormal was clear in his voice. "Back in the early 1800s, there was a cistern where the pool is now. The younger sister, Anna, drowned in it."

"How did she die in it? I didn't think you could fall in one." Cisterns in the city were usually at least five feet off the ground. Not that I had seen one; only a few remained after New Orleans banned them when city water became widely available.

"The older sister, Alice, claimed her sister, Anna, fell in, but you're right, it was too tall for that to happen. The actual story is Alice was jealous of her prettier, younger sister, so she killed her. She thought she would have a better chance at a suitor without the competition."

"Quite the family," I said. "So now Anna haunts the area?"

"Not just her, but her sister, too. One of Anna's suitors drowned Alice the day they found her."

"So their ghosts haunt the hotel?"

"That's what I've been told," Beau said. "Are you sure you didn't see the sisters? Or feel their presence?"

I shook my head. I hated to disappoint him, but the frustration and anger I experienced in the pool was all from Scarlett.

Beau gulped the rest of his martini and placed his well-manicured hands on the bar. "I haven't seen them either. Maybe someday."

"Need another drink?" Rose asked after she returned to our end of the bar.

"Not for me." I stood up, holding on to the bar stool for balance. Between the family fight, the fall into the pool, and the Irish coffee, my body and mind were spent. "Time to go."

"Let me walk you home." Beau pulled out his wallet. "Rose, I'll pay for Sammy's drinks, too."

Before I could protest, Rose said, "No need to; Terry already did."

"Does Connor know he has competition?" Beau grinned as I mouthed "Thank you," to Terry, who appeared to be winning the poker game by the pile of peanuts in front of him.

"Connor has nothing to worry about." Rose laughed. "Sammy and Connor are a great couple."

I wished I had the same confidence in my relationship. Connor and I needed to talk, or rather, he needed to explain why he was talking to Scarlett outside the hotel as I walked up to meet my family. Neither of them saw me, but I watched their animated conversation. Last night he tried to get away from her, so why was he with her today? A group of tipsy tourists blocked my view, so I missed how they left each other.

"Even after last night, you think that?" I asked Rose.

"Yes." She put down the bar towel in her hands. "I know Scarlett threw herself at Connor, but he wasn't interested in her. He didn't even remember her."

I agreed Connor didn't recall the time he spent with my cousin, but she did. She draped her arms around him when she recognized him last night. She had squealed, "It's me, Scarlett! I'll never forget that amazing weekend we had during Mardi Gras two years ago. You declared I was the prettiest girl you'd ever seen!"

I didn't care that Connor had dated women before me, but did it have to be my cousin?

"Rose knows best." Beau held out his arm. I took it and let him lead me out of The Gas Light. "Don't worry about Connor. Listen, isn't that your phone? I bet its Connor professing his undying love to you."

"Wrong. It's Jasper." I stared at the text. "He says *We're really sorry about today. Please come by tomorrow at 9. Don't give up on us."*

"See, your family isn't all that bad. Go see them tomorrow," Beau said.

"I'm allowed back in the hotel?"

"Of course! You're my friend, and you're always welcome. And if the staff gives you a hard time, you let me know."

"Thanks." I tapped a quick message back to Jasper: *I'll meet you in the courtyard at 9.*

Beau continued to make small talk as we walked to my apartment building. I appreciated he didn't insist I chat since I was exhausted from the day. We stopped in front of Andrew's door. Beau knocked and then turned to me.

"Go see your aunt and cousins tomorrow. I know it will be difficult, but give them another chance." He kissed me on the cheek as Andrew opened his door. "Just stay away from the edge of the pool."

"Samantha, what happened?" Andrew stared at me with his intense blue eyes. "Weren't you visiting with your family?"

"I'll explain everything," Beau said. "Sammy's had a long day and by the yawn she's stifling, she needs to rest."

"And shower," I said. "Thanks, Beau, for filling Andrew in and for the towel. I'll bring it back in the morning."

"Good." Beau gently pushed me toward my apartment. "It will all work out."

"Andrew, I'll be at the store tomorrow afternoon like we planned," I said.

I was thankful Beau would tell Andrew what had happened to me. We'd have a lot to discuss tomorrow, and I wanted us to focus on our plans with Lagniappe Books, not my family or romantic woes.

A chorus of meows met me as I entered the courtyard.

My cat, Nubi, and his feline friends, Cleopatra and Nefertiti, lounged by the stairs to the second-floor balcony, probably waiting for Sissy. Although she denied it, I was positive Sissy gave them treats. She claimed not to be partial to animals after a childhood incident with her family cat, Mr. Nibbles, but she had a soft spot for the Thibodeaux Mansion kitties.

"Hi, furry friends," I said as I hurried to my door, hoping I wouldn't run into anyone else.

No such luck.

5

———

"Cleopatra! Nefertiti! Time to come inside, my sweets," Ruby cooed from her open doorway. When she saw me, her voice dropped. "Samantha, you startled me."

"Sorry," I mumbled as I tried to find my keys in my backpack. I wanted to get inside my home without explaining myself to my next-door neighbor. Again, no such luck.

Ruby stepped out of her doorway and looked me up and down and sniffed. "You look and smell like a Bourbon Street tourist. I sense you found trouble today."

"Yes, and her name was Scarlett."

Ruby snorted and then put up her hand to cover her mouth. Well, at least someone enjoyed my problems. "I assume Scarlett is your doppelgänger cousin. Aren't you carrying the crystal I gave you?"

While Ruby never joins our group when we meet outside, it was apparent she kept up on the comings and goings of her neighbors. If confronted with that statement, I'm sure she would say it's the spirits talking to her. Ruby

21

was Thibodeaux Mansion's resident spiritualist, tarot card reader, and grumpy neighbor.

After my aunt and cousins left last night, Ruby came into the courtyard and stopped me before I joined my friends back at the table. She had stepped closer to me and held out her hand. Nestled in her palm was a shiny black oval stone. It was obsidian, which she said was supposed to protect me from emotional and physical negativity.

It obviously didn't work.

The towel around my shoulders dropped to the ground, and my cat, Nubi, sniffed at it. "I need to carry it for it to protect me?"

"Of course you do! Do I have to spell everything out for you?"

Apparently she did. Then again, it would be easier to find a book on crystals at the shop tomorrow than to be lectured by Ruby.

"Carry the obsidian stone with you while your family is here." Ruby followed her cats back to her doorway. "It's obvious that disruptive forces are at play with your relationship with your aunt and cousins. Protect yourself, but more importantly, protect your neighbors."

The firm close of her door signaled the end of her lecture, with no chance for me to refute her claims. I couldn't say she was wrong. So far, my interactions with my aunt and cousins were not heartwarming. I hoped we'd get past today's fight, and it would become a story to tell like Terry's. But the water sloshing in my ears reminded me that Scarlett had no interest in being family, so I doubted she'd be my maid of honor at my wedding, whether it was my first or my third.

I picked up my towel and saw an empty beer bottle holding a single red rose by my doorstep. The attached note said *Hope it went well with your family. I'm going to jam with my friends, but I'll see you tomorrow. Missed you today, Connor.*

"Do you think he really missed me?" I asked Nubi as he followed me into our apartment. Nubi meowed in response, but I'm sure he meant "Feed me now" instead of yes or no.

I did as he commanded and watched with a smile as he ate. Oh, to be a sleek black cat without a care in the world. I don't know where Nubi was before he claimed me as his own, but my apartment was more comfortable than the cemetery where we met.

"Nubi, I'd rather be you than me. Can we switch?"

This time his meow was a definite no as he took his last bite of food and jumped onto the loveseat. He curled up into a tight ball and closed his eyes. I dumped my wet clothes on the floor of my bathroom and took a ridiculously long, hot shower. Feeling as if I washed off the crud of the fight, I crawled into bed. Nubi joined me immediately and meowed at me as I checked my phone one last time before turning out the light.

"Sorry, Nubi, I'll finish up on this phone quickly and we can go to bed." I softly scratched the little spot of white fur on his head. He turned away as if he didn't believe I would be off my phone anytime soon.

After confirming there were no urgent emails to answer, I checked my text messages. There was a new one, a Mississippi number, so I braced myself for a long-winded message from Charlene. To my surprise it was from my pool-pushing cousin.

This is Scarlett. Sorry about today. Meet me at the pool at 8 and we can talk. Please.

What? Did her mother force her to do this? I didn't think so since she wanted to talk before our scheduled meeting at 9 a.m. She had some nerve summoning me to her hotel that early. I stared at the message. It wasn't the grandest of apologies, but if she took the time to send it at 10:30 p.m., the situation must weigh on her. I needed to be the bigger person, so I texted back: *I'll be there at 8.*

I set my alarm for 7 a.m., and after waiting a few minutes to see if she responded, I finally turned off the light. Maybe we would work things out tomorrow, but I planned to put Ruby's crystal in my pocket, just in case.

6

———

I woke up earlier than my alarm and couldn't get back to sleep. When Nubi realized I was awake, he meowed incessantly for his breakfast. After feeding him, I decided I might as well start my day. Unlike my hungry cat, I didn't want to eat, since my stomach tossed and turned in anticipation of meeting Scarlett this morning. Would she apologize for yesterday, or would she just demand the tomb key again?

The key lay on the kitchen counter where I left it last night. Deciding it would be safest to leave it here, I put it back inside my favorite Nancy Drew book, *The Clue of the Black Keys*. If I agreed to turn over the key to Scarlett, I'd come home for it. But there was still that nagging feeling in my head and in my heart that I should keep it. I wasn't ready to give up part of my St. Martin family heritage yet, if at all.

"Wish me luck, pretty boy." Nubi and I headed outside. It was just after 7 a.m. so the sun was rising. Nubi slunk to the back of the courtyard and jumped into the lush plants that filled the former water fountain. I wanted to hide with

25

him, but I slunk off in the other direction and left through the front gate.

The rumble of an overflowing garbage truck broke the silence as I walked toward Hotel Jeanne. A few other pedestrians were out, and we nodded at each other, but kept on our own paths. I took a sip of chicory coffee from my travel mug as I passed my landlady Libby's cafe, Artistic Coffee & Creations. My stomach growled as the smell of freshly baked scones wafted out the door. But I didn't stop. I considered popping in to buy a few for my relatives, but I'd risk running into Libby. While she always meant well, I wasn't in the mood for her opinion on my family. And of course, she'd put in a kind word for her son, Connor. I couldn't deal with one of Libby's pep talks this morning.

As I walked up to Hotel Jeanne, I stopped to admire the beauty of the building. Actually, it was two buildings. The original owner combined a one-story Creole cottage with the three-story townhouse next door. Both houses were painted a pale yellow with dark green shutters. With the additional outbuildings of both properties, the hotel offered thirteen guest rooms and suites. Beau had said, "I don't need an unlucky number of rooms in my first hotel." And he was already working on a way to add another room or suite.

By taking down the brick wall in between the homes' courtyards, the hotel had a large courtyard that included seating areas and a pool in the back. Next to the cottage was a gated parking lot for guests.

The lobby entrance was through the original townhouse; I took a deep breath and opened the door. It was a small foyer, as the staircase to the second floor was only a few feet away. To my left was the doorway to the reception area.

"Welcome to Hotel Jeanne! How may I help you on this

beautiful morning?" asked the man behind the registration desk. His name tag said, "Mr. Ambrose Fortner, Manager." Ambrose's unnaturally white teeth blinded me when he smiled. His slicked back hair shined brightly, too, due to black dye and a dollop of gel, was my guess.

"Good morning. I'm here to meet someone," I said.

"Who are you visiting?"

"My, um, family, um, the St. Martins," I stuttered. It was going to take some work getting used to calling them my family.

"Yes, Mrs. St. Martin and her children."

Just then a gray-haired woman in a crisp housekeeper uniform walked through. The stack of fluffy white towels she carried hid her face from the manager, but I saw the eye roll she made at the mention of the family. She picked up her pace after realizing I caught her reaction. From the scene last night, I could only imagine what kind of hotel guests Charlene, Scarlett, and Jasper were.

He studied me. "You and the younger Ms. St. Martin look alike."

I wished everyone would stop comparing the two of us, but for now I would just grin and bear it. "They're my aunt and cousins."

"How nice." While his tone sounded authentic, I caught the slight frown he made before he continued talking. "Are you the woman who fell into the pool yesterday?"

"Yes, that was me. I'm so sorry for any water I left on my way out." I gulped my coffee, praying the mug covered most of my face.

"Mr. Boudreaux explained everything." Ambrose smiled with his mouth, but not his eyes. Whether his disdain was for me or for Beau, I wasn't sure.

"Beau told me how thrilled he is to own this beautiful

hotel," I replied, hoping we wouldn't have to discuss yesterday. My prayer was answered when a twenty-something bearded man dressed in a dull brown suit entered the room from a door marked "Private."

"Ambrose, I've made my notes, so I'm going to head home," the man said. "Sorry to interrupt."

"This is a relative of the St. Martin family," Ambrose said. "I didn't get your name, miss."

"I'm Samantha Richardson." I walked over and offered my hand.

"Daniel Lane, the assistant manager of the hotel. It's nice to meet you." He shook my hand vigorously. "Were you the one who fell in the pool yesterday? Everyone's talking about it."

"I'm sure Miss Richardson does not want to discuss the event, Daniel," Ambrose admonished.

"I'm sorry, I didn't mean to embarrass you." Daniel fiddled with his name tag. "I'm glad to see you're OK."

"It's fine. It was an accident," I lied.

"Of course," Ambrose said. "Shall I call Mrs. St. Martin's suite for you?"

"No, we're going to meet at nine. Sorry, make that eight," I said. "I woke up early, so I thought I'd drink my coffee and enjoy your beautiful courtyard."

"Yes, it is a spectacular place in the morning." Ambrose smiled. "Please help yourself to the coffee and pastries in our kitchen. It is open to guests."

"Thanks. I appreciate the offer."

"Let me show you." He walked out from behind the reception desk to the hallway. "Daniel, please wait for me. We must discuss the noise complaints we received yesterday."

"You mean the ghost complaints?" Daniel grinned at me. "The hotel is haunted, you know."

"So, I've heard." I smiled at him, but not at Ambrose. His frown made me think he was not amused. "No need to show me the kitchen, Mr. Fortner. I have enough to drink."

I doubted I would like their coffee. One of the many things Beau planned to change about the hotel was the generic brand of coffee they served. Ambrose must have wanted breakfast for himself, as he kept walking. Or he could have been making sure I was doing what I said I was there to do.

The courtyard entrance was in the same direction, so I followed him. But I stopped when we got to the end of the corridor; I could never pass up a library. Yesterday I didn't see it on my way in, and definitely not on my way out.

The room had a double-wide entry with a small wood desk and straight-back chair in the center. The only other furniture was two sets of faded blue velvet wing chairs. What caught my eye were the wooden bookcases that lined the walls. The shelves went from the floor to the ceiling and featured a carved fleur-de-lis pattern across the top of each one.

Only books filled the shelves. I was too far away to read any titles, but from the variety of sizes and colors of the books it appeared to be an eclectic selection. The book lover in me wanted to rush over and inspect each book; the book-shop salesperson in me wanted to dust and organize the shelves.

"That's our famous library. The original owner of this portion of the hotel started the collection, and every owner has added to it," Ambrose said. "Are you a bibliophile?"

I turned to face him again, although I was more interested in the library. "I love books, and I work at Lagniappe Books."

"You do? That is a splendid shop." Ambrose's sincerity rang true. "It's beautifully appointed and curated."

"Andrew will be thrilled to hear that. What type of books do you read?"

"History, biographies, and literary fiction." He lowered his voice and said, "But my guilty pleasure is hard-boiled detective novels."

"Like *The Maltese Falcon*? I loved that book, although I prefer cozy mysteries."

"Yes, that's my favorite. While I haven't read many cozies, I have the utmost respect for Agatha Christie. She was a delightful storyteller."

"I agree. Is the library open for your guests?"

"It is, but it's not in the best shape, I'm afraid." Ambrose sighed as he looked around. "I would love to have the books organized and have the room be a place to read and relax."

"I like my idea of an office center better." Daniel now stood next to Ambrose. "We could cater to more business customers if we had computers and a copy machine in here."

The look of horror on Ambrose's face made his thoughts about the subject obvious. "I don't think so. Daniel, why have you left the desk unattended?"

"The guests in room four want to speak to the *real* manager about the noises that woke them up last night. They're concerned there are rats in the walls."

"Please tell me you didn't say the sounds were ghosts," Ambrose said.

"Wouldn't a ghost be better than a rat?" Daniel smirked. "Don't worry, I didn't say either. But they didn't want to talk to me, so you need to call them back."

"Of course. Miss Richardson, please excuse me." Ambrose bowed slightly and then he left the room.

"Wouldn't you like ghosts instead of rats? I know I would," Daniel said. "And a business center would be better than these dusty books."

Not wanting to spend the next twenty minutes explaining the importance and value of books to Daniel, I just smiled. "Don't let me keep you. You must be on your way home if you've been here all night."

Daniel yawned, stretched his long arms over his head, and then ran a hand through his cropped brown hair. "Yes, we're short a manager, so I'm working seven to seven these days. Well, actually even later, since Ambrose doesn't get here at six-thirty like he says he will."

"That's a tough schedule. I'll go out to the courtyard now. Nice to meet you."

"Enjoy the rising sun out there, Samantha. Especially before your family shows up." He shook my hand and then left the room.

Now I had no doubt that the St. Martins had established a reputation. And I guess that included me. While I would have loved to explore the library, I needed to take the time to settle myself before Scarlett showed up. I opened the door to the courtyard, taking in the warm morning sunshine and the scent of jasmine. Peace and quiet appeared to be waiting for me outside — at least until Scarlett made her entrance.

7

L ight bounced off the figure of Joan of Arc as I crossed the slate patio to the center of the court-yard. Yesterday I had rushed in and out of the area so I hadn't noticed it or much of anything. Now the hotel name made sense; Jeanne was French for Joan. In 1972 France gifted a Joan of Arc statue to the city of New Orleans, and they eventually placed it at the French Market. The piece featured the Maid of New Orleans (as she is called here) riding a horse with a flag in her hand.

Hotel Jeanne's version of the statue topped a three-tiered water fountain. The cascading water soothed my nerves until the overpowering scent of chlorine hit me. I sniffed at the fountain, but the offending odor wasn't coming from there. Another breeze came by and lifted the chemical smell away.

Joan and her horse faced the rear, so I followed her lead. I could use some of her bravery to deal with Scarlett. Hope-fully, we wouldn't battle again, but at least I was more prepared for her. This time I would stand far from the pool's edge.

While the courtyard appeared neat, everything was threadbare. From the faded yellow seat cushions to the chipped glass tables, Beau needed to do a lot of updating to bring Hotel Jeanne up to his standards. "Old doesn't mean worn out and I'm not just talking about me," he liked to say. From his well-groomed eyebrows to his polished shoes, Beau always looked put together, and he would expect no less from the hotel and the staff.

Miniature potted palm trees defined the pool area in the back of the courtyard. Surrounding the rectangular pool on three sides were lounge chairs and two tables with four chairs each. The yellow theme and shabby condition continued with the furniture in this section. A brick fence loomed behind the pool. Jasmine vines dripped down trellises mounted to the wall.

Beau would replace the furniture, but also the garish florescent yellow plastic sign that said, "Pool Closed for Cleaning." That explained the chlorine odor in the courtyard. Did my dip in the pool fully dressed require a complete scrub-down? My curiosity got the better of me and I sidestepped the sign, supposing I'd find a cleaner.

I found someone all right.

Through the crystal blue water, there was a body at the bottom of the deep end of the pool.

I stared at the person before my senses kicked in. "Hey! Are you OK?" I shouted, not really expecting an answer.

I dropped my mug and backpack on the ground and jumped in feet first. It took just a few strokes to swim to the body. I dived to the bottom and grabbed the woman's arm and pulled her to the surface.

"Scarlett," I whispered after I turned her over.

She was dead.

8

The low-cut violet blouse and tight denim skirt that Scarlett wore yesterday clung to her lifeless body. Most of her make-up appeared washed off by the pool water except for her glossy blood-red lipstick. Now I could see that we had the same smattering of freckles on our faces, but I didn't hide mine. She still had on the four-inch black stilettos that made her tower over me.

Did she trip over her heels and land in the pool? I looked over to the edge of the deep end, which was closest to the guest lounge. There appeared to be drops of blood, but also dirt. Where did it come from?

My grip on Scarlett's body loosened as I shivered. The water was warm yesterday, but now it was cold. I grasped my cousin and pulled her over to the steps in the pool where I could sit and still hold on to her. Keeping one hand on Scarlett, I used the other to wipe my stinging eyes. I'd found the source of the overwhelming chlorine smell.

I needed to get help, but my instinct was not to let her go. Fortunately, Daniel and Ambrose entered the courtyard, and their voices grew louder as their feet hit the slate tiles.

"Ambrose, I'm positive I locked the lounge door," Daniel said. "The guests in room six couldn't have heard anyone in there."

"Do you think they're lying?" Ambrose said.

"Maybe it was the ghosts." Daniel laughed. "Whatever the case, let's check this out so I can finally go home."

"Yes, and I have much to do today."

I gathered my nerves and started yelling, "Help! Ambrose, Daniel, please help me!"

"Who is there? Where are you?" Ambrose called out.

"In the pool!" I screamed back.

"Miss Richardson, what are you doing in there?" Ambrose demanded, but then put his hand up to his mouth and stared.

"What are you two doing in there?" Daniel asked. "Is something wrong?"

"It is obvious there is, Daniel!" Ambrose berated him. "Call 911."

"She's dead." My voice cracked.

"Are you sure she's dead?" Daniel asked.

"Yes, she is. It's Scarlett St. Martin." I stammered.

"Your cousin." Ambrose said flatly.

"You mean the cousin you fought with yesterday?" Daniel said.

"This isn't the time or the place to discuss that," Ambrose snapped. "Call 911 and stand out front and wait for the police. I'll phone Mr. Boudreaux."

"Shouldn't we help her out?" Daniel started toward me, but Ambrose grabbed his arm.

"I will handle things here. Go do what I told you to do."

Daniel glared at Ambrose, but he hurried toward the main building.

"Now, Miss Richardson, why don't you get out of the

pool?" Ambrose said. "There's nothing you can do for her, I'm afraid."

I looked down and realized I still had Scarlett's body in my arms. Closing my eyes, I said a quick prayer for her. I let her go, and she sank back down to the bottom.

I got out of the pool, but stayed near the edge, searching for any signs of Scarlett slipping into the pool. Besides the blood drops and scattered dirt, there was nothing else except the cleaning net propped up against the back wall. I started toward the net, but Ambrose coughed loudly, so I stopped. While his face was devoid of emotions, a vein in his neck pulsed. I imagine he had faced many crises as a hotel manager, but I bet a death in the pool wasn't one of them.

Ambrose took out his cell phone. "I'll call Mr. Boudreaux now. Are you all right by yourself?"

I nodded, and Ambrose walked over to a glass table that was wet with the morning dew. He spoke briefly and then put his phone away. Immediately, he took his phone back out of his jacket pocket and made another call. He turned his back to me as he talked, but he stopped speaking when the gate from the parking lot to the courtyard was flung open.

"Thank God I was parking my car when you called, Ambrose!" Beau said. The wrought-iron gate slammed behind him and he jumped. "Why isn't this locked? Oh, my goodness, Sammy, why are you wet again?"

Beau stood still and stared at the pool, then at me. "That is your cousin, isn't it? I'm so sorry. What happened to her?"

"I don't know. I found her at the bottom of the pool."

"Did anyone try CPR? Should we do it now?" Beau asked.

"It's too late." I stared back at her body. "She was cold when I got to her."

"Oh, dear. I assume you've called the police."

"Yes," Ambrose said. "They should be here any moment. May we speak privately?"

"What?" Beau turned his head away from the pool. "Yes, of course. Excuse me, Sammy."

They spoke in hushed tones so I didn't hear what they were saying, but it was obvious Ambrose and Beau were at odds with each other. I wrapped my arms around my trembling body as I stood at the side of the pool, staring at Scarlett's body. Without her heavy make-up, we did look alike.

"It must be strange seeing yourself dead," said a voice from behind me.

9

———————

I whipped my head around to find a young housekeeper standing behind me. The name tag "Shelby" was pinned to her gray uniform. She held a pair of bulky white tennis shoes in her hands while black high-tops dotted with fuchsia skulls were on her feet. A well-worn backpack, also featuring skulls, hung from one of her shoulders.

"That sounds like a line from a horror movie," I replied.

"I'm sorry. That didn't sound nice once I said it." Her face reddened as she shuffled her feet in place. "I should have said, what's that phrase? Yeah, I'm sorry for your loss."

"It's all right. We do look alike," I replied. "And don't take this the wrong way, but you seem very calm for someone coming across a dead body."

"I worked in a nursing home before here, so dead bodies don't bother me." She giggled, but then coughed as if she remembered she should be serious. When I was a teenager like her, I would have done the same thing. "But this is my first murder."

I wish I could say the same. "Why did you say murder and not accident?"

"Those chairs are out of place and I bet those are drops of blood over there." Two of the chaise lounge chairs were sideways instead of facing the pool. Dark spots dotted one chair and the ground next to it. "And a potted plant is missing from that table." She pointed to a low square table that stood in between the sets of French doors that lead into the lounge.

"I agree that is suspicious," I said. "Anything else?"

"I hope you won't take offense, but Miss St. Martin was the type of person to get murdered."

"You're very observant," I replied. For someone so young, she knew an awful lot about human nature. "I'd say it comes with your job to be detail-oriented, but I have a feeling that's just your personality."

She blushed and smiled. "My momma says it will get me into trouble, but my nana says it makes me smart. I'm saving up to study criminal justice."

"That sounds like a good path for you."

"I hope so." She shifted her backpack to her other shoulder. "I better go get ready for my shift before Mr. Fortner finds me out here. Sorry for your loss, Miss..."

"I'm Sammy. Nice to meet you, Shelby."

"Nice to meet you, too. Can I get you a towel? I have keys to the lounge and I can grab a towel from there."

Before I answered, Ambrose and Beau walked toward us, both with grim faces and cell phones in their hands.

"Miss Jones, you need to get to work." Ambrose's voice was stern, but it didn't bother Shelby. She nodded and shuffled away, after taking a quick glance at Scarlett's body.

She only made it a few steps when Ambrose called out

to her, "And please keep this situation to yourself. We'll have a staff meeting as soon as possible."

"Yes, Mr. Fortner." She unlocked the door marked "Housekeeping." Before she went inside, she looked over at me and smiled. I returned her smile. She was a smart kid, and I bet she could tell me more about the hotel and the guests. And I suspected her version would be more truthful and less tactful than Ambrose's.

Voices from the main building headed my way. I took a deep breath and braced myself for the police. Today was going to be a long day.

Before the police arrived, I turned to Beau and said, "I didn't kill her."

"I would never think you were a murderer, Sammy!" Beau insisted. "I bet you don't even kill spiders in your apartment."

This wasn't the time to tell him I killed any and all spiders and bugs that crossed my threshold.

"I can't believe your cousin is dead." Beau bit his lip as he surveyed the scene. "And in my pool."

I watched Ambrose's face tense as Beau said, "My pool." He quickly made his face blank when he saw me staring at him.

"I'm so sorry," I said. "For everyone."

"It's not your fault, honey." Beau grabbed my hand. "You're shivering. You need a towel. Let's walk over to the guest lounge."

"I'll wait here for the police," Ambrose called.

"Oh, yes, thank you," Beau said.

"Certainly, Mr. Boudreaux."

"Ambrose, please remember to call me Beau." He smiled at Ambrose, who smiled in return. But as soon as Beau turned around, Ambrose grimaced. Beau had a lot of work to do with Ambrose, it appeared. And now he had a murder to deal with, too.

"This should be locked. Did Ambrose open the room up when he got here?" Beau asked after opening the French doors to the lounge.

"No, he and Daniel came right over to me in the pool. He stayed in the courtyard while Daniel went back inside the main building to call the police."

"Ambrose has some explaining to do." Beau sighed. "He told me he runs a tight ship, but two unlocked doors is a big problem."

Especially if it led to murder.

"At least the room looks OK," he said.

Everything looked in order, but this was my first time in the lounge, so I had to take his word for it. We had entered through a set of French doors and I sat down at one of the four round tables. The doors provided the only natural light into the room, as the other three walls were brick. On each table sat a vase of yellow tulips with a laminated list of wines.

Beau grabbed a fluffy blue and white pool towel from a wicker shelf. He sniffed it before putting it around my shoulders. "I thought these towels were off yesterday. We need new ones or better washing machines. These are not soft enough."

"Add towel shopping to your long list of things to do, including dealing with a murder."

"I will, but sweetie, let me get one thing off my list — making sure you know I don't blame you one bit for this.

You've got a big heart and you'll feel responsible for this even though you had nothing to do with it."

Beau walked over to a glass cabinet along the wall to the left of the doors. He tried to open the cabinet door. "Well, at least this is locked. Not that anyone with any taste would want any of these wines."

"Is this room open all day usually?" I asked.

"No, it's supposed to be open from nine in the morning until ten at night. We offer a happy hour of drinks and light appetizers from five to seven."

"So this room should have been locked at ten? And the guests are aware of this?"

"They should. Why do you ask?"

"I was just wondering if Scarlett came down here for a glass of wine."

"Perhaps she had a drink or two and then fell in the pool. Then it would be an accident." Beau's face relaxed. "Accidents happen all the time at hotels. Oh, Sammy, I'm sorry, I'm a terrible friend!"

He put his arm around me. "It's OK, Beau. You have every right to be worried about the hotel. Trust me, I hope it was an accident, too."

"You don't believe that, do you?"

I shook my head. As much as I wanted it to be an accident, the blood drops away from the edge and the dirt made me doubt it.

"It's you again?" Detective Christine Gammon said as she opened the door. "Sammy, we have to stop meeting like this."

"Trust me, I didn't want to see you like this either."

Christine and I met when I first moved to New Orleans and discovered a body. I wasn't related to that poor victim, though.

"I understand she was your cousin." Christine's voice softened as well as her face. Her tall stature and authoritative voice intimidated most people, but her kindness showed in her eyes when the situation called for it. "I'm sorry for your loss."

"Thanks."

Christine took a notebook and a silver pen out of her navy blue blazer pocket and flipped to a blank page. "Let's start at the beginning. When did you arrive this morning?"

With Beau listening intently, I explained to Christine that I was scheduled to meet my aunt and cousins here at nine, but Scarlett asked me to come earlier, at eight. Since I couldn't sleep, I had brought my coffee to the courtyard to wait for Scarlett.

"What made you go to the pool? Especially after you fell in yesterday." Christine flipped to another page in her notebook and arched her eyebrows at me.

"How do you know about that?" Beau asked before I could.

"A friend told me about it. He was at The Gas Light when you came in after your dip in the pool," Christine said.

So she already knew about the fight. Beau frowned, and I guessed he realized how bad this looked for me, too. Not that I planned on lying to the police, but I had hoped to downplay the argument.

"Yes, I slipped into the pool. It was an emotional visit yesterday. I just met my family two days ago."

"You slipped? That's not what I heard." Christine's stare made me uncomfortable, but then again, that was her job.

"Fine. Scarlett wanted me to fall into the pool after our argument." How did people lie to the police? Here I was feeling guilty, and I didn't even kill Scarlett. But I did say I'd keep the key over her dead body in my drunken anger.

"She wanted the key to the family mausoleum, but it's mine."

"A tomb fight. Yes, those are messy." Christine made more notes. "You agreed to come back today. You even agreed to get here early to meet with Scarlett alone."

"That's my fault. I told her she should meet them," Beau insisted. "I'm so sorry, Sammy. This wouldn't be happening if I didn't force you to meet your relatives..."

"Beau, would you grab a cup of coffee for Sammy?" Christine interrupted. "I'm sure she could use it."

I hoped it was my shivering that made Christine ask Beau to get coffee, but I saw through her ploy. She wanted to talk to me alone. At least she wasn't dragging me to the police station... yet.

10

———

"No! No! No! It can't be my baby girl!"

Charlene's cries awoke painful memories. When the police called to say my parents had been killed in a car crash, I barely made it off the phone without wailing. Charlene had lost her husband a few years ago, and now her daughter.

Christine's partner, Rob Armstrong, opened the lounge door. I also met Rob at a crime scene, but now I knew him better as Sissy's boyfriend. While he looked imposing with his muscular body and serious face, his gentle eyes and slow Southern drawl put everyone at ease.

Rob gently ushered a sobbing Charlene inside. She wore a long floral robe, pink slippers, and a turquoise scarf wrapped around her head. "Mrs. St. Martin, please take a seat. After you have a moment to gather yourself, we'll talk."

"Here, take this chair." Beau stood up. "You and Sammy should be with each other."

Charlene looked over at me with wide eyes. Did she know I found Scarlett? I began shivering again, so I pulled the towel around me tighter.

"Sarah Jane, what are you doing here?" She didn't take the seat next to me; she stayed where she was, holding on to Rob's arm. "And why are you wet? Did you…"

Rob interrupted her. "I'm sorry, Mrs. St. Martin, I didn't get the chance to tell you that Sammy found your daughter this morning."

"What?" she squealed. "Why are you here so early? We were getting together at nine."

"Scarlett texted me to meet her at eight," I said. "I woke up early, so I came here to wait in the courtyard until she joined me."

"And then you found her." Jasper stood in the open door. He was already dressed, unlike his mother. He wore jeans, a green polo shirt, and tennis shoes, although his brown hair was sticking up from the back of his head. I tried to read his face, but I couldn't place his emotions. Sadness? Confusion? Guilt?

"Let me get coffee for everyone." Beau rushed out of the room, but I wished he had stayed. From the stony stare from Charlene and the inquisitive looks from Rob and Christine, I already felt like I was on trial.

"Sammy, are you OK? You actually went into the pool?" Jasper guided his mother to a seat at another table. But then he came over to me and put his hand on my shoulder. "Was she alive when you first found her?"

"No. I'm so sorry," I said.

Charlene sobbed into a tissue that Rob handed her. "Why was she in the pool? I thought she was in her room all night."

"I saw her leave our suite." All eyes turned to Jasper.

"What time was this?" Rob asked.

"Um, I think around ten. She said she was going to get more wine," Jasper said.

"She must have come to the lounge. Remember how she liked that wine we had at happy hour." Charlene blew her nose.

"She liked it because it was free," Jasper mumbled, but I heard it, and so did Christine. She jotted down more notes and gave a nod to Rob.

"Sammy, did you see Scarlett's cell phone anywhere?" Rob asked.

"Sorry, I don't remember seeing one. Is it missing?"

"She always carried it with her. I told her she'd get brain cancer if she didn't put it down," Charlene said.

"Why don't we go to your suite and search for it?" Rob offered his arm to Charlene.

"The police in our suite? I don't know about that," Charlene stammered, but she took Rob's arm and walked with him to the door.

"Momma, they're just doing their job. We have nothing to hide," Jasper said. "Sammy, we'll talk later, right?"

I nodded and watched him leave. While he declared they had nothing to hide, the look between him and his mother said otherwise.

As they exited, a woman in a jacket marked CSI poked her head inside. "Detective Gammon, can I see you for a moment?"

"Please wait here, Sammy," Christine said.

She and the CSI spoke for a minute, and then Christine turned to me. "Sammy, let's go to the station where we can talk in private."

I opened my mouth to ask her why, but the stare she gave me changed my mind. What in the world did they find out there? Christine held the door open, so I pulled my towel around me without a word.

I didn't want to go to the police station, but Christine

hadn't asked me; it was a demand. And by the looks from the coroner and crime scene investigators, the detective had a lot of questions for me. I hoped I had the right answers.

Christine let me sit in the front seat of her unmarked police car. She didn't put on the siren, so that was a good sign. Fortunately, it was a short drive from the hotel to the station.

I would have preferred to go to Cafe Beignet, which was right next door to the police station. Christine must have seen me looking wistfully at the cafe. "I'll send someone to get coffee for us. Do you want beignets, too?"

"Just coffee, thanks." My stomach was too upset to even consider putting food in it. The caffeine would soothe me. Some people drink coffee to be alert, but coffee calmed me down. And I needed all the help I could get.

I'd been to the police station before as a witness, and while I hoped I was here in that role again, I wasn't sure. Christine didn't have me in handcuffs, but she wasn't as talkative as usual. She apparently saved it for the interrogation room.

"Let me grab some dry clothes for you. You must be cold," Christine said. "And we'll take your clothes. Just your shirt and pants."

"Why?"

"Sammy, you've read enough mystery novels to know the answer."

I didn't know if she was joking or not. I took a chance and answered her with a non-serious response. "Sorry, I haven't read any mysteries where a woman finds her cousin dead in a hotel pool."

While I tried to come across as funny, my words fell flat.

"That didn't come out right. Sorry, what I mean is do you expect to find something on my clothes?"

"We'll talk when I get back."

Christine returned to the room with a towel, a pair of yoga pants, and a NOPD t-shirt. She also brought in coffee and a blueberry muffin. "You said no food, but I thought you could use something."

After changing and handing my wet clothes to Christine, I sipped my coffee and took a bite of the muffin. "Thanks. I didn't eat this morning."

"Did you plan on having breakfast with Scarlett?"

"No, she texted me around 10:30 last night asking me to meet her before getting together with the entire family."

"Can I see your phone?"

I handed my phone to Christine, and she clicked on my texts. After scribbling in her notebook, she gave it back to me. "Thanks. I'm surprised you agreed to meet her after the fight you had. Did you plan on giving her the tomb key?"

"First, we didn't fight. We just disagreed," I insisted. "And no, I left the key at home. I wanted to hear her out before I decided what to do."

"Would you have turned over the key? Or do you want to keep the tomb?" Christine closed her notebook and crossed her hands on top of it. "It's worth a lot of money, at least $50,000, is my guess. Maybe more, since your family mausoleum is unique with its key design."

"No!" I took in a deep breath and exhaled. "It didn't matter how much the tomb is worth. I don't plan to sell it, but I wouldn't kill anyone to keep it."

"Sammy, you know I have to ask." Christine stared at me with those penetrating eyes that must make suspects confess — if they're guilty, which I wasn't.

"I understand." I sighed. "So Scarlett was definitely murdered?"

"Her death is suspicious."

"Come on, Christine, you can tell me more than that, can't you?" I asked. "You didn't bring me here for no reason."

"Someone struck your cousin before she ended up in the pool. Did you have anything to do with it?"

"No!" I gave up on trying to calm myself down. "When I left yesterday, she was alive. When I came back today, she was dead. I had nothing to do with her death."

"You didn't come back last night? Perhaps you thought you two could hash it out, and it got out of hand."

"Absolutely not. I didn't kill her."

Christine took out her notebook again. "Can anyone vouch for your whereabouts last night? How about your boyfriend?"

I bit my lip before I spouted off that Connor and I weren't at the "staying at each other's apartment overnight" stage in our relationship. And at this rate, we wouldn't get there. Especially if he was chatting up Scarlett yesterday. But I didn't share that with Christine. I wouldn't throw Connor under the bus — at least until he explained his side of the story.

"No. The last person I saw was Ruby when I came home from the bar."

She wrote Ruby's name. "We'll just confirm that with her. No one else? Did you make any calls?"

Great. Now Ruby had something else to dislike about me. How much sage would she need to cleanse the area she shared with a murder suspect?

"No calls. I was with my cat until I left my apartment this morning around seven."

Rob came into the room and took the chair next to

Christine. He gave me a quick smile, but then ignored me as he opened his notebook and showed it to his partner. I wanted to lean over the table to read it, too, but I restrained myself — barely.

After Christine looked at Rob's notes, she asked, "One last question. How tall are you?"

"I'm almost five-five."

"Did you wear high heels last night?" Rob said.

I looked at my now second pair of pool-soaked Converse sneakers. "I wear them on special occasions. But, no, I wasn't wearing high heels last night."

"OK." She and Rob looked at each other. As long-time partners, they could communicate without a word. I wished they had spoken out loud.

"Why did you ask about my shoes?" I didn't move while Christine stood up and reached for the doorknob.

"Sammy, we'll talk again later if I have questions. I'll get your clothes back to you as soon as possible." Christine gestured toward the open door, so I got up. Pestering her for an answer didn't seem like a smart idea, and I wanted to go home.

"Rob, how are Charlene and Jasper?" I said as the detectives walked me to the front of the station.

"As good as can be expected," Rob said. "They're still in shock, but Jasper asked about you."

I said nothing. Was Jasper's concern for my well being or did he believe I killed his sister?

At least one person thought I was innocent, and she was waiting for me by the NOPD t-shirt vending machine. I wondered how many t-shirts they usually sold, but this morning no one was buying them. The woman standing in front of the machine most likely kept anyone away.

11

"Finally!" Sissy put her hands on her hips. She directed her frustration at Rob and Christine with a pointed look at them. Her eyes softened at me, and she pulled me in for a hug.

"Hi, Sissy. Here for Rob or for a t-shirt?" Christine said in a deadpan voice.

"No, I'm here for Sammy, not a t-shirt." Sissy crossed her arms and stared at her fiancé. While she was almost a foot shorter than Rob, her stance and firm voice made her a force to be reckoned with. "Or Rob. You should have sent her home right away. She'll catch a cold."

"As a nurse, you know she won't get a cold from being damp." Rob sighed. "Also, it's May in New Orleans; it's not cold outside."

Weather wise it wasn't cold, but the air was chilly between the newly engaged couple.

"I'm OK. They offered me towels, and I got this lovely t-shirt." I grasped Sissy's hand and gave it a squeeze. "Let's go home."

"Fine." Sissy smiled at me, but turned to Rob and Christine and glared. "We'll leave so they can do their jobs."

"Sissy..." Rob said, but Sissy was already pulling me toward the door. I looked back to see Rob shaking his head, but he perked up as I smiled half-heartedly at him. He was used to Sissy's defensiveness of her friends, but he always took her annoyance with him to heart, it seemed.

"We'll be in touch, Sammy," Christine said after checking her phone. "Come on, Rob, the coroner wants us."

"That was quick." Rob followed Christine back to their office. I wanted to go with them, too, but hopefully I'd find out something soon. And if they were getting info that would clear me, all the better.

"Sammy, what in the world happened at the hotel?" Sissy asked.

"First, tell me how you knew I was at the station. Did Rob call you?"

Sissy blew wisps of blond hair out of her face. "That man should have, but no, Andrew did. Beau called him and explained that you went to the police station."

"That was kind of Beau."

"Yes, he's a good fellow. Andrew wanted to come with me to get you, but he said he had to wait for a delivery. I told him we'd call him when we got home."

"I completely forgot about that shipment today." A big order from a new vendor was coming today, and I'd promised Andrew I would be there to help. I was turning out to be a lousy business partner already.

"Don't worry! Andrew said he can handle it and the shop. Neal will pop in to help Andrew in between tours.

And Rose will check in with Beau to see if he needs help at the hotel."

I rested my head on Sissy's shoulder as we walked toward Thibodeaux Mansion. Of course everyone pitched in; that's what our group of friends, our family, did for each other.

"And Sammy, Connor is beside himself. He wanted to come to the station, but he's meeting with his boss today. His old boss, right?"

"Yep. He gave notice before he left Baton Rouge. Today is just the exit interview."

"I'm sure he tried to reschedule. Connor was so worried about you when I called him."

"So he knows Scarlett is dead?"

"Yes, but Sammy, he's concerned about you, not your cousin." Sissy put her hand on the gate before I opened it. "You're the one he loves, not her."

I nodded and followed her into the courtyard. Maybe he didn't love Scarlett, but was he worried about me or the murder? Did he have something to do with it? Or did he think I killed her?

12

────────

I didn't know what Connor was thinking, but I soon found out his mother's view on the situation. Libby was sitting at my bistro table outside my door.

"Sammy, I am so sorry! You just met your cousin and now she's gone," Libby said. "What a dreadful thing to happen, darling."

I accepted Libby's hug, thankful she didn't accuse me of murder. She saw firsthand how horrible Scarlett was to me the first night we met. And I was sure she knew about the pool incident yesterday. And she must have heard about my outburst at The Gas Light. Her warm embrace and the box of scones made me relax a bit. She wasn't kicking me out of my apartment, but would she still want me dating her son?

She answered that concern for me quickly. "Connor wanted to be the one waiting for you. He sent me here in his place. And I brought your favorite scones."

I opened the bakery box to find four sweet potato scones. After inhaling the rich scent of cinnamon and sugar, my stomach growled. All I'd had today was coffee and a muffin, and I realized I was actually hungry.

"Thanks, Libby, for everything," I said after taking a bite of the warm scone.

"Of course! We're your family, honey. Don't you forget that." Libby hugged me again. "Now go inside and call Andrew. And Connor will come by as soon as he can. He's worried sick about you."

Libby rushed toward the courtyard gate with her phone up to her ear. "Yes, William, she's OK. I'll stop by your office before I go to the cafe."

My eyes grew watery, thinking of how lucky I was to have such an incredible group of people in my life. Whoever said blood is thicker than water didn't have a family like mine. But I had a biological family, and one of them was dead. While I had no love for Scarlett, part of me wondered if we would have come to terms with the key. Would Charlene and Jasper still want to continue forging a relationship after this morning?

"I see your mind is going a hundred miles an hour," Sissy interrupted my internal ramblings. "Let's go inside."

Sissy took the key out of my backpack and opened my door. She guided me to my loveseat, and I flopped down.

"Call Andrew." Sissy handed me my cell phone. "I'll make coffee."

I would have preferred to text Andrew, but he hated texts. Taking a deep breath, I dialed his number. We had just finished clearing his name in a double murder case, and now it was my turn.

"Samantha, I was so worried!" Andrew said as soon as he answered his cell phone. "Are you OK? No, of course you aren't, but tell me, are you at least in one piece?"

I explained what happened to a silent Andrew. "And now I'm a murder suspect and I'm late to work. I don't want to let you down, but I'm not sure I can really concentrate at the store."

"There is no need for you to be here, my dear. You must take care of yourself." Andrew's soothing voice almost made me cry. "I'll come by tomorrow morning, and we'll stop at Cafe Beignet before we go to the shop."

"Beignets? Are we going to break the 'no beignets in the shop' rule?"

"My dear, I'll always break the rules for you. Now rest. Goodbye."

"I wasn't going to let you go to work, but I didn't think Andrew would allow you to anyway." Sissy put a steaming cup of coffee on the table. The warm mug warmed my hands, but it was Sissy's arm around me that comforted me.

"OK, you've had a scone and coffee, go shower." Sissy pulled me up from the loveseat. "I'll check on you later unless you'd like me to stay. I'm happy to."

"No, I'll get cleaned up and rest for a bit. Then I guess I should call Charlene and Jasper. Assuming they still want to talk to me."

"Of course they will! They know you had nothing to do with Scarlett's murder!"

But did they? It didn't take long for me to find out.

13

—————

A knock on my door woke me up from my nap. After showering, I'd fallen asleep on my loveseat with my cell phone in my hands, trying to gather the courage to call my relatives. Instead, they showed up at my doorstep.

Charlene's face was blotchy, and she held a tissue up to her swollen nose. Jasper rubbed the crescent moon scar on the right side of his face while shuffling his feet.

"Charlene. Jasper. What a surprise."

"I tried calling and texting. We were worried when you didn't answer," Jasper said.

"Yes, we thought the killer might have got you, too!" Charlene began crying so I couldn't leave them on my doorstep.

"I'm sorry, I turned off my phone." That was true. After Sissy left, I set my cell phone to "do not disturb." Rob and Christine could find me if they needed me. But I had hoped they wouldn't.

But Charlene and Jasper needed me — at least they

appeared to as they stood at my door. Since they didn't accuse me of killing Scarlett, I couldn't turn them away.

"Would you like to come in?" I asked.

Charlene walked right in and sat down on my loveseat. She looked all around at my bookshelves and artwork, all New Orleans themed thanks to Libby, who decorated this furnished apartment. I'd added a few of my personal items, including my collection of books. While it wasn't the fanciest of apartments, it was warm and comfortable. It was home.

"What a darling little place." Charlene fluffed a white tasseled pillow that was printed with the saying, "A Clean House is a Sign of a Misspent Life." I don't think she agreed with the sentiment since she straightened my magazine pile and brushed cat hair off the coffee table.

"It's great." Jasper was looking over my book collection. "I loved *Interview with the Vampire*."

"Me, too." I relaxed a bit at the small talk, but it didn't last.

"Now, Sarah Jane, tell me again about this message Scarlett sent you." Charlene patted the seat next to her. "I'm so surprised she did that. We were planning to see you at nine. Jasper said he texted you."

"I did." Jasper's exasperation with his mother was obvious, but Charlene either didn't see it or ignored it.

"He did." I smiled at Jasper. "Scarlett texted me after that, asking to meet at eight. I messaged her back and then showed up this morning."

"That's so unlike her," Charlene said. "Why would she want to talk to you alone?"

I assumed Scarlett wanted to discuss the key or Connor. Or both. Apologizing for her outburst and for "helping" me into the pool didn't seem like something she would do. And Jasper thought the same thing.

"Well, I doubt it was to apologize. That isn't her style," Jasper said.

"Wasn't her style, you mean." Charlene took another tissue from her purse. "She's dead and gone and you shouldn't say cruel things about her."

"Sorry, Momma." Jasper came over to the loveseat and gave his mother a hug. I took the opportunity to get up and grab a glass of water. I was intruding on their grief, and I felt like an outsider.

Nubi sauntered out of my bedroom and rubbed up against my leg. He always sensed when I needed comfort. I picked him up and held him over my shoulder, resting my face in his soft black fur. The rhythm of his purrs calmed me.

"And who's this?" Jasper asked.

"This is Nubi, although his formal name is Anubis."

Nubi jumped from my arms and trotted over to Jasper. He sniffed Jasper's hand and accepted scratches from him.

"Anubis? Like the Egyptian God of the afterlife?" Jasper said. "That's quite a meaningful name."

"You have no idea," I said. "But I didn't name him, my neighbor Ruby did."

"While this is sweet and all, can we get back to talking about Scarlett?" Charlene interrupted. Nubi didn't agree as he meowed and jumped into Jasper's lap. "Put the cat down; I don't want fur on me."

Jasper kept petting Nubi, who purred in response. "As you can tell, Sammy, Momma isn't a cat person."

"I didn't have time to play with pets. I had you, your sister, and your cousin to raise."

"And a husband who didn't do anything," Jasper said.

They glared at each other but didn't say a word. Nubi opened his eyes and looked at me. He must have felt as uncomfortable as I did. And things just kept getting more awkward.

A knock made me jump. I pulled back the curtains from my window to see Frank standing at the door. He had a grin on his handsome face and two grocery bags in his large hands. I had completely forgotten my weekly order from his grandmother's shop was to be delivered tonight.

"Hey, Sammy. I heard the news." He put the bags down on the doormat and hugged me. Usually I had to pull myself out of his tight embraces, but tonight I let him hold me a bit longer. The comfort of a friend eased a bit of my tension.

"Hey, there. Good to see you." I smiled at him after we pulled apart.

Before I could introduce Frank, he said, "I know you didn't kill your cousin, even if she was a piece of work."

"Um, thanks, Frank," I said. "This is my cousin's mother and brother, Charlene and Jasper St. Martin."

His face turned the shade of his grandmother's marinara sauce. Charlene crossed her arms and glared at him. Jasper let Frank off the hook. "Hi. I can help you with those bags."

"Thanks, man. Really, I'm sorry for your loss." Frank exhaled and handed a bag to Jasper. They unloaded the groceries onto the counter. They chatted as they worked, talking about the Saints. When I moved here, I learned that discussing New Orleans' beloved football team was a great ice breaker.

"Wow, this smells fantastic." Jasper opened a container of chicken and andouille sausage gumbo. "Momma, you'll love this. It reminds me of Grandma's."

"I can get more for y'all. This is just your regular order, Sammy," Frank said.

"It'll be plenty." His grandmother's portions were oversized. Her heart was as generous as her food.

"Call me if you need more." Frank hugged me once again and shook Jasper's hand. "Nice to meet you. If you visit during football season, we'll go to a game. Sammy will come, won't you?"

"I'd love to." I smiled. While Frank could be a bit of a flirt, he had a kind heart like his grandmother, Frankie. And they both squeezed you like a boa constrictor when they hugged you.

Frank stood in front of the coffee table. "Ma'am, I'm very sorry about your daughter. I speak for my grandmother that if y'all need anything, let us know."

"Thank you." Charlene offered her hand, and he shook it gently. "How kind of you to deliver food on such a horrible day."

"It's no bother. We think the world of Sammy, and we're happy to help her and her family anytime." Frank left, but first he whispered in my ear, "Now don't you worry about what people are saying in the Quarter. I'm putting them straight."

I hadn't been worrying about my reputation until Frank said that. Great. Were people talking, or was Frank being flirtatious? Thank goodness Frankie had included a bottle of my favorite Merlot with my groceries. It wasn't part of my regular order, but she always anticipated what I needed. And she knew her grandson had a big mouth. Then again, she was a considerable source of neighborhood gossip, although she had more tact than Frank.

"We should leave you to your supper." Charlene stood up and reached for her purse.

"Why don't you stay? I have plenty of food," I said. "I bet you haven't eaten for a while."

"We don't want to intrude," Charlene said.

"You won't be," I said. "Sit down, and Jasper can help me put together our dinner."

Charlene took off the lightweight lilac cardigan she wore and sat before I finished speaking. "It's awfully sweet of you. We had cold sandwiches at the police station, but that's all."

Jasper joined me in the kitchen. He ladled bowls of warm chicken and andouille sausage gumbo and I sliced the loaf of crisp French bread. I poured a glass of wine for each of us without asking. If they didn't want it, I'd drink theirs. I pulled up a side chair while Charlene and Jasper sat on the loveseat.

"Oh, it's dry, isn't it?" Charlene wrinkled her nose, but she took another sip of her wine.

"Would you prefer something else?" I started to get up, but Jasper leaned across the coffee table and put his hand on mine.

"It's fine. Don't mind my mother. Her taste in wine is suspect," Jasper said.

"My taste is just fine, thank you very much." Charlene smiled. "My son thinks he's one of those fancy wine people. What is it called, a summerling?"

"You know it's a sommelier, Momma." Jasper laughed, and Charlene joined him. The sommelier conversation appeared to be a running family joke. It was nice to have a moment of levity and to see that my aunt and cousin had some affection toward each other.

"Are you interested in wine, Jasper?" I asked. "I lived in California for a long time, and I'm still confused about wines."

"Oh, he can tell you all about them. Why don't you do that while I powder my nose? Where's your restroom, my dear?"

I pointed through to the bedroom and watched an off-balanced Charlene go through the kitchen to my bedroom. She stopped at the foot of my bed, apparently surveying everything. I almost got up to make sure she didn't fall on her way to the bathroom, but she hurried off.

Jasper explained all about red wine, and while I was interested, I kept an ear out for Charlene. After about ten minutes, I stood up. "I think I should check on your mother."

Before he could protest or offer to go, I trotted into my bedroom to find her standing over my nightstand. Her hand was on the drawer handle, but she dropped it and yelped when I coughed loudly behind her.

"Oh, you scared me!" Charlene said. "I just had to look at your pictures. Are these the people who raised you?"

She picked up the framed photo of my adopted parents with me at my college graduation. She put it down and grabbed the picture of everyone from Thibodeaux Mansion, except Ruby, sitting around a table in the courtyard at one of our regular dinners. "You look so happy with all these people."

"Yes, they're all my family." I took the frame out of her hands and placed it on the nightstand. "Do you need anything?"

"Oh, yes, more tissues. I looked in your bathroom, but didn't see any." She scurried out of my room, but called back, "Do you have more out here?"

"I'll get some for you." I popped my head into my bathroom to find the cabinet doors open. Was she really looking for tissues? There was no reason for her to look for them in my nightstand, either. She must have been snooping. Or then again, she might have been searching for the tomb key. I hadn't removed it from its hiding place in one of my Nancy

Drew books, so I doubt she would have thought to look there. She hadn't asked for it, but if Scarlett was so obsessed with it, Charlene could be too.

After grabbing a box of tissues from my pantry, I joined Charlene and Jasper in the living room, where they talked in hushed tones. Jasper's exasperation was written all over his face as his mother clenched his arm.

"I was telling Jasper what a lovely bedroom and bathroom you have," Charlene said as I sat down and handed her the tissues. "You seem to have a place for everything."

Did she mean the tomb key? If so, she didn't say, but she looked around the apartment more intently than before. Jasper continued his explanation of grapes, and I finally relaxed after Charlene stopped searching the room and ate her gumbo. She even asked Jasper questions and complimented him on his knowledge. While the wine and gumbo warmed my stomach, listening to Jasper speak passionately and seeing his mother's pride warmed my heart.

Just when the tension was subsiding over good food, there was another knock on the door.

14

———

I opened the door to find Connor with a bouquet of pink tulips, a grocery bag, and a concerned look on his face.

"Sammy, I'm sorry I wasn't here earlier for you." He hugged me, but pulled away quickly. "Oh, I didn't realize you had company."

"I wouldn't call us company; we're Sarah Jane's family." Charlene put her bowl on the coffee table and dabbed at the corners of her mouth with a napkin. "We needed to be together after my baby girl's death."

"I'm very sorry, Mrs. St. Martin," Connor said. "Hi, Jasper. I'm sorry about your sister."

"Thanks. You're the second grocery delivery tonight." Jasper pointed to the bag.

"Second? Oh, Frank must have been here." Connor beelined to the kitchen and took a vase out from a cabinet. Charlene studied him as he filled it with water and arranged the flowers in it.

"Did he bring dessert?" Connor asked. "I hope not since I have bread pudding."

"With bourbon whipped cream?" I took out four small plates and forks.

Connor kissed me on the cheek. "Of course. I thought you'd need it after today."

"Yes, we all need some comfort after losing our Scarlett." Charlene handed her bowl to her son and pointed at her empty wineglass.

"Here, let me take that, Jasper." I took the bowl from him and handed him the wine bottle to refill his mother's glass.

Connor looked at me and opened his mouth, but he shut it. Charlene's glare made me uncomfortable, and when Connor took out his trumpet mouthpiece, I realized he was nervous.

I carried the dessert plates to the living area, and Connor brought over another chair and sat next to me. We ate in silence until Charlene put her plate down and took a big gulp of her wine. She stared at Connor and said, "You knew my Scarlett, didn't you?"

Well, that was unexpected, at least to me. She knew he did; she was there when Scarlett threw herself at Connor. My face grew warm, and it wasn't just from the wine. Was Charlene doing this to embarrass me or Connor? It appeared to be both, as Connor's face was flushed and his eyes were downcast.

"Yes, ma'am," Connor answered after swallowing the last bit of his bread pudding.

"Momma, don't start on him." Jasper sighed. "I got the impression that they barely knew each other."

"Scarlett would beg to differ if she was still on this earth." Charlene folded her hands in her lap, looking demure, but her eyes were anything but subtle. "I just want to hear about their relationship. Stories of my baby are what I need right now."

I scraped my plate for the remaining crumbs and whipped cream and kept my mouth shut. Like Charlene, I was curious about what Connor had to say about Scarlett. But I would have preferred to have that conversation just with Connor.

"Scarlett and I met during Mardi Gras two years ago. We enjoyed each other's company..."

Jasper's snort interrupted Connor's explanation. "I'm sorry, please continue."

"OK, well," Connor stammered. Jasper's snort threw Connor off, but he said, "She was a lot of fun, but we didn't keep in touch after the weekend."

"That sounds like Scarlett," Jasper said. "She was the love 'em and leave 'em type."

"Jasper Elvis St. Martin, you watch your mouth!" Charlene picked up a throw pillow and whacked her son on his arm. "Do not talk that way about your sister."

"Sorry, Momma." Jasper's face turned red, and I poured more wine into his cup.

"I'm sure the distance made it hard to keep in touch." Charlene took a tissue out of her purse. "Scarlett was a busy girl with her job at the insurance agency and all her friends."

"It sounds like she had a great life, ma'am." Connor relaxed a bit, but he continued to twirl his trumpet mouthpiece. "And again, I'm sorry for your loss. I'm sure y'all will miss her."

"We will. I'm so sorry Sarah Jane and Scarlett didn't have the chance to get to know each other. They would have been wonderful friends," Charlene said.

Thankfully, I wasn't drinking or eating when she said that, or I might have choked. I managed to smile at Charlene. "It's all very sad."

She reached across the table and squeezed my hand. "Yes, but we'll soldier on, won't we?"

"Yes, we will." Jasper stood up and offered his hand to his mother. "And now we should soldier on back to the hotel. It's been a long day for all of us."

"Can I call you a cab?" I asked. "Do you want to take any food back with y'all?"

"It's not that far to walk, and we could use the fresh air." Jasper shook his head as his mother reached for the wine bottle. It was empty anyway, and I couldn't help but feel sad for Charlene. If there was ever a night to drink, this was it.

"Yes, I guess a walk would be good." Charlene went over to Connor, who immediately stood up. By the shocked look on his face, he hadn't expected the hug she gave him. "Connor, you take care. Be sure to tell my niece all about Scarlett. You had the pleasure of knowing her longer than Sarah Jane."

Jasper opened the front door. "Let's go, Momma."

"Family has to stick together." Charlene squeezed me tight. "We'll talk tomorrow."

"Thanks, Sammy, for dinner," Jasper said. "See you later."

As I went to close my door, I saw Charlene's sweater on the loveseat. I grabbed it and started toward the gate, hoping to catch them. I stopped just before the entryway and hid around the corner when I heard Charlene speaking.

"If I find out that girl killed my baby, I'm going to make sure she goes to jail for the rest of her life," Charlene sputtered.

"Momma, Sammy had nothing to do with Scarlett's death," Jasper said. "She wouldn't do that."

"But what if she's like her brother? He was no good, like

his parents. They always did what they wanted, not what was best for the family."

"I don't think she's like her brother at all. Aunt Anna Grace and Uncle Sawyer were decent people." Jasper put his arm around his mother's shoulders. "You're just upset about Scarlett."

She rested her head against her son. "Yes, I'm upset. But the police better find out who killed my baby. And if Sarah Jane, I mean Samantha, didn't do it, I wouldn't be surprised if it was her brother."

My brother? Did Charlene actually believe Joey came back to town and killed Scarlett?

I leaned against the brick wall, trying to catch my breath. Once it slowed down, I staggered back to my apartment with Charlene's sweater in my hand.

"Sammy, what's wrong? You've still got your aunt's sweater and you're white as a ghost." Connor put down the kitchen towel. "Here, sit."

I flopped onto my loveseat and closed my eyes. I sat up and searched through the mail on my coffee table. Bills, magazines, and a postcard from my best friend in San Francisco was all I found. "There's nothing from my brother."

"I'm confused. Why are you looking for mail from Joey?" Connor held my hands. My head didn't trust him, but my heart needed to at that moment.

"I overheard Charlene saying my brother might have killed Scarlett. What if he's back?" After he disappeared a few months ago, he began sending me photographs from our childhood before Hurricane Geoffrey separated us. The last one included my aunt and cousins and on the back it said, "Trust No One."

"Should we call Rob?" Connor asked.

Could my brother really be back? The most recent envelope was postmarked from Huntley, Mississippi, where Charlene and her children lived. Did he know they were coming to New Orleans and followed them?

"I'm sure he's already considered it," I said. "If Rob has any concerns, he would tell me."

"Yes, he would, but aren't you worried?"

"Part of me is, but I decided after the postcards starting arriving not to let it rule my life." I let go of Connor's hands and stood up. "I'm always cautious, but I'll protect myself even more."

He got up and pulled me in for a hug. I let him because I needed it as much as I acted tough. "I could sleep here. On the couch of course."

"Quite the gentleman." I laughed. "I'll be fine."

"If you say so."

His sour tone annoyed me. Was he just disappointed I didn't want him to stay, or did he believe I couldn't handle myself? Either way, I was ready for him to go.

"I do say so." I picked up the empty cups. They clanked as I dropped them into the sink. "It's been a long day, and I need to sleep."

Connor started to say something, but he stopped when I walked over to my front door. And while I meant what I said about Joey, I was also thinking of protecting my heart from Connor.

"Fine, Sammy. You can take care of yourself. I just want you to know I'm here for you."

His puppy dog eyes almost got to me, but I stood firm — mostly.

"Thanks, really, I appreciate your concern." I accepted his hug and gave him a chance to tell me about meeting my cousin. "I'm sure this is awkward for you. Seeing Scarlett again must have been strange. She seemed eager to talk to you."

Connor opened the door before he said, "It was weird to see her."

"That's all?"

"Yes, what else could it be?" Connor cocked his head and looked blankly at me.

"Nothing, nothing at all. My brain is just spinning after everything today." I gave a fake smile. "Good night."

"I'll see you tomorrow." He twirled his trumpet mouthpiece as he headed toward his apartment.

What else could it be? Maybe Connor had been interested in Scarlett again. Or had he been telling her to leave him, or even me, alone? Or could it have been a murder?

15

—————

"Good morning, Samantha. Based on your work ethic, I had no doubt you'd be ready to go to the shop."

Andrew stood in front of my doorway at 8:30 a.m. wearing his usual dress pants, white Oxford shirt, and a pink polka-dotted bowtie. His warm smile and intense blue eyes were always a comfort to me, and this morning was no different.

"I may have bags under my eyes, but I'm dressed and caffeinated." A cup of coffee, a long shower, and my comfortable outfit of black jeans, a black silk t-shirt, and my black flats, and I was as ready as I would ever be for the day.

"You look well, considering yesterday's circumstances." Andrew offered his arm after I locked my front door. "I assume you had a quiet evening after we spoke."

"Far from it." I recounted yesterday's events as we walked.

By the time we arrived at Cafe Beignet, Andrew experienced the same emotions I had last night — disbelief, horror, and disappointment. After we placed our order for cafe au laits and beignets, Andrew asked, "Are you sure it was Connor you saw with Scarlett? It could have been another handsome man in the Quarter."

"True, but do you know any other men who twirl a trumpet mouthpiece when they're nervous? Or spent a 'magical' weekend with my cousin?"

"I see your point." He grabbed a handful of napkins from the table next to us. "You won't learn the truth until you ask him. Don't make up stories until you talk to him."

"Easier said than done."

"Especially for you, my imaginative friend." Andrew handed me my coffee, and I followed him out the door. "And Samantha, everyone knows you can't let anything go, but be cautious."

"With Connor?" My eyes widened. "Do you think he had something to do with Scarlett's murder?"

"No, of course not!" Andrew shook his head. "What I meant is don't investigate on your own. Talk to Connor about your relationship, but do not play Nancy Drew."

"You're no fun." I pretended to pout, but I couldn't keep a straight face. "Fine, I'll try to be good."

Andrew raised his eyebrows at me, but let it go. We walked quietly down Royal Street until the shop's next-door neighbor, Suzy of Suzy's Surprises, stopped us.

"Howdy, neighbors!" Suzy leaned her broom against her door and waved.

"Good morning, Suzy. Ready for another busy day?" Andrew said.

Our neighbor's shop always had customers as she offered something for everyone. From fleur-de-lis jewelry to New Orleans themed t-shirts to tchotchkes of questionable taste, Suzy's store was constantly packed.

"Ready as I'll ever be!" Suzy's laughter made me smile, along with her outfit. While her shop lacked a clear identity, she did not. Without fail, every time I saw Suzy she wore a 1950s-style dress with a rhinestone peacock pin on the lapel.

Suzy stepped over to us and lowered her voice. "Now, Sammy, I know you're innocent. Everyone on the street knows it, too."

"Everyone?" I croaked.

She explained she had run into most of the other shop owners on the block at Artistic Coffee & Creations. Not only was Libby my landlady and mother to my boyfriend, she owned my favorite cafe. Between showcasing the work of local artists and selling the best coffee and scones, Libby heard all the neighborhood gossip, just like Frankie at her corner store.

Libby told them that yes, my cousin was killed, and I had found the body, but I had nothing to do with it. While I appreciated the support, I had hoped my name wasn't connected to the murder. But who was I kidding? This was the French Quarter, and gossip abounded.

"I'm sure Samantha is relieved the neighbors are rallying behind her." Andrew put his hand on my elbow and gently pushed me toward Lagniappe Books.

"We've got your back, Sammy! Just like we did when they said Andrew had killed those people." Suzy stopped me and grabbed my hand and gave it a squeeze. "You'll be okey-dokee."

"Thanks." I managed to smile before Andrew opened the door and ushered me inside. We walked past the floor-to-ceiling mahogany bookshelves and the long dining room table that served as our sales counter to the back of the store. I plopped down on the burgundy loveseat while Andrew placed our beignets on the low marble coffee table.

He sat in one of the matching armchairs and sipped his coffee. We knew each other well enough to recognize when we needed some peace and quiet.

"I'm going to eat all these beignets if you don't grab one now." After eating two of the fluffy, powdered sugar dusted New Orleans style donuts, I finally spoke. "Save my thighs from these calories."

"Oh, please, beignet calories evaporate in the air, just like gossip." Andrew tucked a napkin in the collar of his shirt and bit into a beignet.

"Didn't you hear Suzy? The entire neighborhood knows about the murder," I whined. "It's horrible."

"I have no idea what that's like." Andrew arched his eyebrows.

"Ugh, I'm such a lousy friend. Forgive me, please." I pushed over the other bag of beignets to him. Only a few days ago, Andrew was the prime suspect in two murders. He was exonerated quickly, but it wasn't a pleasant experience, especially for someone as private as he was.

"It's all right, my dear." He smiled. "But Suzy and our other neighbors will most likely come by to visit. Two suspected murderers at one shop in a week are quite the novelty."

"Better them than Rob and Christine."

"We'll get through this," he said. "You know what would make today better?"

"A Pimm's Cup and a muffuletta at Napoleon House?" Comprised of lemonade, 7-up, Pimm's syrup, and a slice of cucumber, a Pimm's Cup was my favorite drink. Sitting on the patio at Napoleon House with a glass in my hand and a muffuletta sandwich in the other always made me happy.

"That wasn't what I had in mind, but muffulettas for lunch would be good — after we work on our plan to have you become a full-fledged partner here." Andrew went to the private office and returned with his leather-bound planner. "Let's talk about when we should go to the attorney and start the paperwork."

Between that and the customers coming in, the day flew by. And the muffuletta and jambalaya from Napoleon House helped. We skipped the Pimm's Cups, as we had a lot of work to do. Although day drinking wasn't frowned upon, with my exhaustion it would only take one cocktail to put me to sleep.

As we tallied up the day's sales, Beau burst through the door without his usual perkiness.

"Aren't you two a sight for sore eyes!" Beau hugged us both and then took a seat in the back. "Please tell me you're done for the day and can commiserate over a drink at the Carousel Bar."

"My head is spinning, so I don't think I can handle a carousel." I laughed. Andrew and Beau were becoming semi-regulars at the Hotel Monteleone's famous bar. While the bar stools weren't horse-shaped, they were mounted to a slowly spinning base.

"Ha, ha, fine, we can go somewhere static as long as I get a drink," Beau said. "I don't know which was worse — dealing with the police or my hotel staff."

"That's a tough call," I said. "Ambrose and Christine both have that intense stare that makes me nervous."

"Now, now, Ambrose means well," Andrew said. "Hotel service is more a vocation than a career for him."

"I didn't realize you knew Ambrose," I said.

"We met at a few Chamber of Commerce events," Andrew said. "He is stiff, but he also contributes excellent suggestions at the meetings. He just doesn't understand how to relax around people."

"I can see that." I said. "But I have an idea how you can get on Ambrose's good side, Beau."

"How? I'm open to any ideas. It would make my life a thousand times easier if Ambrose was on my side."

"I'm your solution."

16

"You?" Beau and Andrew exclaimed in unison.

"Yes, me. I can…"

"Sammy, honey, it's sweet of you to think you can charm Ambrose, but that won't work on so many levels." Beau giggled. "To start, you're not his type."

"I don't believe anyone is," Andrew said with a slight smile.

"You two are as bad as teenage boys. I'm not going to try to seduce him," I admonished them over their laughter. "Ambrose told me he would love to have the hotel library cleaned and organized. He wants it to be a place for guests to relax."

"Really?" Beau said. "He's said nothing to me about the library."

"Ambrose is dealing with so many things," Andrew said. "Between building a relationship with the new owner and the increasing complaints about ghosts, he is busy."

"Me and the ghosts — we're the problems?" Beau said indignantly.

"You know what I mean," Andrew said. "Redoing the

library might be his desire, but Ambrose is focusing on the most pressing issues."

"You're right," Beau said. "I should be more sympathetic to Ambrose."

"The library renovation is the perfect way to get in his good graces," I said. "And it would be an added attraction for your guests. I can go through the bookshelves and organize them."

Beau nodded, so I kept going. "Who knows what's on those shelves? Historical papers about the hotel? First-edition books?"

"And Lagniappe Books could handle the sale of any valuable books," Beau said.

"It would be a win-win for all of us." I grinned.

"Andrew, you could do talks there!" Beau started talking a mile a minute. "The room is huge. Sammy's right, it is a win for all of us. What do you think?"

"It's a wonderful idea, except for the part that has Samantha at the scene of the crime. Would that look good to the police?"

"Technically, the pool was the scene of the crime." I smiled, but Andrew didn't in return. "I'll be careful, I promise."

"Sammy will be safe. You have my word," Beau said. "And I'll have you sell some of the first-edition books I'm sure are hiding on those dusty shelves."

"Hmm..." Andrew stared up at the ceiling and pursed his lips.

"See, it benefits everyone," I said. "Maybe I can find the source of the ghostly sounds, too."

"You mean like finding which old pipes are making noises?" Andrew said.

"You mean contacting the ghosts?" Beau said.

I loved that the two of them had totally opposite ideas about the noise problem. I tried to remain neutral whether it was noisy pipes or spirits from the great beyond. "I can look into both areas, but my focus would be the books."

"And finding out who killed your cousin." Andrew didn't say it as a question. He knew me all too well.

"If you fix the library and solve the murder, I will forever be indebted to you." Beau grasped my hand and kissed it.

"I promise just to concentrate on the library, but if I happen to learn anything..."

"You'll share it immediately with Rob and Christine." Andrew finished my sentence.

"Cross my heart and hope *not* to die." I put my hand over my heart.

"It is a win-win for everyone." The tension in Beau's face disappeared, but it appeared in Andrew's face. "Andrew, I promise I'll watch out for Sammy."

"Let's try it as long as you both keep safe." Andrew sighed.

"Hurray! Let's go out for a drink to celebrate." Beau clapped and headed to the door.

"You two go on. I'm exhausted," I said. "I'll close up here and you two get on your horses and sip your Vieux Carre cocktails in my honor."

"Are you sure?" Andrew asked.

"Yes, I should really call Charlene and check on her." Assuming she wanted to talk to me. Did she still wonder if I had something to do with Scarlett's death? The only way to find out was to chat with her.

"I hate to leave you alone..." Andrew said, but Sissy interrupted him as she entered the shop.

"Alone? Sammy's got me for the night." Sissy put her

arm around my shoulder. "I'll keep her company. Don't you worry."

"I say we head to the bar where we can discuss business and pleasure." Beau kissed Sissy on the cheek, and then me. "Sammy, I'll meet you at the hotel in the morning. Say ten o'clock? Does that work for you, too, Andrew?"

"Yes, that's fine," Andrew said. "I can manage the store in the morning by myself. Let's reconvene here for lunch to go over your findings."

"Thanks. And before you say it, I'll be careful." I waved to Andrew and Beau as they closed the door behind them.

"So, you're here to keep me company?" I raised my eyebrows at Sissy, whose twinkling eyes and mischievous grin told me she had a plan.

"Yes, I am. We're going to do a little investigating of our own!"

17

"You want to go to the pool?" I turned the shop sign to "Closed" and rested against the door.

"Not the pool, just the hotel," Sissy said. "I bet your aunt and cousin know more than they're saying."

"Why do you say that?"

"Rob said they were elusive about Scarlett's intentions here in New Orleans." Sissy stood next to me at the front door. "Of course he wouldn't tell me more, and Lord knows I tried."

I laughed. "I can't help but wonder if Rob doesn't keep things from you so he can enjoy you trying to wheedle it out of him."

"Maybe that's why he put a ring on it." Sissy flashed her engagement ring. My knowledge of jewelry was lacking, but the center diamond was rectangular and shone brightly, even in the dwindling sunlight. "But seriously, isn't it odd she was killed after demanding your tomb key?"

"Yes, and that makes me a suspect." I grabbed my little blue backpack and ushered Sissy down the steps. "You'll visit me in jail, right?"

"Of course I would, but it won't come to that." Sissy looped her arm through mine. "Rob and Christine will solve the case, but knowing you, you have some ideas of your own."

Sissy didn't say a word as I recapped the conversation I overheard last night. Charlene's theory that my brother was the murderer still nagged at me. Could he have come back just to kill Scarlett? Did he plan to murder Charlene and Jasper? And what about me?

"I can't discount the idea he's here," I said. "The key and the mausoleum are the only connections I see between Scarlett and Joey."

"Did Joey have anything in the tomb when y'all talked there?" Sissy put air quotes around the word "talked." Yes, my brother and I spoke at the family mausoleum, but he also tried to kill me there.

"Not a thing but bone dust and sad memories." I sighed. "But let's get back to why you want to go to the hotel. I can just call them."

"That's not the Southern way!" Sissy shook a finger at me. "And it's not the detective way, either. We need to see their facial expressions, the looks your aunt and cousin give each other, and we should check Scarlett's room."

"The police must have searched it."

"True, but they might not think something is important, and we'll know if it is. And I bet your cousin was good at hiding things. It's worth a try."

As tired as I was, I agreed to go to the hotel. I couldn't imagine that we would find anything, but what if we did? Clearing my name was worth an impromptu visit with my relatives.

18

"Here are my beautiful girls!" Frankie Fortuna exclaimed as Sissy and I walked through the door to her store to buy flowers before we went to the hotel. "Come here!"

She squeezed both of us. Frankie's advanced age and small stature were deceiving; she could hug the breath out of you. Not only did Frankie give out her affection, she had everything and anything a French Quarter resident needed. Her store was a one-stop shop for groceries, prepared food, sundries, and gossip.

"First, Sammy, let me tell you how sorry I am about your cousin." Frankie made the sign of the cross. "And don't you worry about people talking. Anyone who knows you, knows you wouldn't hurt anybody, especially your kin."

I smiled, then turned my attention toward the flowers. A bouquet of mixed flowers in shades of red seemed like the right gift to bring in honor of Scarlett. The bottle of wine Sissy picked out seemed appropriate, too.

"Sammy, you have a new admirer," Frankie said as she rang up our items.

"I do?" Not that I wanted any other romantic complications, but I was curious.

"She's taken," Sissy said. "Not like me, but just give it time."

I rolled my eyes. Connor and I were far from being engaged. And until he told me what he and Scarlett were talking about, I wasn't sure if we were even dating.

"Silly girls, I didn't mean in the romantic sense." Frankie laughed. "Shelby Jones came by this morning."

"Shelby from Hotel Jeanne?" I said. "I only met her briefly."

"That's the one. She's a sweet kid. Her family has lived in the neighborhood as long as I can remember," Frankie said. "Shelby is a hard worker, just like her momma. And both of them love Moon Pies."

"What did she say? Does she know anything about the murder?" Sissy put two Moon Pies on the counter. "I love these things too."

"It wouldn't surprise me if she did," Frankie said. "Housekeepers are invisible. People say crazy stuff in front of them. Kind of like being a shopkeeper."

"You're not invisible to anyone." I laughed. "But what did Shelby say that makes you think she likes me?"

"She said you were so nice even though you were sopping wet from finding your cousin. I said you are also kind no matter what the situation you find yourself in." Frankie tied a red ribbon around the flower bouquet. "She wants to be a detective. I suggested she ask you about the cases you've solved."

"Now, Frankie, you know I'm not a detective. You should send her to Rob and Christine." I protested.

"No, Frankie did the right thing. You get more done than Rob and Christine."

"Sissy, don't say that about your fiancé!" I said.

"Well, at least tell her that PIs can do things cops can't do." Sissy winked.

"But I'm not a PI," I said. "Shelby mentioned she wanted to go to school for criminal justice, so she really should talk to Christine and Rob. But I'm happy to chat with her about other subjects. I'll be at the hotel tomorrow, working in the library."

"Oh, that's wonderful!" Frankie put her hands up to her cheeks. "The last time I was inside Hotel Jeanne, the library was filled top to bottom with books, but it was so dusty, I didn't stay in there long."

"I hate to say not much has changed, but I'm going through the collection to see what's there."

"You might find a ghost or two or ten." Frankie handed the flowers to me and the wine bottle and Moon Pies to Sissy. "A place that old is full of history, good and bad."

Before I could ask Frankie about the ghosts, three neighborhood boys bounded into the shop. "Hey, Miss Frankie! Did you get in those new sour candies? We got cash!"

The tallest boy stretched out his hand to show Frankie his crumpled dollar bills. His friends did the same, and she peered into their hands. "That's enough money, but have you had your dinner? No candy if you haven't."

Frankie's ghost stories had to wait for another day. Sissy and I took our peace offerings and made our way to the hotel. I hoped we would find some answers, but not Scarlett's ghost.

19

———————

Sissy grabbed my arm as I reached for the hotel's door. "Hold on, let's get our stories straight before we go in."

"Good idea. We'll give Charlene the flowers and wine, and then you do that thing you do with your good Southern manners."

"What do you mean?"

"You know what I mean. Remember how you sweet-talked those cops so I could try to sneak into the park? Do that."

Sissy laughed. "I didn't realize it was a Southern thing. My normal personality isn't full of sweetness and charm?"

"I've overheard you talk to your patients — sweetness isn't the term they'd use." I grinned.

"Hey, I'm only tough on the ones who don't listen. When I say take your meds, I mean it." Sissy put her hands on her hips and frowned.

"I'm teasing. Although I've seen you give Rob that look, too."

"Maybe." She fluttered her eyelashes. "But I'll need to

use that supposed sweetness if your aunt calls the cops on us if she catches you snooping."

"It shouldn't come to that, but thanks." I opened the door and almost ran into Ambrose.

"Good evening, ladies." He held the door for us. "Miss Richardson, I hope you have recovered from the *incident*."

Did the word incident cover everything from falling into the pool to discovering a dead body in the world of hotel management? I gave a quick smile and answered, "Yes, I'm fine, thanks. We're here to visit my aunt and cousin."

"We brought flowers and wine." Sissy held them up as if she had to prove to him we were here for a reason and not trying to snoop.

"How nice. Have a good evening." Ambrose smiled as he rushed out the door. He muttered under his breath, "You should have bought cheaper wine."

I bit my lip not to laugh, as I was sure Ambrose would have been mortified if he realized I'd heard him. Although it was good to see he had a sense of humor. He was joking, wasn't he?

The Creole cottage portion of the hotel offered the only suites, and access to that building was through the courtyard. Jasper opened the door to their suite with an empty bottle of cheap Rosé wine in his hand. I shuddered, remembering drinking it in college with less than desirable results.

"Looks like we're here just in time," Sissy said to a surprised Jasper. "I'm so sorry about your sister. Sammy wanted to see how y'all were doing."

"Yes, I'm sorry we didn't call first," I said. "Is this a bad time?"

"Y'all must be psychic." Jasper sighed. "I was going to buy another bottle of wine, but here you are with one. And a great bottle to boot."

"I remembered you said you like the Chardonnay from this vintner," I replied.

We stood there awkwardly for a moment; I wondered if I should give him a hug. Sissy took it upon herself to fix the situation.

"Well, let's try it out!" Sissy put her arm around Jasper and led him away from the door.

We walked into the living room. Some might call it shabby chic, but the dull yellow lumpy couch appeared to be anything but chic. A low oval coffee table and two pink side chairs made up the rest of the furniture in the space. Empty wine glasses and coffee mugs covered a built-in wet bar.

An air of weariness filled the room, but it wasn't just the furniture. The St. Martin family's belongings were strewn about. A mound of men's clothes and sneakers was in one corner and stacks of official-looking papers were piled on top of the coffee table.

"Oh, my sweet niece, you came to see your aunt!" Charlene squeezed me, but before I could wiggle out of her embrace, she stepped backward. "Do you have any news about my baby girl?"

"My fiancé is working day and night on your daughter's case." Sissy handed the bouquet to Charlene. "We're all so sorry for your loss, Mrs. St. Martin."

"How kind of you!" Charlene smelled the flowers before she placed them on the cup-ringed table. "Now, you just call me Aunt Charlene. I hope Sarah Jane will do the same."

I ignored Charlene for two reasons. One, I wasn't ready to call her aunt although it was the polite thing to do; I didn't feel that kinship with her just yet. And two, she called me by my birth name and I needed her to stop doing that.

While it might comfort her to use it, the name only brought me sadness.

Jasper seemed to pick up on that. "Momma, remember it's Samantha or Sammy now."

"I'm sorry, I just keep forgetting." Charlene sat down on the couch while Sissy and I each took a chair. "Your momma just loved your name. She sang it whenever she woke you up from a nap. Of course, that was if your brother hadn't already picked you up out of the crib. He sure did love you."

"Yes, he did. We all did, and still do," Jasper said.

"Yes, we do," Charlene agreed. "Why don't we drink that lovely wine you brought with you?"

"I'll get some fresh glasses," Jasper said. "They'll have to be plastic. I think we've gone through all the glassware."

"You can try the front desk," Charlene said. "But no one answered when I called about an hour ago."

"It might be the shift change," I said. "Ambrose was leaving as we came in."

"He actually left the building?" Charlene grabbed the plastic cups from Jasper. "I thought he must have a coffin hidden somewhere in the hotel. He's as pale as a baby's bottom and is always stumbling about."

"Now, Momma." Jasper shook his head as Sissy and I giggled.

"Ambrose is dedicated to the hotel." I jumped at the sound of the wine cork popping. "But why did you say he's stumbling around?"

"When he's not at that reception desk he's always lurking around," Charlene said. "But you know, that younger fella, what's his name?"

"Daniel?" I said.

"Yep, that's him. He pussyfoots around the place, too."

"Do you think they both are up to something?" Sissy

asked. "We should make Beau aware if they're not doing their jobs."

"Oh, they're fine. Momma is just used to having everyone wait on her hand and foot." Jasper laughed, but there was a strained undertone to his voice. "But honestly, they've been very kind, considering the circumstances."

"Yes, your friend, the owner, has been especially thoughtful," Charlene agreed.

"He'll be glad to hear it," Sissy said. "Now, Mrs. St. Martin, sorry, Charlene, tell me about you. Are you from Mississippi originally?"

Sissy nudged my foot as Charlene began telling her life story, starting from her birth at the Huntley Community Hospital. I took this as my hint to go snoop in Scarlett's room. After gulping down my glass of wine, I whispered to Jasper, "May I use your restroom?"

"Sure, I'll show you," he answered, but I was already up and headed toward the bathroom.

"No need to." I smiled as I rushed off.

There were only two bedrooms in the suite, and it was easy to see who was staying where. Charlene's potent citrus perfume wafted out of the master bedroom. Two over-flowing suitcases laid in front of the king-size bed. I opened the door to the other bedroom and by the clothes draped over the white duvet cover on the queen-size bed; I knew this was Scarlett's room. Where did Jasper sleep? He must be on the lumpy couch in the living room, poor guy.

Scarlett's belongings were scattered around the room in a haphazard manner. Her nightstand had six bottles of red nail polish and a half-empty water bottle. An assortment of her tiny skirts and low-cut blouses were heaped on top of the chair that went with the vanity table. More make-up, along with a framed picture of a man with a little girl, covered the dresser.

I picked up the frame and read the handwriting below the image, *Scarlett and her Daddy on the farm.* My uncle had been handsome in a rugged way. His brown hair was shaggy, but his jeans and red t-shirt were clean. With a lanky arm around Scarlett, Preston smiled directly at the camera. A toddler-aged Scarlett, in a smocked green gingham dress and white cowboy boots, gazed at her father.

Preston looked happy and confident, but I noted an intensity in his eyes that scared me. Was I just seeing things because I knew he had blackmailed my adoptive parents and that my brother claimed he mistreated him? And did my birth father look like him? Scarlett loved her father enough to bring a framed photo of him when she left home.

I put the picture back down quickly; I couldn't get distracted by images of the past. I needed to find anything that would tell me what Scarlett had been up to in the present. The police would have taken anything obvious, but I hoped I could find something they overlooked.

Starting with the bed, I lifted the mattress up at each side, sliding my hand underneath, hoping to find a secret diary. Nothing. Same for the nightstand and the dresser drawers. I checked under the bed and even lifted the floral print rug that covered the wide-planked wooden floor.

I didn't find any clues, and I learned little about Scarlett. From her belongings, I concluded she liked expensive brands of make-up, but her clothes were a mix of high-end and low-end brands. Not one pair of shoes had less than a two-inch heel. She didn't have any books in the room unless the police took them away. But I doubted that. The only personal item was that photo.

The bedroom door was slightly open, so I listened to them in the living room. Sissy's voice filled the moments when Charlene stopped talking. Jasper added in a word here and there, but Charlene dominated the conversation. Sissy could write Charlene's biography after tonight. Poor Jasper probably knew these stories by heart; his mother sure did like to talk.

I needed to get back before they got suspicious, so I took another look in the closet. After searching the pockets of each pair of jeans and even the pocket of the hotel-supplied bathrobe, I closed the door. I jumped as I turned around to find Jasper standing in the bedroom doorway.

"I think I have what you're looking for."

20

"Jasper, you scared me!" I smiled, but it didn't hide my flushed face. "I was just..." My words trailed off. There was no legitimate reason for me to be in his dead sister's room.

He closed the bedroom door and handed me a large manila envelope. "I found this in her suitcase and hid it in mine before we left with the police. When the cops showed up, I assumed it wouldn't be good news."

I took the envelope from him and sat on the bed. "You knew where her hiding place was?"

"When Scarlett's your sister, you learn to hide anything you don't want her to see." He sighed. "She read my entire journal to our church youth group one summer. I retaliated by doing the same to her."

Growing up as an only child, I couldn't imagine having my privacy invaded by someone, especially not your sibling. "But you could still find her stuff."

"Oh, we both got better at hiding things, but Scarlett was pretty transparent." His laugh was sad, not malicious. "She fussed over that suitcase more than usual, so I checked it first. She hid the envelope in the lining, underneath loads of underwear."

I paged through the sheets of papers from the envelope. They were weekly reports from a private investigator starting the month after my brother left Huntley until last week. The investigator followed rumors and sightings of Joey that matched the postcards he sent me, but the investigator hadn't found him in person. In the last letter, the investigator asked Scarlett if she wanted to continue. If so, he needed to be paid.

"So she kept her search for my brother a secret?" I asked. "I wonder why?"

"Scarlett always did everything on her own. She wasn't the sharing type."

"But what did she want with him?"

"Revenge is my guess." Jasper looked away when he spoke. I bet there was more to the story than he was sharing. But he started talking before I could question him.

"Have you seen your brother since he left? Or heard from him?"

I stuffed the papers inside the envelope to give myself time to answer. Should I trust Jasper? I took a leap of faith. "He's sent me postcards, and they line up with the cities where the investigator says Joey, sorry, Samuel, was spotted."

"You can call him Joey." Jasper took the envelope from my hands and put it on the bed behind us. "You knew him as Joey more than Samuel. Do you remember anything about him before the hurricane?"

I shook my head. "Not really. I wish I did. I bet he was a kinder person then."

"He was a sweet kid before the storm took everyone away. And before he moved in with us." His shoulders sagged, and he rubbed his scar.

"No offense, but your father was a horrible man."

He sat up straight and looked me dead in the eyes. "You don't know the half of it. But Scarlett didn't see our father the same way. She was as bad as him sometimes."

"Does her hiring a PI have something to do with your father? Why was she so eager to find my brother? And why was she so insistent that she have the mausoleum key?"

Jasper's mouth opened and closed as if he couldn't decide if he should answer me. It took all my patience not to tell him to talk.

"Sammy, it's like this..."

"There you are!" Charlene burst into the room with a smile plastered on her face, but her eyes darted back and forth from me to Jasper. "Oh, how sweet to see y'all together. Jasper must be telling you all about his sister."

Sissy mouthed, "I'm sorry" behind Charlene's back. I was the one who should have said sorry; I'd left Sissy alone with my aunt too long.

"Yes, we're just catching up." Jasper stood up and put his hands on his mother's shoulders. "Let's go back to the sitting area and have a drink."

"A good idea." I put my hands behind me as if I needed to push myself up from the bed. Instead, I pushed the clothes, hoping they covered the envelope. "I'm sure you have other stories about Scarlett."

Instead of turning around, Charlene came over to the bed and reached behind me. Jasper stiffened as his mother's hand hovered over the fuchsia blouse that covered all but a corner of the envelope. I waited for Charlene to grab it and grill Jasper and me about it.

She didn't. Instead, Charlene moved the fuchsia blouse, so it was completely over the envelope, and turned back to me.

"You should have something of Scarlett's." Charlene looked me up and down. "Well, not the clothes, but perhaps a pair of shoes."

I bit the inside of my cheek so I wouldn't defend my physique, as I suspected Charlene wouldn't care. "That's sweet of you, but I'm fine. I'm sure her friends would be a better fit for them."

Charlene put a green and gold scarf around my neck. "You should take this scarf at least. But you're right, Scarlett has so many friends, and they would love to have some of her beautiful things as mementos."

The cheap polyester scarf was itchy, but I kept it on so as not to offend Charlene. Her stack of bracelets hit my hand as she grabbed me to lead me out of the room. Jasper poured the remaining wine into our cups. Sissy and I huddled on the couch together and listened to Charlene talk... and talk... and talk.

"... so I told my husband, 'Preston, that's not a cat, that's a possum!' We laughed and laughed. Right, Jasper?"

"I don't recall it that way..." Jasper stammered.

"Oh, you just forgot!" Charlene stuck her cup in Jasper's face. "Pour me more wine and I'll explain..."

"Momma..."

"I'm sorry, but Sammy and I need to go." Sissy looked at her cell phone and stood up, pulling me up with her. "We're meeting my fiancé."

"Your fiancé?" Charlene asked in a voice that was an octave or three higher than normal. "Has he solved my baby's murder?"

"I don't think so," Sissy said. "He'll call you as soon as he has any information, I'm sure."

"And make sure if you think of anything, anything that might help him, you tell him," I said directly to Jasper.

Charlene looked at Jasper and me, but before she spoke, Jasper said, "We'll do that, I promise."

"Yes, we want to help." Charlene tried to push herself off her chair, but she fell back. "Oh, my, I am so tired. I'll rest here while Jasper walks you out."

As Jasper opened the door, Charlene called out, "Sarah Jane, sorry, I mean Sammy. Since you have the key, can you take us to the mausoleum?" Charlene asked.

"We don't need the key to go pay our respects." Jasper stared at his mother while he rubbed his crescent moon scar.

"You'll think I'm crazy, but I need to make sure everything is OK before we put my sweet Scarlett in her final resting place." Her eyes watered as she reached into her dress pocket for a crumpled tissue. She dabbed her eyes. "I want everything perfect for her."

"Momma..." Jasper slumped against the door and shook his head.

"I'm happy to take you there." I said. "We can go tomorrow after I finish work, about five."

"Isn't the cemetery closed at night?" Charlene said.

"My friend is a security guard there, so I'll call him to see if he can let us in," I replied. "If not, I'll change my schedule at work. I'm sure Andrew will understand."

"Thank you, darling." Charlene waved goodbye and then reached for the bottle of wine. "Jasper, grab another bottle and..."

We didn't hear the rest of her demands as Jasper shut the door quickly behind us. "Sorry about Momma. She's a little demanding."

"Well, it's my turn to be demanding." I grabbed Jasper's arm. "Why was your sister trying to find my brother?"

"Scarlett was trying to find Joey? Sorry, I mean Samuel.

Oh, you know who I mean," Sissy said. "I thought she didn't care about him."

"She hired a private eye to find him." I let go of Jasper's arm, but glared at him. "I don't think she did it because she had any family affection for him."

"No, she didn't like him." Jasper walked to the Joan of Arc fountain, so Sissy and I followed. "She wanted to find him for..."

Jasper didn't get to finish his sentence since someone who was much chattier than him joined us.

21

"Hi, Jasper. Hi, Sammy," Daniel said. "I hope you're having a nice evening."

"Yes, thanks," I said. "Just catching up."

"It's good to see you both together after the drowning. No hard feelings then?" Daniel said.

"What do you mean?" Jasper took a step closer to Daniel. "Why would either of us have hard feelings? My sister's murder had nothing to do with me or my cousin."

"I'm sorry. That came out all wrong." Daniel stood his ground, but his face had paled. "Tragedy can tear families apart, but obviously that's not the case with you two."

"OK," Jasper said, but from his tone, I don't think he really meant it.

"My apologies. Now let me fix my second faux pas of not introducing myself to your other guest." Daniel reached out his hand to Sissy. "I'm Daniel Lane, the night manager of the hotel."

Sissy shook his hand. "I'm Sissy Covington. It's a pretty place here."

"I agree." Daniel's eyes lit up as he looked around the courtyard.

"Well, I'll say goodnight here. Momma must be waiting for me." Jasper replied. "Sammy, call me about the cemetery tomorrow. Bye."

Jasper rushed off before I could protest. As much as I wanted to chase him down and ask more questions, I didn't. Sissy's imploring look and her gentle grasp of my hand made me stay put. She had to be just as curious as I was about what Jasper knew, but she stopped me for a reason. My tense body and elevated breathing gave away my frustration and lack of patience, and even I had to admit I wasn't in the best state of mind to talk to my cousin.

"Poor guy. His mother calls for him almost as much as mine." Daniel took out his ringing cell phone and stared at the screen. After stroking his beard with one hand, he put his phone away. "Well, almost."

We followed Daniel to the main building. He chatted away with Sissy as they discovered they both went to Louisiana State University (LSU), although Daniel graduated five years after she did.

"What made you pick LSU? You aren't from Louisiana," Sissy said.

"How did you know?" Daniel asked. "You're right, I'm from North Carolina."

"Your Southern accent is pretty good, but you slip now and then." Sissy laughed. "I bet those years at college helped your accent."

"And my mother." Daniel smiled. "She's from Louisiana originally, and her accent is strong. I thought having a Southern accent would help in the hospitality industry here. Northerners find it charming and Southerners feel at home."

"Well, your accent is better than mine." I laughed. "I think it might take me a while to get one."

Daniel pulled his ringing cell phone out of the pocket of his beige pants and sighed. "Speaking of mothers, mine is calling again. I hope I'll see y'all again soon."

We left the hotel, but not before we heard Daniel talking with his mother. "Yes, Momma, I'm working hard. I promise. Yes, Momma."

"His mother sounds like Charlene." Sissy giggled as we stood outside the hotel.

"Did you need to meet Rob?"

"What? Oh, no I said that to escape," Sissy said. "Your aunt would talk for days if you let her."

"Thanks for saving us."

"That's my job, but now fill me in! What did you find in Scarlett's room? What did Jasper tell you?"

"Not enough." I sighed. "First Charlene interrupted, then Daniel kept me from interrogating Jasper."

"Sounds like you'll see him tomorrow at the cemetery. What's with your aunt asking you to bring the key?"

"I was going to ask you if there was some strange Southern tradition I didn't know about. Please don't tell me the family cleans inside the tomb for the burial?"

"Not that I know of." Sissy shuddered. "Your tomb is different since you have a key to open it. To get into my family's mausoleum, they have to take off the marble nameplate to bury the body."

"I wish mine was like that; my brother couldn't have put me inside then."

"Oh, honey, that's an awful memory." Sissy hugged me. "Are you sure you want to go with them? I'm sure they could go by themselves."

"I'll be OK." I wiped a stray tear. While I didn't want to

visit the cemetery with them, I needed to find out what Charlene was up to. And I would make Jasper tell me why Scarlett wanted to locate my brother. I had the key to the tomb, and I wasn't giving it up without answers.

"How about a drink at my place? You can tell me what Jasper said and we'll flip through the stacks of brides' magazines my mother sent over."

"And so it begins." I laughed. "Your mother must be beside herself to get to plan a wedding."

"You have no idea. But first I have to find a place for Rob to live or we're going to share my apartment."

"I totally forgot about that." Rob's rental home was up for sale, and he didn't want to buy it because of all the problems with it. I kept a smile on my face, but inside I was frowning. Sissy's engagement meant she would probably move out of Thibodeaux Mansion, as her one-bedroom apartment didn't seem like the ideal newlywed home. What if she moved out of town?

"Don't worry, I'm not moving away," she said, as if she read my mind. "Rob and I will stay around for a long, long time. I'm not leaving you."

I was about to protest that I wasn't worrying when we were interrupted by a man in a teal suit with a blinding smile. He waved to us from the doorstep of the building to the right of the hotel. "Hello, there, beautiful creatures! You're going the wrong way!"

"Sammy, you're about to take part in a rite of passage in New Orleans — meeting Gideon Pearce," Sissy said.

"What do you mean?" I asked. "He looks like any other older eccentric French Quarter gentleman." Actually, he looked a bit like Mark Twain, with his bushy white hair and mustache. But his tight teal suit with the day-glow pink pocket square made it seem as if he was trying to look thirty years younger than he was.

"Just you wait." Sissy grinned.

"Are you here for the party? You must be art lovers." He trotted over to us. "The name is Gideon Pearce, and I'm hosting the show for renowned artist Cherry C."

"No, we were visiting at the hotel," Sissy said. "Have a splendid party."

"Oh, but you're more than welcome to come." Gideon didn't hide the fact he was looking us both up and down. "I can tell you all about New Orleans."

"We live here and we're on our way home." I took a step backward. And so did Sissy. Overly friendly people aren't uncommon in the neighborhood, but his overbearing manner was off-putting.

"How have I missed you two scrumptious ladies here in the Quarter?" His voice was as smooth as his shiny suit. "Lucky for me you left the hotel when I was here."

"Yes, lucky for you," Sissy said in the fake sweet tone she used when someone annoyed her.

"I like you." Gideon laughed, either oblivious or ignoring her condescending tone. "Please come to the party. You'll want a drink after being in there." He cocked his head toward Hotel Jeanne and grimaced.

"There's nothing wrong with the hotel," I snapped. "It's a beautiful place."

"Now, hold on. I didn't mean to upset you. Redheads do have tempers, don't they?"

I glared at him and turned to walk away.

"Don't go! I think the hotel is charming, too. In fact, I tried to buy it," Gideon said.

"That's right. Beau outbid you, didn't he?" I said.

"You know him?" Gideon's shoulders slumped.

"Yes, he's our good friend," Sissy said. "Beau will do wonders for the place."

"If you say so, but I could do better with it." Gideon puffed his chest out and winked. "I'm better at everything. For instance, I would get you a bigger ring than that, my dear."

Sissy's beautiful engagement ring was nothing to sneeze about, but before I could defend my friend, and her fiancé's choice in rings, she did it herself.

"Fortunately, for my future husband, I care more about substance than flash," Sissy said. "You know what I mean, don't you?"

"Gideon! Leave those women be and get in here! Cherry is having a conniption!" A young woman wearing a black jumpsuit and a look of frustration popped her head around Gideon's door. "She wants to move all the furniture out of the room so it doesn't distract from her art."

Sissy didn't hide her amusement as she laughed. "Gideon, I think you've got your hands full."

"I better get inside, but y'all are welcome to join us. It's not just an art show. We're donating the proceeds of a painting to charity."

"Well, then we hope you'll have a great turnout." Sissy's voice was sincere. But I couldn't help but wonder if Gideon made that up to persuade us to come inside.

He took a step toward his house, but then stopped. "One last thing, ladies. Tell your friend Beau Boudreaux that running a hotel isn't that easy." Gideon lowered his voice. "Between the ghosts and a modern murder, it might be more than he can handle. I'm happy to take it off his hands."

He winked at Sissy. "Same goes to your fiancé."

"Gideon, get in here now before she throws your furniture in the pool!" the young woman shouted.

"I must save my furniture!" Gideon yelled as he rushed back to his door. "I hope you change your minds!"

"Not on his life." I shook my head. "What a piece of work. So, everyone goes through this when they meet Gideon?"

"Oh, yes, he doesn't remember, but I met him at a fundraiser at the hospital two years ago. He drank so much that security had to carry him out." Sissy laughed. "But he donated a ton of money that night. Actually, he donates to a lot of charities."

"I wouldn't have expected that."

"His boorish behavior is tolerated since he does some good with his big old trust fund," Sissy said. "Yes, he's obnoxious to say the least, but I've dealt with worse."

"You're more gracious about him than I would have been," I said. "Even an engagement ring didn't stop him."

"I doubt anything stops him when he wants something."

Did that also apply to the hotel? What would Gideon do to get it?

22

———————

"Sammy, darling, be careful!"

I looked over my shoulder at Beau standing below me. "Beau, I'm fine!" He stepped away as I climbed down the wooden ladder with three books in my arms. "The ladder is sturdy. It's attached to the shelves and slides to each one easily."

Beau and I were to meet at ten o'clock, but once again I couldn't sleep. After a quick jog around the neighborhood, a hot shower, and a long stare at my phone, I came to Hotel Jeanne instead of replying to Connor's earlier text. Starting on the library organization appealed to me more than wondering what his message *we need to talk* really meant.

I'd arrived at the hotel at nine and headed straight to the library. Ambrose was busy with guests, so I snuck past the reception area. The dim lighting and dusty shelves didn't keep me from exploring the room. I ran my hand over the beautiful mahogany shelves. They extended from floor to ceiling and fit the wall perfectly. A talented artisan must have made these bookcases just for this space. With a bit of polishing, these shelves would shine like new. First, I needed to organize the books and judging by the layers of dust, no one had touched them in years.

"I'm not sure about that old ladder. Let me have Ambrose find a proper one for you. Ambrose!"

"No, it's fine. I can reach all the books. I'll bring them down when I want to inspect them."

"Did you call for me, Mr. Boudreaux?" Ambrose came into the library.

"Yes, can you get a regular ladder for Sammy to use in here?"

"An industrial ladder? Inside the hotel?" Ambrose's face puckered. "Is that necessary?"

"No, it's not." I put the books down on the small table in between two armchairs. Ambrose's face relaxed. "The library ladder works fine."

"Good. A regular ladder inside the library while guests are coming in and out would be unsightly," Ambrose's face puckered again.

"But safety is more important." Beau went over to the ladder and put his hands on each rung. "I guess this is tough enough."

"I'll make a note in the manager's notebook to monitor the ladder," Ambrose said.

"Shelby, did you need something?" Ambrose asked Shelby, who stood in the library doorway. She looked like any other hotel housekeeper, except for her pierced ears. With her henna-dyed hair in a loose ponytail, I could see she had four earrings on each ear. I flinched when I got my ears pierced with only one hole in each ear, so I couldn't imagine sitting through it that many times.

"No, Mr. Fortner, I was just curious about what was going on. Hi, Mr. Boudreaux. Hi, Sammy." Shelby said.

"Hello, Shelby, call me Beau, please. I'm glad you're here.

I want your opinion on the laundry detergent. It seems rough."

"Um, sure, Mr. Boudreaux. Sorry, Beau." Shelby blushed. "But I'm only a part-time housekeeper, don't you want to ask Mrs. Wright?"

"I have asked her, but I'd also like your views. Do you have a moment? Great, come with me." Beau led a stunned Shelby out of the room.

Ambrose's posture stiffened, more than usual, as he watched them leave.

"Beau likes to include everyone in his businesses," I said. "My guess is most owners don't ask the housekeeper for her opinion."

Ambrose straightened his tie and cleared his throat. "Yes, you are correct. Mr. Boudreaux is the first owner I've worked with who is this hands on."

"You've been at the hotel a while?"

For the first time, I saw a genuine smile from Ambrose. He took a good five minutes telling me his history with the hotel. Starting as a desk clerk twenty years ago, he worked his way to assistant manager and then the last owner made him the general manager.

"I had hoped to become the owner of Hotel Jeanne, but that dream died," he said.

Ambrose's sad declaration explained some, if not all, of his animosity toward Beau.

"Oh, I'm sorry. It's difficult to lose your dream."

"Well, yes, for now it's out of my hands." Ambrose brushed the invisible dirt off his jacket. The sadness in his eyes made me change the subject.

"Since you've been here so long, can you tell me about the ghosts in the hotel? Have you seen any?"

Not only was I getting a smile today, Ambrose offered a

rolling laugh. "Ghost stories are just marketing tools, but that's just what they are — stories."

"So you haven't met the Abernathy sisters at the pool?"

"Sorry, but the answer is no. Not that I believe in ghosts. There is always an explanation for supposed sightings."

"I've heard that there are noises at night. Any idea what causes them?"

"No, but I will get to the bottom of it. I don't like loose ends, especially in my hotel." Ambrose gave a nod and left the room.

Ambrose didn't own the hotel, but he sure acted as if he did. Was his dedication going to be an asset or a hinderance to Beau? My friend needed to watch his manager.

I spent the morning coming up with a game plan for the library. With six bookcases, there were hundreds of books to go through. Off the bat, I could tell that some of them were mass market paperbacks that wouldn't have value, monetary or historical. A set of encyclopedia made me smile, as I hadn't seen a set since elementary school.

As tempted as I was to pull down the older looking books on the top shelves, I stopped myself. I wanted gloves before I started going through these books. And I needed cleaning supplies as a layer of dust covered everything. It was such a shame, as the woodwork was beautiful.

On one shelf, the books jutted out just a hair more than the others. I put my hand on the back of the shelf to find a raised daisy pattern there. I moved the ladder to the other shelves to check for this same pattern, but it wasn't there. A sneezing fit made me climb down, and I decided to wait until I had cleaning materials to go back to the odd shelf.

I sat at the small desk, which was empty on top and had hotel stationery and pens in the lone drawer. While the wood matched the shelves, I was positive the bookshelves' carpenter did not make the desk. It didn't have the same level of detail or craftsmanship as the shelves. I made a note to ask Beau if there was any of the original furniture from the library elsewhere in the building.

I jotted down a list of supplies I needed before I headed back to Lagniappe Books to go over my ideas for the library with Andrew. Beau wanted to know if any of the books were valuable, so he could decide whether to sell them or display them. And much to Ambrose's surprise, Beau agreed that the library should be a relaxing reading room, as Ambrose suggested. A clunky copy machine and rows of utilitarian computers invading the hotel horrified Beau, too. While Beau hoped this would be a good step in his relationship with Ambrose, so far there had been no change.

"Sammy, hey, what are you doing here?" I looked up from the desk to find Jasper standing in the doorway.

"Hi. I'm going through the books." I smiled. "The library hasn't been inventoried for a while, if ever."

"Cool. Looks like you're busy."

"I'm just getting started. But how are you? How's your mother?"

"As good as she can be. She's hoping we can go to the cemetery today. Did you have time to call your friend?"

"Yes, sorry, I meant to text you, but I got wrapped up in the books," I said. "Mr. Hugo will let us in after five. Does that work?"

"That's great." I heard apprehension in his voice. "Um, about last night, the reports from the private investigator. Do you think I should give them to the police?"

"Yes. While it might mean nothing, they should have

them," I said. "I'm glad you asked because I was going to mention it tonight."

Sissy and I talked about the reports last night. We both agreed that Rob and Christine should be told about them. I wanted to give Jasper a chance to hand them in on his own. It would be better for me if he did it, so it wouldn't look like I was just trying to clear my name. Although if the reports made my brother a suspect, I wouldn't be that upset. I wasn't a murderer, but we all knew he was one.

"OK, I'll take them by when Momma takes her daily siesta as she calls it." Jasper didn't sound happy, but he seemed resigned that he needed to do it. "It'll be quicker if I go by myself."

"Did you mother know Scarlett hired a private investigator?"

"I doubt it, but I haven't told her yet."

By the fleeting glance and the movement of the blouse over the envelope, I suspected Charlene was aware of Scarlett's search for my brother. But what would she think about Jasper giving it over to the police?

"Rob and Christine will be glad you're turning it over, but be ready for a reprimand." I warned Jasper, but he was prepared.

"I expect a good verbal thrashing. I'm used to them." His face turned red, and I guessed he didn't mean to say that last part out loud.

"Don't worry, they're actually kind people. And they'll offer you coffee from Cafe Beignet, which is fantastic." I hoped my words were making him feel better. "Just be honest with them and you'll be fine, really."

"It might be worth it if I get beignets." Jasper grinned. "I love them."

"Me, too, although pralines are my favorite treat."

"I'll remember that."

Jasper smiled just like my brother, and the memory of Joey bringing pralines made me shut my eyes so I wouldn't cry. There was a kindness they both had, but also a sadness that lived deep within. I opened my eyes quickly and grinned, hoping my sorrow wasn't obvious.

"We'll have to get some. Maybe after the cemetery," I said. "Can you and your mother meet me at Lagniappe Books around 4:45? I need to work at the shop before we go."

"We'll see you there. Thanks again, Sammy."

He left the library, but my memories of my brother didn't leave with him. Joey and Jasper shared many wonderful qualities. I just hoped Jasper didn't have Joey's bad ones — like being a murderer.

23

Before I left for the bookstore, I wanted to tell Beau and Ambrose I was heading out for the day. I ran into Shelby, coming down the stairs with an empty box.

"Hi, Shelby. Busy day?"

"Hey, Sammy." Shelby put the carton on the ground and wiped her hands on the white apron of her uniform. "No, it's actually slow, which is fine by me. I needed to restock our supplies upstairs. You can't imagine how many soaps and shampoos we go through."

"Oh, I bet it's a lot." I laughed, remembering how my first college roommate only bathed with hotel toiletries her mother collected for her. "How was your chat with Beau?"

"Great! He's so different from any of my other bosses." She lowered her voice. "And he's the complete opposite of Ambrose. I'm not even sure Ambrose remembers my name half the time."

"Beau cares about people and means what he says," I replied. "Ambrose is, well, more formal than Beau."

"That's putting it mildly." She grinned and took a step

closer. "Ambrose acts like he owns the hotel, but Daniel does, too. He's just more *friendly*."

"What do you mean friendly? Like inappropriately friendly?"

Shelby laughed. "Ew, no! I mean, Daniel chats you up whenever he sees you. He asks everything about your day, and he has tons of questions about the neighborhood."

"OK, but you know to tell Beau if anyone makes you uncomfortable, right?"

"I can take care of myself, but thanks for the concern." Shelby smiled, so I must not have offended her. At eighteen, I wasn't as self-assured as she appeared. I might not be at thirty either.

"Well, I better run. Time to go back to the bookstore."

"Me, too. I need another box of soap. See you around!" Shelby walked down the hallway toward the courtyard door. I recalled seeing the door marked housekeeping by the pool. The staff must get a workout going from building to building.

I entered the reception area to find the desk empty. The office door was ajar, so I went over to say goodbye to Ambrose or Beau, or whoever was inside. I pulled my hand back from the doorknob when I heard Ambrose say, "No! It is not working out like we expected."

I waited for a response, but it was quiet. Ambrose must be on the phone.

He spoke again. "Fine, we can talk later about this. Goodbye."

He could have been talking to Beau, but I doubted it. Even if he was giving his notice, I doubted he'd speak so angrily. His professionalism seemed to be engrained in his personality. And when Beau entered the reception area, my hunch was confirmed.

"Sammy, darling, there you are!" Beau said, louder than I would have liked. I didn't want Ambrose to know I overheard him, but no luck. Ambrose opened the office door and almost ran into me.

"Samantha, did you need something? I was on the phone, but I am at your assistance now." Ambrose's voice returned to normal, but I caught a flash of anger in his eyes. Was it residual anger from his phone call, or did he realize I was snooping?

"I wanted to let you and Beau know I was leaving for the day. I'm working on a plan to catalog and organize the books."

"That's wonderful. I can't wait to have the library as a great place for our guests like Ambrose suggested," Beau said. "Ambrose, make sure you tell Sammy if there's anything particular you think needs to be done."

"Of course, Mr. Boudreaux." He bowed slightly at both of us. "If you'll excuse me, I have some reservations I need to attend to."

Beau put his arm around me and led me out of the hotel. Once outside, he asked, "OK, what was that about? Ambrose was stiffer than usual."

I opened my backpack and took out my sunglasses. "He must have realized I heard him on the phone." I told Beau what I overheard.

"Isn't that interesting?" Beau tapped a finger against his nose. "I'm going to be nosy over the next few days and find out what he's up to."

"Maybe it's nothing." I regretted telling Beau, as I could see how agitated he was at my revelation. "Anyone who is that uptight needs to vent sometimes, right?"

"You're trying to make me feel better, aren't you?" Beau said. "Let's just watch him, but now let's grab coffee and head back to the bookshop. We can play detective tomorrow."

I agreed about getting coffee, although I had put playing detective on my agenda for later that night. But for the moment, a cafe au lait was the only thing on my mind.

24

We arrived at Lagniappe Books, and Andrew welcomed us and the coffee with open arms.

"It's like you read my mind." Andrew took a sip of his cafe au lait. "It's been crazy today. A gaggle of tourists from Omaha rushed through the door when I opened. I spent most of my morning working with them."

"I bet you sold every one of them at least two books." I looked at the empty spots on all the shelves.

"Yes, I did as a matter of fact." Andrew smiled. "And then I handed them over to Neal. He is taking them on a tour with a special emphasis on French Quarter architecture. Turns out they're here for a construction convention."

"Your day sounds more productive than mine." Beau sat down on the loveseat in the back. "Shelby, the sweet house-keeper, was the most helpful person today. Besides Sammy, of course."

Andrew joined him, and they filled each other in on their day. I restocked the shelves, answered emails, and helped more conventioneers. The earlier group had spread the word about Lagniappe Books, and our New Orleans architecture books were selling in droves.

"I must run. No rest for the wicked." Beau stood by the front door. "Sammy, I'll see you tomorrow at the hotel?"

"I'll be there with gloves and dust rags," I said. "Hopefully we'll find some treasures."

"Fingers crossed!" Beau blew a kiss and headed out of the shop.

"He's so worried about the hotel," Andrew said once the door closed. "He's having a hard time connecting with Ambrose and Daniel."

"I don't think it's a problem on his part." I explained about Ambrose's desire to own the hotel and the conversation I overheard. I also told him about Shelby's opinion that Daniel acted like he owned the hotel, too.

"He has his hands full, but he's purchased other businesses where he's had to deal with disgruntled employees." Andrew said. "Running a hotel is more complicated than he expected."

"That's why I like book shops. We only deal with each other and a few crazy customers."

"I agree, except we have an annoying vendor who won't stop calling about a line of Voodoo dolls he insists will sell well here." Andrew cringed. "I am happy we carry religion books, but I draw the line at Voodoo accessories, especially ones not made in New Orleans. That's just disrespectful."

"And you don't want to compete with Papa, do you? Or are you afraid he'll put a curse on you?" I laughed.

Papa Gede was Andrew's friend, and after solving two murders together, he became mine. He owned a Voodoo shop, and was a historian of the religion and its most famous practitioner, Marie Laveau. While he could put on a show for the tourists, Papa's serious devotion to Voodoo was second to none.

"I'm not worried about Papa. He likes me almost as much as you," Andrew said.

"Ha, Ruby is his favorite. She likes an actual person and not just ghosts."

"They do have a connection, don't they? But let's not talk about them or ghosts," Andrew said. "We need to concentrate on the land of the living and talk about the newsletter for this week."

"There goes my idea for a ghost story themed newsletter." I pretended to pout. "You're no fun."

"We have different ideas of fun, my dear." Andrew raised his eyebrows at me and gestured for me to follow him to the seating area. "Stop pouting and grab your laptop. We have work to do."

It was good to focus on the bookstore instead of the library. I even forgot about my evening trip to the cemetery until Charlene threw open the shop door.

"Sarah Jane, it's your Aunt Charlene!" She called out. But I'd recognize that perky Southern drawl anywhere. And no one else called me Sarah Jane.

"Momma, it's Samantha." Jasper sighed. "Hey, there. We're a bit early, but I wanted to see the store."

"Come on in," I said. "You remember Andrew."

"Hello, sir." Jasper shook Andrew's hand. "What a great place. I can see why Sammy loves working here."

"Thank you. I'm glad to hear Samantha enjoys her job." Andrew smiled. "Especially since she'll be my partner soon."

"Partner?" Charlene's voice rose an octave. "Aren't you dating that Connor boy, Sarah Jane?"

"Business partner, I assure you." Andrew put his arm

around me. "And good friends. Actually I consider Samantha my family."

"Well, now, we're her family, you know." Charlene smiled slightly. "But it's sweet y'all are so close — platonically, that is."

"Yes, she's all Connor's on the romantic front." Andrew squeezed me before he took his arm off my shoulders. "I understand Samantha is taking you to St. Louis Cemetery. Are you interested in graveyards or history?"

Charlene pulled a tissue out of her bag and dabbed her eyes. "Not particularly. I just want to see if the mausoleum is in good enough shape to bury my baby girl."

"Of course." Andrew said. "Have you been there since your husband passed away?"

"My father is buried in Huntley, not New Orleans." Jasper said.

"Oh?" Andrew said. "Since it's the family tomb, I assumed he was interred there."

"I hate to say it, but my nephew took the key before we could bury my beloved husband." Charlene let out a sob, but there were no tears.

"Momma, it wasn't the missing key that kept you from burying Dad here." Jasper glared at his mother. "You wanted him in your family plot."

"Well now, it all worked out, didn't it?" Charlene stuffed her tissue in her purse. "Grief can be so overwhelming. You just do the best that you can. I am doing my best, Jasper."

Jasper looked down at the floor and said, "I know, Momma."

Feeling like I was in the middle of a family therapy session, I didn't care that I was obviously changing the subject. "So, what kind of books do y'all like?"

"It would be my honor to show you around, Mrs. St. Martin," Andrew said.

"How lovely," Charlene said. "Jasper, why don't you have your cousin show you around?"

"I would love to." I stood by Jasper, who smiled at me. "What do you say, Jasper?"

"Sounds good," he said. His body relaxed when his mother smiled at him. "Momma and I both do love to read."

"Now tell me, what type of books do you enjoy?" Andrew asked Charlene.

"Do you sell any romance books?" Charlene lowered her voice. "Not the smutty kind, but actual romance?"

"Yes, I do, let me show you." Andrew offered his arm to Charlene, who giggled. She went with him to the romance section, where Andrew would find the right books for her. He had a knack for picking the perfect book for everyone who came in. I was getting better at it, but nowhere near Andrew's level.

"It's good to see Momma smile," Jasper said, watching his mother chat with Andrew. "Scarlett's death is killing her inside."

"It's got to be hard on you, too."

He nodded and then headed to the history section. "There are a ton of books just on New Orleans history."

"It's Andrew's specialty. He knows everything about the city's history. He's even teaching a class at Tulane this semester."

"Wow, I'd love to take it. History was my favorite subject in school." He took a book off the shelf and leafed through it.

"Did you study it at college? What do you do? I never asked you about your job."

"No college for me." He closed the book and put it back

on the shelf. "I wanted to, but my father said he needed me on the farm. But eventually he didn't, so I've been a bartender, construction worker, and office temp."

"You're a jack of all trades, then. Nothing wrong with that. I'm on my second career here with Andrew and the shop. You have plenty of time to find a job you like."

He smiled, but the sadness in his eyes broke my heart. Now that his father and sister were gone, would he be able to do what he wanted? Charlene appeared dependent on her children, and now that Scarlett was dead, would Jasper feel responsible for his mother? From the dejection in his eyes, he seemed to believe that.

I grabbed the book that he had looked through and handed it back to him. "Take this as a gift from me. Think of it as the start of your formal history education until you go to school. If that's the path you decide to take."

"Thanks. Maybe I'll make a change." He took the book, but I don't think he believed what he said. I wished I had the right words to say, but I really didn't know what his situation was at home. Standing in a bookshop with his mother within earshot wasn't the best place to have a heart-to-heart talk about his future.

As much as I wanted to ask Jasper about Scarlett's investigation, I didn't have the chance. Even though Andrew had Charlene completely engaged, she seemed to sense when I was going to ask about Scarlett. She turned her head every time I tried to broach the topic with Jasper. It must have been a coincidence, unless she was psychic. Or was I just paranoid?

Andrew found the perfect books for Charlene and charmed her so much that she was laughing by the time they came to the seating area where I left Jasper reading the history book. I waited on customers while the three of them talked. By the time I finished, Andrew had won Jasper over, too.

"You should leave now so you can have a leisurely walk through the Quarter," Andrew said when I joined them.

"Let us pay for our books before we go." Jasper stood up and took out a brown leather wallet.

"No, these are a gift." Andrew waved off Jasper's credit card. "It's been a pleasure getting to know Samantha's family."

"You are just the sweetest." Charlene gave a surprised Andrew a hug. "I'm so happy to have these books to read. It will help take my mind off the horrors of this week for a little while."

Jasper shook Andrew's hand. "Thanks, Andrew. We appreciate your kindness."

I kissed Andrew on the cheek before following Charlene and Jasper out of the store. "You know you're my family, don't you?"

"Yes, but that doesn't mean they can't be your family, too." Andrew squeezed my hand. "But keep an eye on your aunt. She's a little too interested in your tomb."

I agreed, and as we walked through the busy streets of the French Quarter, Charlene peppered me with questions about the mausoleum. What in the world was it about the St. Martin tomb Charlene was interested in?

"Hello, Sammy. I'm sorry to see you here under these circumstances."

"Thanks, Mr. Hugo. We appreciate having privacy."

My friend and favorite security guard, Mr. Hugo, opened the gate and ushered us into the cemetery. With his brown uniform stretched across his belly and his twinkling eyes, he reminded me of Santa Claus. He gave me a peck on the cheek before turning his attention to my aunt. Taking off his brown cap, he nodded at her. "I'm very sorry about your daughter, Mrs. St. Martin. What a tragedy."

"Yes, it is." Charlene dabbed at her eyes with a tissue. "Thank you for your condolences. Hopefully visiting my angel's eventual resting place will bring me comfort."

"I'm sure it will, ma'am," Mr. Hugo replied. "I'll walk over with you, then I need to make my rounds."

"You're here early today," I said as I followed him to the mausoleum. Mr. Hugo usually worked at night.

"Now I'm working the day shift and only twice a week.

My wife wants me home more." He hiked up his belt and laughed. "I can't imagine why."

"I can," I said. "Your wife loves you. Marie Laveau won't mind if you're not here as much."

Marie Laveau's tomb drew visitors and locals to this cemetery. As the most famous Voodoo practitioner in history, her family mausoleum was always surrounded with tour guides telling stories about her in varying levels of fact or fiction.

Mr. Hugo grinned. "I told her to keep looking out for me, though. My wife is gonna get tired of having me around. Then what will I do?"

"You could always take Neal up on his offer to work as a tour guide."

"I have to admit, I've been thinking about it." Mr. Hugo tapped a finger on the side of his head. "I'd still be able to visit Miss Laveau."

"You'd be an amazing guide. Neal would be lucky to have you."

And Neal needed the help. He'd been without a partner since losing his first two to very different, but unfortunate, circumstances.

Sunset was a few hours away, but there was already a chill in the air. I pulled my lightweight black jacket tighter, thinking it was my anxiety about bringing Charlene and Jasper here. But then a breeze blew through the row of tombs.

"This wind is going to blow my hair to bits and pieces." Charlene patted her head.

With the amount of hairspray I smelled when she squeezed me while we waited for Mr. Hugo, I didn't think any part of her blond bouffant hairdo could move.

"Don't you worry, Mrs. St. Martin, the breeze will die

down in a minute," Mr. Hugo said. "We'll get a bit of sunshine soon enough."

"I hope God will shine down on where my baby will rest for all of eternity," Charlene said.

We walked through the rows of tombs, each one different in their own way. From the condition of the mausoleums it was easy to tell which ones were taken care of by the owners or by local preservationists. Whether it was a fern growing out of the exposed brick, the remnants of a bouquet, or the gleam of a newly plastered facade, each tomb had something that gave them character and a sense of history.

My heart skipped a beat as we approached the St. Martin tomb. It always happened when I visited. I had only been here a handful of times, but I would close my eyes and take a deep breath. And when I would open my eyes, Mr. Hugo would be next to me with a sympathetic smile on his face.

"Breathe, dear child," he would say before leaving me, singing *Amazing Grace* in his beautiful, baritone voice.

And today was no exception. After he performed his ritual, Mr. Hugo took his time walking down the row of mausoleums, picking up abandoned tour brochures and dead flowers.

I wished I had asked him to stay as I watched Charlene and Jasper huddled in front of the mausoleum. I may have been born into their family, but I didn't grow up as a St. Martin. Seeing their closeness made me ache for my own family. I waited off to the side until they were ready to include me.

"It looks a lot better than it did the last time we were here." Jasper gave his mother a quick hug and joined me.

"Joey, I mean Samuel, cleaned it up," I said.

"That's so unlike your brother," Charlene said. "But at least he did one thing right."

Mr. Hugo told me that before my brother cleaned the tomb, layers of dirt coated the large cross, intertwined with roses that topped the structure. The family name was etched on the top, but the elements had worn it down so it was barely legible. On the right side of the mausoleum was a nameplate of those buried inside, including me since it was assumed I had died in Hurricane Geoffrey. A door with a keyhole was on the left. I grasped the key that was once again around my neck, trying not to let the memories of the first time I opened the tomb overwhelm me.

Charlene placed a bouquet on top of the wilted flowers from my last visit. I made a mental note to order flowers for my adopted parents' graves in Florida. Compared to New Orleans, I'd have to say their cemetery had no soul. It was generic, unlike the cemeteries here. Yes, there were crumbling tombs, ones that no one visited, or even knew about, but there still was a sense of history, a sense that at some point someone had cared enough to build a place to bury their family.

"Darling, you brought the key with you, didn't you?" Charlene reached out her palm.

"Yes," I replied, but I didn't take the necklace off. Something told me if I gave her the key, I'd never get it back. I wasn't ready to give it up now, perhaps ever.

Charlene put her hand down and said, "You must think I'm crazy, but I need to see inside the tomb."

"Momma..." Jasper ran his hands through his hair and for a minute I thought he might start actually pulling it out.

"Hush now, Jasper. Your momma just wants to make sure there's room for your sister."

"Trust me, there is plenty of room for her..." I began, but

Charlene skittered over to me and gave me one of her signature hugs.

"Oh, honey, this must be hard for you! I'm sorry."

Yes, it was hard for me. I didn't want to open the mausoleum and relive one of the worst nights of my life. After my brother tried to knock me unconscious, he placed me on the top shelf and closed the door. I still hadn't decided if he left the key on purpose so I would be found or if he had to run. It really didn't matter, since the act of putting me while I was alive into the tomb was enough to damage my heart and soul.

"Yes, we should go for Sammy's sake." Jasper pulled his mother away from me. "This must be stressful for her."

"Let me have a moment!" Charlene glared at her son. "Sarah Jane, can I have the key?"

Wanting to get this over with, I took the key necklace off, but I didn't hand it to her. I inserted it into the lock and opened the door. The musty air hit me immediately, making me cough. I didn't look inside; I turned around to face Charlene and Jasper.

"There you go. I hope this brings you peace," I said, hoping I'd kept the irritation out of my voice.

"It will, I'm sure. Thank you, darling!" she gushed as she popped up the steps to look inside. "Jasper, why don't you tell your cousin about everyone who's buried in here?"

"What? I don't think she wants a history lesson." Jasper went over to his mother, who pushed him away.

"Go talk to your cousin!" She put her large purse up to her face and let out a sob. "I need a moment to myself."

"Jasper, why don't you fill me in on the family history?" I decided this would go faster if I agreed with Charlene's plan. I wanted to keep an eye on her, though. What was she up to?

I stood by Jasper, who begrudgingly began telling me

how the St. Martins came to New Orleans in the early 1900s. Our great-great-grandfather, Clarence, moved to the city from Mississippi. His son, Walter, was born days after the Great Hurricane of 1915. Our great-grandfather had a son, Edward, who left New Orleans to take up farming back on the family's land in Mississippi. Edward and his wife, Tillie, raised our fathers, Sawyer and Preston, in Huntley.

Jasper shared how our grandmother who was originally from New Orleans, took our fathers to visit the city whenever she could. "It wasn't a big surprise when your parents moved back to the city," he said. "New Orleans was in their blood, and with your parents being the creative types, they belonged here. And after seeing you in the bookshop and with your friends, it looks like you were meant to be here, too."

"Thanks," I whispered, holding back tears. Hearing the stories of my birth family instead of just reading their names on a worn marble plaque gave me a sense of connection I didn't have before Jasper arrived. "I wish I could remember them, all of them."

Jasper told me about the time our fathers stole a tractor to ride into town to get milkshakes at the drugstore. As he recounted the story, I forgot about Charlene. That was until a muffled cry came from the mausoleum. We both turned toward the sound.

Jasper's eyes grew wide, and he covered his mouth with both hands. My eyes widened, too, and I didn't know whether to laugh or cry.

Charlene was head first into the mausoleum and apparently stuck.

26

Charlene's butt wiggled frantically from the middle shelf inside the tomb.

She kicked her legs up and down, but she was too short to reach the step that led to the door of the mausoleum. From the frantic screams and the jerking of her legs, she appeared to be wedged in tight.

"Momma, what are you doing?" Jasper ran over to his mother. "Are you stuck?"

"It's pretty obvious she is," I snapped. "Unless she's imagining what it's like to be locked inside."

What in the world possessed her to climb into the tomb? Having been shoved into this very mausoleum, I knew first-hand it wasn't a pleasant experience. But I was put on the top shelf, which had more room with its vaulted ceiling. Charlene was lying on the middle shelf. Apparently she was larger than the coffins that went inside the tomb; at least when it was made in the early 1900s.

"Charlene, you've got to stop moving so we can pull you out," I yelled into the tomb. "I know you're scared, but we can't help you until you calm down."

Jasper gave me an appreciative smile. "Listen to Sammy, Momma!"

Charlene mumbled a few indecipherable words, and then she stopped kicking. I grasped one leg and Jasper took the other and we pulled. Her body moved a few inches out, but she started yelling again.

"Momma, shut up!" Jasper's face was as red as the shiny plastic flowers on the next tomb over. He took his hands off his mother's leg and wiped them on his jeans. "We can't help you if you keep screaming. Make yourself as small as you can by sucking in your breath."

"Do you think that will work?" I whispered.

"We need to try. I don't want to chisel her out of there," he said, but then he laughed. "I'm sorry, but this is ridiculous."

"True dat," I said, which just made us giggle. My memories of being stuck inside evaporated as Jasper and I watched Charlene's plump legs kick up and down, like a ladybug who was flipped over and trying to right herself. We both covered our mouths with our hands to hold in our laughter.

Charlene screeched and kicked her legs, almost hitting both of us. Standing up straight, I inhaled and exhaled slowly to take the situation seriously.

Jasper yelled, "OK, OK, we'll try again. Stop moving, please, Momma."

We pulled once more, and she slid out. Once we could see her shoulders, we each kept one hand on her leg and placed the other on her shoulder. She wiggled the closer she got to the edge of the shelf.

"Charlene, you need to slow down or you're going to land on your face." I gently squeezed her shoulder. "Let's get you out safely."

"Listen to Sammy, Momma." Jasper followed my lead,

and we inched Charlene out of the tomb and pulled her up on her feet. We held her up while she blinked in the bright sunlight. She was in one piece, although her fake eyelashes were halfway off both eyes and dust covered her yellow floral-print dress.

"I can't believe that happened." Charlene ripped her eyelashes off and looked around her. "Oh, my purse is still inside the tomb!"

"Don't!" Jasper pulled his mother back.

I started to reach into the mausoleum, but hands grabbed me around the waist and yanked me from the entrance. Thinking it was Jasper, I was about to yell at him. Instead, I was facing an anxious-looking Charlene.

"Honey, let Jasper get it. You don't want to go in there. Trust me."

"Momma, she knows what it's like in there. Remember?" Jasper gritted his teeth as he pulled his mother away from me.

Charlene opened her mouth, but then closed it tightly. She glared at her son, but put on a smile when she faced me. "I'm so sorry, sweetheart. I hope you're not having some horrible flashbacks. How thoughtless of me to bring you here."

I wasn't having any flashbacks until she said that. Staring inside the tomb, the memories of the gritty bone dust and my gasping breaths hit me. Waking up in the mausoleum after my brother shoved me in there, I had to fight to keep awake and find a way out. And I had, with the help of my friends, my New Orleans family.

"I'm fine," I lied. "It's all behind me."

"Oh, darling, come here," Charlene embraced me once again. "Jasper, get my purse."

"I'm fine." I tried to pull away from her, but she wouldn't let go.

"Here's your bag," Jasper said.

Charlene practically pushed me aside and rushed to Jasper. She whispered in his ear, and he shook his head. She snatched her bag from her son and stomped off, but stopped to lean up against the tomb across the aisle. Taking a compact out of her purse, she touched up her makeup, ignoring us.

"What was that about?" I asked Jasper.

"Oh, nothing."

"I don't believe that," I snapped. Before I could demand answers from him, Mr. Hugo came up.

"I heard the commotion. Is everything all right? Sammy, are you OK?" he asked.

"Sorry, Mr. Hugo, it was my momma stuck in the tomb." Jasper glared at his mother.

"My goodness, what in the world were you doing Mrs. St. Martin?" Mr. Hugo took a handkerchief out of his pocket and handed it to Charlene. "Oh, now don't cry. Seeing where your baby is going to be laid to rest is tough."

"Thank you." She accepted the handkerchief and dabbed her eyes. "I don't know what came over me."

"Let's get you some water while Sammy and your son lock up the tomb." Mr. Hugo put out his arm, and Charlene took it.

As he guided her down the row, he turned back to look at me. I shrugged my shoulders and mouthed, "Thank you."

"Jasper, what was that all about?" I bit my lip so I wouldn't yell at him. Now, with his mother gone, I wanted answers.

He ran his hand over the engraved names on the tomb, stopping when he got to my birth name, Sarah Jane. He mumbled to himself and did the sign of the cross. With watery eyes, he looked at me.

"Jasper?" His reaction surprised me, but I realized that my birth parents and the toddler version of me were his family. He might feel their loss even more than I did.

"Sammy, I'm sorry. We're such a horrible family for you. You deserve better."

"Jasper, I deserve the truth. Nothing more, nothing less." I rested my hand on his arm. My stomach tossed and turned with worry that what he needed to tell me would break my heart. And while he and Charlene were acting odd, I didn't want to lose them.

"I'll tell you everything, if you're sure."

"I'm sure."

Jasper hemmed and hawed as we stood in front of the tomb. He rubbed the crescent moon shaped scar on his face as if he was trying to erase it. I wanted to pepper him with questions, prod him to talk, but I didn't want to push him too hard. Whatever he had to say was painful to him and I assumed to me.

To give him time, I gave one last look inside the tomb. I checked every inch, but I saw nothing that explained why Charlene shoved herself in there. The click of the lock brought Jasper out of his daze.

"Sorry, I should have helped." He picked up the bouquet. "We should have brought a vase or something."

"I doubt our relatives will mind."

He laughed and wiped his eyes. I sensed it was from relief more than my attempt at humor. "I don't know. Grandma Tillie was pretty particular about her flowers. Momma included her favorites."

"You better put them down for her or she'll follow us out of the cemetery," I said.

"She's probably going to follow us, anyway. She thought you were the cutest baby." Jasper sighed. "She died a few years after Hurricane Geoffrey. Losing everybody was just too much for her."

The wind picked up again and carried the remnants of a dead bouquet past us. Withered rose petals landed on my feet. I brushed them off, wishing I could sweep away the sense of melancholy, too. The feeling of loss was smothering, and by Jasper's haunted face, he felt the same way.

But I still needed the truth, no matter how hard it would be for my cousin.

"Jasper, your mother didn't have to see the tomb for Scarlett's burial," I said. "Does this have something to do with the private investigator Scarlett hired? What's going on, Jasper?"

His shoulders slumped, but he looked me in the eye. "This is a horrible story. Are you sure you want to hear it?"

"Yes." And I meant it. My brother's revelations were devastating, and while I hoped Jasper's story wouldn't be as bad, I wasn't so sure.

"I'd rather talk without my momma, but this isn't the most comfortable place to chat."

"I agree. The sun will set soon and trust me, hanging out here in the dark isn't good." I put the key back around my neck and whispered a goodbye to my parents and Grandma Tillie.

"Let's go find Mr. Hugo and your mother. We can take her to the hotel and then we'll have a drink at The Gas Light."

And I would get answers.

27

Charlene was gone when we reached the front gate of the cemetery. Whether she was actually overcome by her experience in the tomb or she was trying to get away before I questioned her, I didn't know.

"I tried to have her wait, but Mrs. St. Martin insisted she could get to the hotel by herself," Mr. Hugo apologized. "I got her a taxi though, so she's not walking back."

"Momma doesn't like walking, especially by herself." Jasper sighed. "Thank you for taking care of her, Mr. Hugo. And thanks again for letting us in tonight."

"Anything for one of my favorite people." Mr. Hugo hugged me and whispered, "Watch out for your aunt. I can tell when a woman is up to something."

Now both Andrew and Mr. Hugo had warned me about Charlene. Time to get Jasper to The Gas Light.

Rose gave a wave as we walked into The Gas Light, but she took one look at my cousin and pointed to an empty table in the corner. Jasper's pale face, wary eyes, and slouched posture told Rose all she needed to know. She brought over two shots of whiskeys and two beers.

"Thanks, Rose," I said. "You remember my cousin, Jasper."

"I do. Jasper, I'm sorry for your loss. Losing a sibling hurts no matter what your relationship was to each other," Rose said.

"Thanks, Rose," he said. "I appreciate it."

"If you need more of that, let me know." Rose smiled before returning to the bar.

I downed the shot of whiskey, but Jasper just stared at his. "We can go somewhere else."

"It's OK." Jasper pushed his shot glass to the center of the table. "I don't do whiskey. It reminds me too much of my father. It was his favorite. Actually, any alcohol was his favorite."

"I assume he wasn't a social drinker."

"That's putting it mildly. Being sober was rarer than being drunk."

"I'm sorry. That must have made for a tough childhood."

"And adulthood." He took a long sip of his beer. "Even now, my father is hurting us from the grave."

I reached for Jasper's shot and threw it back. Bracing myself for Jasper's explanation, I needed all the courage, liquid or otherwise, that I could get.

"Did Samuel, I mean, Joey, tell you anything about my father?"

"He told me a little." My brother, before he tried to kill me, explained that our uncle blackmailed my adoptive parents until they died two years ago. He learned the truth that I was alive right before Uncle Preston "fell" off the porch and died. I wasn't sure if Jasper would want to know that his cousin apparently killed his father.

"Momma says the detectives told you about the blackmail." He began peeling the label of his beer in long, continuous strips. "I'm sorry he did that to your folks, but I'm not sorry you weren't brought to live with us."

If this was any other situation, having your cousin tell you he's glad they kept you away would be hurtful, but I understood what he meant even before he explained himself.

"I hope you don't take offense, Sammy." The concern in his eyes reminded me of my brother before the truth came out. "But it sounds like you lived a better life than we did and I don't just mean financially."

"My adoptive parents were wonderful people, but I still wish they hadn't hidden my past from me."

"They must have figured out pretty quickly that my father was bad." Jasper rubbed his scar and finished his beer. "Our house wasn't a happy place. My sister could be as mean as our father. Momma tried her best, but she mostly made excuses for Scarlett's and my father's behavior."

A server walked by, and I ordered another beer for Jasper. The shots of whiskey were still buzzing in my head, along with his explanation. While no one's childhood is perfect, Jasper's clenched jaw and sad eyes made me think his childhood wasn't even close to pleasant. And while I wouldn't say it to him, having known Scarlett for only a little while, I had to agree she was mean. I hadn't sized up Charlene yet, so no time like the present.

"I'm sorry about your family, Jasper, really I am," I said. "But what does this have to do with your mother climbing into the tomb? I don't believe a word of what she said at the cemetery."

He thanked the waitress, who put down his beer before he answered. Once again, his shoulders slumped and he closed his eyes. I gave him a moment, but then I asked, "Why did Charlene want to go to the cemetery? Does it have to do with why Scarlett was so adamant about getting the tomb key from me?"

"Yes, to both questions." Jasper opened his eyes, and the shame in them broke my heart. "You already know that my father blackmailed your parents."

"Yes, but what does that have to do with the tomb?"

"Hey, can we walk and talk? I need air." Jasper's hand shook as he drained his beer. So I agreed we should go outside.

I jumped up out of my seat and headed to the bar to pay our tab. Jasper's pale face and constant rubbing of his scar made me think he needed a moment to gather himself. As I weaved my way through the tables, Terry grabbed my hand.

"Hey, cher, I got back into town last night and heard about your cousin." Terry squeezed my hand gently. "I'm sorry y'all didn't have time to become family."

"Thanks, Terry. I guess it wasn't meant to be."

"But that guy you're with is your other cousin, isn't he?" Terry pointed his beer bottle at Jasper, who was now talking to Rose at the bar. "You've got a chance with him though."

"Maybe. We'll just have to see."

Terry frowned for the first time since I'd met him. "There's no *just see*, Sammy. You've got to put in a little effort now."

"I am." I crossed my arms and frowned back at him.

"I didn't mean to upset you." Terry stood up and kissed me on the cheek. "Just don't give up on him. Looks like he could use some family, too."

I relaxed a bit as Terry's face softened. "I guess we all

need family. But I'm not fighting him in a swamp, no matter what."

"At least I've taught you one good thing." The laugh lines on Terry's face deepened as he chuckled. "I'll see you later, and next time introduce me to your kin."

"As long as you introduce me to your cousin." I hugged Terry and headed to the bar.

"Jasper asked me to tell you he's waiting for you outside." Rose took my credit card. "Let me guess. Terry told you to introduce him to your cousin? You should. Jasper is a nice guy even though he's going through such a hard time."

"His sister's death brought up a lot of memories."

"Death always does." Rose handed me my credit card and then vigorously cleaned what looked to be a spotless glass. "By the looks of Jasper, the memories aren't good."

"No, they aren't." I said. "This week has brought out a lot of difficult emotions."

"Does that include your feelings about Connor?" Rose asked. "I'm surprised he's not here with you."

Connor probably thought the same thing as I kept telling him I'd call him later every time he texted during the day. "He's been busy. I've been busy..." Rose's trademark stern expression stopped me from lying. "Fine, Rose. I'm not sure what to do about him. I think he's hiding something from me."

"And by something you mean his past relationship with Scarlett?"

Actually, it was his more recent relationship with Scarlett that I was worried about, but I didn't want to get into that with Rose. "He keeps texting that we need to talk. I guess he wants to break up with me."

"Perhaps he's worried you're going to break up with him."

"Oh." Well, now I felt like an idiot. While worrying about my own heart, I didn't even consider Connor's feelings.

"Sammy, Connor didn't hide his party-boy past from you. I mean, he was that way when you first moved in."

"True."

"I bet he's embarrassed that it has come back to haunt him." Rose said, "No one likes to be reminded of their past, especially when they're working so hard to put it behind them."

Leave it to Rose to put everything in perspective. "I see what you mean. Can you add your therapy fees to my tab?"

"This session is on the house," Rose said. "But seriously, Sammy, talk to Connor and figure out what you both want. Life's too short."

I signed my bill and left the bar as Rose picked up another clean glass to wipe.

28

———

"Fresh air helping?" I found Jasper standing on the edge of a crowd surrounding a three-piece band. The color had returned to his face, and he was tapping his foot to the tune.

"Yes, thanks. Music always helps."

"I agree. The street musicians are one of my favorite things about the French Quarter."

"Your brother told me you used to stop at every band when your family moved here."

"I still do."

While I wanted to learn about my life as a toddler in New Orleans, there were more pressing issues. I needed him to give me answers about the present. The streets and side-walks were crowded, so I decided to take him somewhere more private where we wouldn't be interrupted.

"Let's walk down to the river," I said after the band finished their song.

Jasper nodded, and we walked silently down to the Moonwalk, a brick promenade along the Mississippi River. I found it to be a relaxing place even though it was part of the busy French Quarter. Some days, I ran there, but other times I picked a bench to rest on.

My emotions were like the river water rushing back and forth. Jasper's forlorn face stopped me from snapping at him. I wanted him to explain what Scarlett had been up to, but his embarrassment and shame kept me from yelling. To get answers, I needed to be gentle but firm with him.

"Jasper, why was Scarlett really looking for Joey? Was it just revenge?"

"I'm sure revenge was part of it. She assumed he had something to do with our father's death and then when he left with the tomb key, she was on a mission to find him."

"What is it about the key?" I asked. "Charlene wanted it, too. Why did she search the mausoleum? Obviously she assumed something valuable was in there."

"My father used the tomb to hide his money."

"What?" Although there was a breeze coming off the river, my body temperature rose. "He treated it like a safe deposit box?"

"Yes. He put the money that he got from your parents in it."

"The extortion money you mean."

He hung his head. "I'm sorry, Sammy. This is a horrible story."

"Was your mother aware of the bribery?"

"Momma claims she found out after Daddy died."

"Do you believe her?"

"Yes, because if she knew he had cash she would have taken it." Jasper kicked at a stone underneath his feet. "There were times we were dead broke and that money would have solved a lot of problems for us."

"So he kept it for himself then?" My anger grew thinking of my uncle taking money from my parents and using it only for himself. If Preston had helped his family, I would have felt a little better. But not much.

"Yep, my father was a gambler. He'd bet on anything." He kicked another stone, which shot across the sidewalk and down the embankment.

"How did Scarlett discover the blackmail?"

"Momma said Daddy told Scarlett just before he died."

"But not your mom?"

"Nope."

Apparently Scarlett and her father had a close relationship, so close that he would tell her about the blackmail money and his hiding place. My sympathy grew for Jasper and his mother. To find out not only one but two people in your family were keeping secrets must have been horrible. But not bad enough to keep Charlene from searching a dusty tomb.

"OK, so Scarlett learned about your father's hiding place and wanted to look for any money that he might have left." I said. "But I can tell you that when my brother put me in the mausoleum there was nothing inside but bone dust and spiders."

"That's all my mother found tonight." He rubbed his eyes. "My guess is your brother took whatever my father hid in there."

That explained Charlene's disappointment after we pulled her out of the tomb. Did my brother find anything? If he had taken Preston's stash, that would explain how he pretended to be a graduate student without a job when I first met him.

"So this whole trip was to look in the mausoleum? It had nothing to do with me except for getting the key." I gulped down a sob and walked to the edge of the walkway. As much as I tried to deny it, I had hoped my remaining relatives wanted me, not the money. A freight ship passed by and I wished I could go with it. I needed to escape this moment of melancholy.

"Sammy, you must be mad, but I'm here for you, not for the money," Jasper said after standing quietly next to me. "I can't deny Scarlett came for the tomb key, but I wanted to meet you. And so did Momma."

Jasper was teary-eyed, like me. "I believe you, but I don't know about Charlene yet."

"I'm glad you trust me." Jasper smiled. "And I hope you'll trust my mother. She's got her faults, but deep down she's a good woman."

"I'll try to give her the benefit of the doubt."

"That's all we can ask."

He tentatively put his arm around me, and I rested my head against him. We stood together, watching the freighter make its way out of sight. The ship headed to unload its heavy cargo and for the moment, I imagined my pain and disappointment leaving with it.

"Do you have a girlfriend back home?" Jasper and I left the river and walked through the Quarter to my apartment.

"Nope." His shoulders sagged. "I've had a few girlfriends here and there, but nothing lasts."

I nodded. I had a lackluster love life before I met Connor.

"It's hard dating in a small town. We've all known each other since kindergarten," Jasper said. "And then there's my family. No one wanted my dad as their father-in-law."

Jasper sighed, and I bet he was thinking what I was

thinking: no one wanted Charlene as their mother-in-law or Scarlett as their sister-in-law, either. Poor Jasper.

"Have you considered leaving Huntley?" I asked. "A fresh start isn't a bad thing. Moving to New Orleans has been the best thing for me."

"Even with everything your brother did? And Scarlett?"

"You've got to take the bad with the good. Isn't that how the saying goes?" I put my hand on his arm and he stopped walking to face me. "Jasper, I know it's easier said than done. Taking charge of your life is important."

"You make it look easy."

I laughed, and he tensed. "I'm not laughing at you, so don't get mad." Jasper relaxed, so I continued. "Moving to San Francisco was a big risk and while I met some great people, it wasn't home. New Orleans is my home, but I've learned that finding and being a part of a community, of a family, takes work."

Now wasn't the time to go into all my stories of loneliness, bad career choices, and even worse decisions about men while I lived in San Francisco. And he'd heard enough about my troubles with my brother.

"Family is work, I agree on that." Jasper's smile returned to his face. "I've thought about leaving, but I guess I'm not as brave as you are, Sammy."

"Oh, I disagree. If you can pull your own mother out of a mausoleum in one piece with a straight face, you're pretty tough."

It was his turn to laugh, and while I joined him, my heart sank a bit as he reminded me of my brother. Joey had an infectious laugh too, but the last time I saw him, he wasn't that person. While Jasper had similarities to my brother, I had to remember he wasn't him. I wiped the tears from my eyes as our laughter finally subsided. Jasper did the same, then pulled me in for a hug.

"Sammy, I'm so glad we're cousins. I need someone like you in the family."

"Thanks, I'm happy we met again, too." I relaxed into his hug, feeling thankful that Jasper and I had connected. My New Orleans friends were my family, but tonight I wanted to call Jasper family, too. I still didn't trust Charlene, but maybe I just needed time.

We walked back to Thibodeaux Mansion, chatting away comfortably. We said goodnight at the gate, and I watched him walk down the street. A shiver ran through me, out of nowhere. As I looked at Jasper again, I knew what caused my goosebumps. His friendly smile and wave reminded me of my brother once more. I had trusted Joey easily, with no hesitations. Was I making the same mistake with Jasper?

29

I was dead tired and wanted nothing more than to relax in a hot bath with a book, but Connor had other plans. With a bouquet of red roses and an anxious look on his face, he sat at the bistro table by my apartment.

"Sammy, there you are! I've been texting all day."

"I've been busy." I didn't acknowledge the flowers and opened my front door.

Connor followed me inside and put the vase on my coffee table. As much as I wanted to tell him to go, I needed to talk to him. And talk he did.

"Sammy, why are you're avoiding me? Yes, you're busy, but it's more than that," he said. "Is it about Scarlett?"

What else could it be? I didn't say that, instead I said, "Yes, you didn't tell me everything about her." My face was warm and my breathing became heavy. I sat down on the loveseat and Nubi jumped into my lap.

"Oh, that's why you've been hiding from me." Connor said.

"I haven't been hiding from you," I insisted. "But you have been keeping your relationship with Scarlett from me."

"There was no relationship!" He dropped onto my loveseat, causing Nubi to jump down and meow loudly. "Even Nubi is mad at me."

"I'm not mad."

Connor raised his eyebrows at me. Nubi appeared to doubt my words, too, as he stopped grooming himself to look at me.

"I'm not mad, I'm disappointed. I wish you had told me the truth about the time you spent with Scarlett a few years ago." After taking a deep breath, I said, "And what you were doing with her the day before she was murdered."

"What?" He took out his trumpet mouthpiece and started twirling it. "How did you know about that?"

"I saw you talking to her when I was walking to the hotel. It appeared y'all had a lot to talk about."

"Sammy." He dropped the mouthpiece and grabbed my hands. Part of me wanted to pull away from him, but the sincerity in his eyes stopped me. "Yes, I talked to her. She asked me to come meet her the next day."

"And you did what she asked? Just like that?"

"Yes, because I needed to make sure she understood that I'm in a relationship with you." He turned red. "Sammy, I also needed to tell her I wasn't the same guy she met that weekend. I'm embarrassed to say I don't even remember her."

"She remembered you all right." I pulled my hand away, recalling how physical Scarlett had been with him. "Two years isn't that long ago."

"It feels like a lifetime to me." Connor grabbed the mouthpiece again. "I was a different person then. And I'm different from when we first met three months ago."

His partying ways had stopped when I arrived. He hadn't

given me any reason to doubt his interest in me, even when he was away for work.

"Listen, here's what happened. I went to see her after she texted me. I wished I'd changed my number." He sighed. "I met her outside the hotel and explained that I was dating you, but I hoped we'd all get along since you and her are family."

"Did she accept what you said?"

"I can't say she was happy, but I don't think it was really about me." Connor put his mouthpiece in his pocket. "My guess is that no one says no to her."

"I bet you're right."

"I know she was your cousin, but honestly, I didn't care what she thought," Connor said. "I apologized if I had been a jerk to her in the past, but I made it clear there would be no romantic relationship ever. And then I left."

"You didn't see her again?"

"No, I didn't. How many times do I have to say that?"

"Don't snap at me, I just asked you tonight."

"Sorry, I wasn't talking about you. Rob and Christine asked me a few times when I met with them."

"You talked to them?" My face flushed again. How stupid had I been?

"Of course I did. Did you think I wouldn't mention seeing Scarlett before she died?" He huffed. "Sammy, I have nothing to hide."

"I know." But really, I hadn't known. I had jumped to conclusions instead of talking to Connor.

"Sammy, why didn't you ask me about this the other night?"

Because I'm insecure and assumed you were interested in her, is what I thought, but I said, "Because I'm an idiot."

Connor laughed. His handsome face lit up as if I'd told

the funniest joke. "You are far from being an idiot. It's the detective in you that is overthinking things." He pulled me close to him. "And if we're being honest, we've both had bad relationships so we're scared we'll mess this up." He kissed me gently. "Or maybe that's just me. Are we going to be OK?"

I answered him with a kiss. Yes, one thing was finally all right in my life. And I wouldn't let myself ruin it.

30

—————

I woke up with a smile on my face, even though my body ached from yesterday's craziness. The day had its ups and downs, but it ended on a good note. Making up with Connor lightened my heart. Nubi sensed my cheerful disposition and jumped on the bed and wrapped himself around my head.

"Good morning to you too." I reached up and petted my purring cat. "As much as I'd love to stay in bed with you, I need to get ready for work."

Nubi gave a pitiful meow when I grabbed my cell phone to check for messages. The only one was from Jasper apologizing again for his mother's behavior. He returned my smiley face text with a message that he and his mother planned to visit a family friend and he'd call me later. I appreciated having a break from them since I wasn't ready to hear Charlene's trumped-up explanation for her tomb escapade. I doubt she would tell me the truth.

But Ruby was willing to tell me that truth. As I left for work, she stopped me outside my door.

"Samantha, the spirits are swirling around you this

morning." Ruby waved her hands back and forth, as if she was batting a buzzing bee from her face.

"Maybe they're looking for coffee." I laughed. "If I'd known the spirits were around, I would have offered them a cup."

"You are not amusing."

"Nefertiti and Cleopatra disagree."

Ruby's cats meowed loudly as they slinked to the back of the courtyard where my cat sat. The three of them jumped on top of the brick wall that enclosed the courtyard. Standing like statues, they appeared to be waiting to see what Ruby and I were going to do.

"The cats are just more polite than I am." Ruby frowned. "But honestly, Samantha, you must have conjured up these spirits."

"Well, I am organizing the library at a haunted hotel." I giggled. "Did the ghosts follow me home?"

Instead of lashing out at me, Ruby closed her eyes and mumbled a chant. "No, these spirits are connected to Thibodeaux Mansion, not from Hotel Jeanne."

"How did you know I was working there?" Ruby and I hadn't talked about my work at the hotel. And there were several haunted hotels in the French Quarter, so it would have been pure luck to pick the one where I was working.

"I know more than you could ever understand." Ruby smiled, which shocked me, as she had never smiled at me. "While you doubt my abilities, I am good at what I do."

"So, it's not just a lucky guess?"

"Absolutely not." She huffed and returned to her doorstep. "While I may have been able to deduce you are working at Hotel Jeanne from the neighborhood gossip, I wouldn't know that there are spirits there that are watching you."

Ruby kept up with the neighborhood gossip after all. She acted as if she didn't care about her neighbors, but she just outed herself and the source of some of her psychic abilities. Before I could point that out to her, she stopped me cold.

"And Samantha, the spirits said not only to be careful at the hotel, but wherever you roam. Someone is watching you and most definitely not in a good way."

And with that Ruby tightened the belt on her lemon colored chiffon robe and returned to her apartment with a firm slam of her door. The cats took their leave as well, with all three of them jumping off the brick wall into the neighboring courtyard. They left me alone with the jasmine scented breeze and my apprehension that Ruby and her spirits were right.

The spirits didn't appear at Lagniappe Books that morning, but the detectives did.

"You're very comfortable with that box cutter."

I looked up from the stack of boxes I was opening to see Christine and Rob standing inside the shop. "Yes, Christine, I have a degree in advance box cutting. Are you here for the latest bestseller?"

"Did the butler do it?" Rob picked up a book and paged through it. "And is there a pair of bumbling detectives?"

"He means in the novel." Christine took the book out of Rob's hands and put in back in the box.

"Of course he did." I smiled, but this banter was just prolonging the real reason they were here. "What can I do for y'all?"

"We have a few questions," Christine said. "Your cousin

gave us the private investigator's reports his sister had. Did you know anything about it?"

"He told me about it after Scarlett died. I didn't know until then she was searching for my brother," I said. "Did you talk to the PI? Is he still tracking Joey?"

"He lost the trail in Huntley," Rob said. "Have you heard from him?"

"Not since I gave you the postcard last week. Do you think he's in town?"

"Why do you ask?" Christine leaned up against the bookshelf featuring mysteries.

"I assume he and Scarlett didn't get along, so wouldn't he be a suspect?" I asked.

"We're tracking down all leads." Rob picked up the new book again and took out his wallet. "Sissy said she wanted this book, so I'll surprise her with it."

I accepted his credit card and rang up the sale, trying to ignore Christine's stare. Did she know about Scarlett wanting the tomb key for a windfall her father hid in there?

Yes, she did.

"So you didn't find anything in your family mausoleum before you went with your aunt and cousin?" Christine said. "Yes, Jasper told us about the money. Did you and Scarlett argue over it?"

"No, to all your questions." I handed Rob's credit card and receipt to him and walked to the front door, hoping they'd take the hint to go. Not that I had anything to hide, but I didn't feel like talking to them anymore. I had too much work to do before I returned to the hotel in the afternoon.

"You're positive? I mean, the money technically is your inheritance. It's from blackmailing your adopted parents." Christine came over to me and stood a little too close.

Arching my neck, I glared up at her. "I don't have any of the money and I don't want it. There's no point in dwelling on that part of my past."

Christine studied my face and then put her hand on the doorknob. "If you think of anything, call us. And of course, if you hear from your brother..."

"I'll call you," I said. "And you'll let me know anything that..."

"That applies to you." Rob finished my sentence. "Stay safe, Sammy."

I nodded to both of the detectives and shut the door behind them. I would try to stay safe, but I wouldn't stay away from Hotel Jeanne.

31

———

Ruby's warning that someone was keeping an eye on me wasn't accurate. During my afternoon at Hotel Jeanne no one seemed to look at me "not in a good way" as Ruby declared. Although all the interruptions kept me from getting as much work done as I planned.

"Gesundheit, Samantha." Ambrose was the first person to visit me in the library. "May I get a box of tissues for you?"

"No thanks. I have a pack in my pocket." I stepped down the ladder. "These top shelves are very dusty."

"As I mentioned, this room has been neglected. Although I wanted to do something about it." Ambrose's grimace appeared to be in reaction to my statement, which I hadn't meant as a reproach.

"You are so busy as the manager." I smiled. "And that's why I'm here to help organize the library."

"Yes, I am glad you're here."

Was he? His face was expressionless, but I hoped he was happy. Especially for Beau's sake, as he wanted to make a positive headway in his working relationship with Ambrose.

"Thanks. Here, let me show you what I've found so far. You'll like this."

I picked up a copy of *The Maltese Falcon* from one stack of books I had on the desk. "You told me this was your favorite. It's not in the best shape, but it is a great cover."

Ambrose held the book and stared at its faded orange cover with three hands reaching for a black falcon statue. He smiled as he gently turned the pages. Now I recognized genuine happiness on his face.

"This is wonderful. While it's not a New Orleans themed book, it needs a place of honor on the shelves. But if it's valuable, Mr. Boudreaux might have other plans."

"You and I can agree it's valuable, but not dollar-wise." Ambrose put the book back on the desk, but I picked it back up. "You should have this."

"Oh, no, I can't take anything from the hotel." Ambrose shook his head. "And there could be other books like it that make it a valuable collection."

"I see your point." I placed the book on top of a stack that wasn't worth much. "Once I've inventoried the library, you and Beau can decide what to do with them."

"Mr. Boudreaux most likely has a plan in place." Ambrose's shoulders slumped slightly. "But it is thoughtful of you to consider me when you found *The Maltese Falcon*."

He bowed and then left the room. I still hoped that this library re-do would give them common ground. Shelby dashed that idea.

"Ambrose doesn't like anyone who doesn't kowtow to him." Shelby stepped into the library. "It's nothing to do with Mr. Boudreaux. He's actually a cool guy."

"I agree about Beau." He would be thrilled to learn he had at least one friend in the hotel staff. "I take it you overheard our conversation?"

"Sorry, I didn't mean to eavesdrop." Shelby dropped her backpack on a wingback chair and walked toward the desk. "I'm a little early for my shift, so I decided to see how you were doing with all this stuff. Find any treasures?"

"I've found a couple of interesting books, but no mysterious treasures," I said.

"The ghosts took them." Shelby laughed. "If there was something worth a load of money, Ambrose has taken it by now."

"Why do you say that?" I was shocked, but I smiled as I wanted to keep the conversation light-hearted so Shelby would stay. The way she hung about undetected must mean she noticed a lot more than people realized. "Do you think he's taken something? Besides those little square soaps the hotel uses?"

Fortunately, Shelby found it funny and kept talking. "Ha, ha! Have you smelled Ambrose? I bet he buys a fancy, over-priced soap."

"Oh, so he's the one who smells like peppermint and eucalyptus? I thought it was the cleaning products y'all used."

We laughed until we heard footsteps coming down the hall. Daniel popped his head around the doorway.

"Hi, Sammy. How are things in the spooky library?"

"Nothing spooky yet," I replied. "Aren't you here early for your shift?"

"Wow, you remembered," Daniel said. "I'm just here for my paycheck so I can run some errands before I need to be here."

Daniel looked over at the desk. "Whoa, are all those books worth a lot of money?"

"I don't know yet." I said. "If not, I'm sure they'll have some historical value."

"Oh, well, that's cool, too." Daniel turned around to leave, but then asked, "Have you found anything else? People say there's a secret treasure hidden here."

"Really? Does that explain the ghost stories? Are the ghosts protecting the treasure?" I said.

"Maybe." Daniel winked. "Gotta run, Ambrose is coming, and I don't want to get into last night's noise complaints."

He slipped out, and the courtyard door squeaked, so I assumed he left that way. Shelby came out from the corner where she had quietly stood the entire time Daniel talked.

"Oh, please, there aren't any ghosts here." Shelby picked up her backpack. "It's just to get tourists to stay here."

"You don't believe in ghosts?"

"Nope. I bet there's a real live source behind the ghosts."

"Oh? What do you think it is?" I asked.

"You mean who?" Shelby grinned. "I have my theories, but no proof yet."

"Shelby, be careful..." I started to ask her who she suspected, but she put her finger up to her lips.

"I'll tell you later, I promise." She headed out of the library and ran straight into Ambrose. "Sorry, Mr. Fortner."

"Hello, Miss Jones. Shouldn't you be in your uniform?" Ambrose looked down at Shelby, whose face was now red. "Your shift starts in five minutes."

"Yes, sir. I was just checking with Sammy in case she needed any help."

"I appreciate your offer, Shelby." I hoped she wouldn't be in trouble for stopping by the library.

"If Miss Richardson needs any assistance, she will ask me and I will notify you, Miss Jones." It sounded like Ambrose was talking to me, not Shelby. "Please go get ready. Mrs. Wright is behind on the laundry."

Shelby nodded at him and gave me a smile. I would have folded towels to listen to her, but Ambrose wanted to chat.

"Now Samantha, we should discuss how the library should look while you're not here." Ambrose pointed at the stacks of books on the desk. "I prefer not to have books cluttering up the furniture when you're not working."

Before I could interject, Ambrose droned on, "And the rope and sign must be on the ladder, so none of our guests use it. We don't want anyone getting hurt."

"I agree on all counts." I picked up three books and went to the ladder. "These are going back on the shelves. I'm taking a few with me to Lagniappe Books to get Andrew's opinion."

"Very good."

"Would you like me to give you a daily list of books I take to the shop?"

"Yes, thank you." Ambrose gave a slight smile. "I must admit I am excited for what you might find."

"You'll be the first to know if I discover any more detective novels. Sam Spade might lurk on a shelf somewhere."

My foot slipped off the rung of the ladder at the sound of Ambrose's loud chuckle. Hearing his genuine laughter was a surprise. It lifted my hopes again that the library organization was a great idea.

"I look forward to seeing what you unearth in these long neglected bookcases," Ambrose said.

Ambrose left, his well-polished shoes clicking on the wooden floor toward the front of the hotel. I heard the squeaking courtyard door and waited to see if Shelby or even Daniel came back inside. No one did. Did someone change their mind about entering the building or had someone listened to my conversation with Ambrose?

32

After putting a few books in a bag to take back with me, I shelved the remaining the books and roped off the ladder. I sat at the library desk and wrote up my notes to go over with Andrew. After rubbing my eyes and yawning, I texted Andrew, asking if we could talk tomorrow. I rested my head in my hands until my ringing cell phone woke me up from an involuntary nap.

"Samantha, haven't I taught you to use your phone as an actual phone?"

"Hi, Andrew. Sorry, I keep forgetting you can't teach an old dog new tricks."

I heard his indignation over the phone. "Touché. I received your text and yes, let's talk tomorrow. You sound exhausted."

"And I look it." I took my compact out of my backpack and looked at my tired reflection and messy hair. I used the powder to touch up my eye concealer and redid my ponytail after I hung up the phone. Andrew insisted I go home to rest, and I planned to take his advice.

I waved to Ambrose at the reception desk before I left.

Fortunately, an elderly couple from New York kept him occupied with a list of questions. "No, ma'am, we do not have a most haunted room," Ambrose said as I shut the front door behind me.

I started toward home, but a voice stopped me.

"Hey, you! Yes, I'm talking to you!"

"Hello?"

I looked up at the balcony of the building on the other side of the hotel's parking lot. Through a curtain of lush, hanging ferns, I spotted a slight woman with a large gray braid wrapped around her head. She held a cigarette in her knotted hands as she leaned over the wrought-iron railing.

"Are you the girl asking about the ghosts in the hotel?" She leaned farther over, making me nervous. Her voice was powerful, but her body looked otherwise.

"Um, yes, I guess that's me." I answered quickly, hoping she wouldn't fall over the rail. "Who told you that?"

Her croaky laughter spilled down to the sidewalk. "Oh, honey, I know everything that happens on this street. The door's open, come on up."

I couldn't resist an invitation like that. Opening the door of the two-story townhouse, I stepped back in time. It reminded me of the Gallier Historic House, which was a museum set up as a home would have been in Victorian times. As much as I wanted to explore the home, I rushed up the stairs before the owner yelled for me.

A Siamese cat wearing a rhinestone collar stretched her body across the open doorway to the balcony. "Hello, pretty kitty. May I come in?" I kneeled down to scratch her on the head. She opened her eyes and stared at me, but she accepted my affection. When she gave me a long meow and then trotted outside, I assumed her answer was yes.

The woman sat at a black painted wrought-iron table

with the cat weaving in and out of her legs. From the clumps of brown fur on her white pants, this must be a regular routine.

"Good girl. You made it," the woman said.

"Yes, ma'am," I answered, although I wasn't sure if she was talking to me or the cat. "Your kitty let me through."

"Lady Clementine doesn't like many people, but she took to you right away. That's an excellent sign." She pointed to the other chair across from her. "I'm Myrtle McBride, but you may call me Momo."

I sat and smiled at Momo and Lady Clementine. Momo reminded me of her cat. She was thin, but not frail. Her cat's fur extended to the white blouse she wore and the lime green shawl wrapped around her shoulders. Her wrinkled face gave away her advanced age, but even her thick-lens glasses couldn't hide her alert eyes.

"I'm Samantha Richardson, but my friends call me Sammy."

"Well, Sammy, as you can see, I have an excellent view of the hotel from here through my ferns." Momo waved her hand with the lit cigarette, sending ashes to the floor. She must do that all the time, as I noticed black spots on the wood slats of the balcony. "Lady Clementine and I have watched you coming and going, especially after the murder."

I took a deep breath, waiting for her to interrogate me about my cousin, but she surprised me.

"I asked Frankie about you, so I know you're not a murderer. Francesca Fortuna may be a gossip, but she is the finest judge of character." Momo dropped her cigarette in a porcelain teacup. "Frankie says you're good as gold, so I invited you up here."

Frankie was the best reference I'd ever had. Even if

Momo had nothing to tell me, I was going to have an interesting time talking with her.

"I'm happy Frankie put in a kind word for me. But I must admit, I'm not sure why you invited me here. Although I'm glad you did. Your place is lovely."

"Yes, I do have a wonderful home. Been here all my life except for those awful years up north. Do you know they don't serve sweet tea?"

I laughed as Sissy complained about the lack of sweet tea there, too. "So I've been told."

"I just hate thinking about that time." Momo shivered. "But you're not here about tea. You're investigating the ghosts, aren't you?"

"I'm helping Beau Boudreaux, the new owner, out with the library."

"Oh, yes, I've met him. He brought me a lovely bottle of bourbon to introduce himself. While I never say no to good liquor, he didn't need to smooth things over with me. I don't mind the hotel, unlike his other neighbor."

"You must mean Gideon Pearce."

"I do." She picked up Lady Clementine, who sat in her lap. "He's tried to buy that hotel for years. When it finally came up for sale, Beau outbid him. Thank goodness, because Gideon has no taste."

"Beau wants to maintain the style of the hotel, so you don't need to worry."

"I'm sure he'll make it better. Gideon would have turned it into a tacky place with his girlfriend of the week decorating it." Momo rolled her eyes. "And Gideon doesn't believe in ghosts like Beau."

Momo and Beau must have hit it off over bourbon and ghost stories.

"You know about the hotel's ghosts?"

"Oh, yes, my family has lived here for years so we have passed the ghost stories down from generation to generation."

Momo handed Lady Clementine to me, and then she stood up. The cat settled into my lap so I didn't move.

"Lady Clementine likes you. Now let me go get that bourbon. We'll have a drink while I tell you the tale of the Lovelorn Ghost."

While Bourbon wasn't my favorite, I would guzzle swamp water to hear her story. Momo returned to the balcony with a wooden tray holding two crystal glasses filled with a healthy dose of alcohol. Cheese straws were stacked on a silver platter that she placed close to me. Whether it was out of politeness or she assumed I needed to line my stomach, I wasn't sure. I put my hands around my glass and waited for Momo to settle back into her chair.

After taking a sip of her drink, she began, "The Lovelorn Ghost is a young woman who lived in the townhouse part of the hotel in the 1920s. The story goes her father hired a carpenter to make some additions to the home."

"The library shelves?"

"Yes, the father, Julian Fuller, was quite the bibliophile. He turned a parlor into the library and hired a young carpenter to make the shelves for his extensive collection. He supposedly did other work through the building."

"It is a spectacular library," I said. "Let me guess, Mr. Fuller's daughter fell in love with him."

"A tale as old as time." Momo smiled. "They were in love and hid it well until they couldn't anymore."

"A baby bump gave it away?"

"Bingo! The father sent his daughter to live with relatives to have the baby. He fired the carpenter, badmouthing him to everyone in the city. The young man was penniless and heartbroken."

I picked up a cheese straw and nibbled it. I knew there would be no happy ending for the two lovers.

"I can tell from your sad eyes that you've already figured out the ending." Momo patted my hand. "The two never really had a chance. The carpenter drowned in the Mississippi River. By accident or suicide, no one knows."

"How awful." I took a sip of my drink. "What happened to the woman? Please don't tell me she drowned, too." I'd had enough of drowning stories over the past few days.

"No, she returned home after having the baby. She had nowhere else to go."

"With the baby?"

"Oh, no, her father made her give the infant to another family to raise. She didn't live long after coming back to New Orleans."

"What happened to her?"

"The official cause of death was tuberculosis. Of course, this is a ghost story, so heartbreak is the real reason for her demise."

"And now she roams the house, but why does she make trouble? Is it anger or just sadness?" I looked through the ferns at the hotel. Losing the love of your life and your child would make anyone angry. If ghosts existed, I understood why this woman haunted her old home.

"She hid treasures throughout the house before she died, so the rumors are that she's protecting them."

"Treasures? Has anyone found anything?"

"Not that I've heard, so I'd say no."

The chattering of pedestrians filled the air as we sat in companionable silence, sipping our drinks. After they passed, I said, "I can see why she haunts the hotel. Have you ever seen her?"

Momo's hands shook as she cackled. Lady Clementine raised her head up and glared at her owner.

"I'm sorry, my precious." She put her glass on the table and reached over to pet her cranky cat. "She hates when I laugh while she's resting. No, Sammy, I haven't. I don't believe in ghosts."

"Really? I assumed you did. You said that it was a good thing that Beau believed in ghosts."

"Spirits and goblins make for marvelous tales. As much as we like to drink here, I'm not surprised at the number of stories told about ghosts."

This time I laughed. "I can't argue with that. Everyone has a tale about ghosts or other paranormal activities."

"Now, I'm not saying there aren't ghosts, but they come from people's minds. A person's belief in spirits makes them real, at least to them. They make for marvelous stories and ghosts make for good excuses for strange occurrences." Momo finished the last of her bourbon. "I'm glad Beau believes in them, as he'll keep the history of the buildings alive. We should remember the past. If it's through ghost stories, so be it."

"I'm sure they'll say my cousin Scarlett roams the pool deck calling out my name."

Momo reached over the table and put her warm hand on my cheek. "Sammy, we're all haunted by someone or something. Don't let the past keep you from living."

Lady Clementine meowed, I assumed, in agreement. I gave her a final scratch on her head and placed her on the floor. "Thank you for inviting me here. I'd love to visit you again."

"Come see me anytime, Sammy." Momo's spunky energy appeared to be waning. "I enjoy your company."

As I took a step inside, Momo said, "Lady Clementine, leave my cup alone!"

The sneaky Siamese cat now sat on the table with one paw on the side of Momo's teacup, which was perilously close to the edge. Momo picked up her teacup while clucking at her cat, who gave her the "Who me?" look that Nubi often used on me.

"She can be such a naughty kitty. It's her way of telling me to stop smoking since she only does that when there's a cigarette butt in the cup."

I smiled at Momo, but also at Lady Clementine, who I could have sworn winked at me from behind her human. "She's one smart kitty, isn't she?"

"She is, but at my age I'm not giving up my vices." Momo definitely winked at me, but her cat turned her back and washed her paws. "To be honest, I should stop using these cups as ashtrays. I don't have many left."

I hadn't noticed earlier that the teacup had a delicate flower pattern all around it. "It's a beautiful cup. Are those daisies?"

"Yes. Aren't they pretty?" She handed me the cup. I inspected the tiny white and yellow daisies. "They were my mother's favorite flowers, although I'm partial to roses."

I gave it back to her, watching as her eyes grew watery. Whether her sudden melancholy was from remembering her mother or the lack of roses, I decided not to pry.

"It is a beautiful pattern on the cup. Do you have an entire set of this china?" I asked.

"Yes, my mother bought it when the first hotel owner sold a few of the Fuller family possessions. When the family sold the house, they sold it furnished."

"It's a unique pattern."

"My mother told me that Mrs. Fuller purchased it when she was pregnant with our Lovelorn Ghost. It was for her daughter's name."

"Her name was Daisy?"

"Actually, her name was Marguerite, but Daisy was her nickname. Marguerite is a French name, the oxeye daisy, I think. It's been a while since I studied the language."

"Me, too." I laughed. "Thank you again."

She kissed me on the cheek and walked me to the top of the stairs. "I hope I'll see you soon. I have plenty of Bourbon."

Closing the front door behind me, I made a note to bring Momo a bouquet soon. Should it be daisies or roses? I had seen daisies somewhere recently, though. I ambled home, trying to remember where I'd seen them.

"Oh, sorry!" I apologized to the surprised man I ran into when I spun around.

"Where's the fire, lady?" he shouted as I rushed down the sidewalk in the opposite direction I had planned to go.

There was no fire, but I knew where to find a daisy — not just a flower, but also possibly a ghost.

33

"Hello, Sammy! Back so soon? Or are you here to see your family this time?" Daniel called from the reception desk. I had hoped to sneak in unnoticed, but he was an attentive employee. Rushing into the hotel gave me away, I imagined.

"Not now. I left something in the library," I lied. "I'll just find it and be on my way."

Daniel nodded and answered his cell phone as I walked down the hall, trying not to attract anyone else's attention. I wanted to explore the shelves on my own. After placing my backpack on a chair, I moved the ladder over to the bookcase on the far left. I stepped onto the top rung and grabbed the edge of the shelf to steady myself.

I found the book that jutted out a hair and pried it out from the rest again. There was the mark I had discovered earlier. Three small daisies were centered on the back of the shelf. They were beautifully carved and obviously hand-crafted. I ran my hand over them, imagining the Lovelorn Ghost's true love placing these flowers here for her.

While the romantic notion was lovely, what if the daisies

were more than a token of affection? I tried pushing the three flowers all at once and then individually, but nothing happened. I'd always hoped to find a secret passageway, but nothing opened.

This time when I ran my hand over the flowers, I did it slowly, feeling for any differences in the flowers or the wood. When I got to the flower on the right of the bunch, I noticed a slight divot on the outside edge. Hooking my finger on it, I pulled to the left and with a groan, the section of the back shelf slid open.

I gasped and grabbed the top of the ladder as I almost fell off. The panel was wafer thin and the edge of it was undetectable from the other pieces. Finally, a secret hiding place! My enthusiasm waned when I saw nothing in it. I dug my phone out of my pocket and turned on the flashlight. The corner of a yellowed piece of paper peeked out from the bottom of the shelf.

After putting my phone away, I used one hand to balance myself on the shelf while with my right thumb and pointer finger I pinched the edge of the paper. Slowly, I pulled on it and discovered it was a small envelope. Written in cursive was the word *Daisy*.

I grasped the ladder with my left hand as my right hand shook so hard that I had to put the envelope down on the shelf. After wiping my hands on my jeans, I picked it back up. I flipped it over and found the back flap wasn't sealed but tucked in. Daisy, or someone else, must have read the letter. I took a deep breath, trying to contain my excitement. Instead, I had to control my annoyance when Daniel arrived.

"Hey, Sammy. How's it going?" Daniel leaned against the doorway with his arms crossed and his eyebrows raised. "Do you need me to help?"

I kept one hand on the ladder, but turned to face Daniel. "No, I found the book I needed."

I put the envelope inside the book that had hidden the daisy. It was Agatha Christie's *The Mysterious Affair at Styles*, which I loved. I wanted to close the panel, but I needed Daniel to leave. Beau deserved to be the first to know, and then Ambrose.

"That's good. I'm going to make a cup of coffee. Do you want one?" Daniel took a step into the room.

"No, it's too late for coffee for me." That was a complete lie, as I could drink coffee before I went to bed with no problems. But I didn't want the hotel coffee, and I didn't want to chat with Daniel. I wanted to read the letter.

"Yeah, it's the end of the day for you, but I have a long night ahead." He yawned and then checked his beeping cell phone.

"Sounds like you've got a message, so I'll let you go. I need to clean up here. I wouldn't want Ambrose to find it a mess." I turned back to the shelf and pretended to straighten the books.

"It's just another text from my mother." Daniel sighed and shoved his cell phone back in his pocket. "But you're right, Ambrose will notice if a book was off by a hair. If you change your mind about the coffee, give me a holler."

"Thanks. Good night!" I waved my hand, but didn't turn around. I counted to ten and faced the doorway to make sure Daniel had left. While the coast was clear, I slid the panel back and pushed the remaining books on the shelf toward the center, covering the daisies.

Not wanting to risk running into Daniel, I grabbed my

backpack, clutched the book to my chest, and rushed out the front door. I looked ahead, up at Momo's balcony, but she and Lady Clementine weren't there. Which was just as well, because I wouldn't be able to keep this news from her. From the way she told the story, she was invested in learning about the Lovelorn Ghost's past, too.

I picked up my pace until two voices from the parking lot caught my attention. What were they doing together?

34

Ambrose and Gideon were chatting, and it appeared cordial by the looks on their faces. It didn't surprise me they were talking, but their friendly nature was unexpected. Beau told me they didn't care for one another.

Could Gideon be getting information from Ambrose about Beau and the hotel? Ambrose wanted to own the hotel, and so did Gideon. Were they working together to get Beau to sell the hotel to them? Beau had enough trouble without the two of them plotting against him.

Of course, I had no proof they were up to no good. Neighbors talked to each other all the time in the French Quarter. Ambrose turned toward the sidewalk and gave me a polite wave. Gideon leered at me, but Ambrose re-engaged him in conversation, so I dodged that bullet. I brushed aside my paranoia for the moment, but I would tell Beau about them later.

I ran around the clumps of pedestrians on the sidewalk until I made my way to an empty corner. As much as I was dying to open the envelope, I wanted Beau to be a part of the discovery. I took out my cell phone and called him.

"Beau, hey it's Sammy. Yes, everything is fine," I said before Beau could even say hello. "Where are you?"

"I'm actually at The Gas Light. Sissy dragged Andrew here, so I joined them. Rose is currently bringing over my second delicious martini."

"Stay there. I'm on my way with something you'll want to see." I ended the call, but not before Beau said, "What is it? Tell me!"

I entered The Gas Light to find Beau, Andrew, Sissy, and Neal waiting for me at one of the back tables.

"It's about time." Beau pulled out the chair next to him. "Sit! We're dying to know what you have to show us!"

"Let her take a sip first." Rose had silently appeared next to me with a Pimm's Cup. "Sammy, you look exhausted, no offense."

"None taken." I gulped my drink. "It's been a long few days."

"I think that's an understatement," Sissy said. "But we can't wait any longer! What do you have?"

I opened my backpack and took out the envelope and handed it to Beau. "This was in a secret panel in one of the library's bookshelves. It's addressed to Daisy, who was Marguerite Fuller."

"A secret panel?" Beau gasped. "My hotel has a secret panel!"

"Where do you think the ghosts hide?" Andrew said dryly, but there was a twinkle in his eye.

"Don't tease me. This is exciting!" Beau fumed at Andrew, but relaxed once he saw his smile. "Fine, I'm excited, but I bet Sammy is, too."

"It was pretty cool, especially after Momo told me the Lovelorn Ghost's story." I said.

"You met Momo McBride?" Beau asked. "She didn't tell me about the Lovelorn Ghost, just the Abernathy sisters. And to think I brought her a fine bottle of bourbon."

"The bourbon you gave her is wonderful," I said. "Yes, I was lucky to get a drink, her stories, and the approval of Lady Clementine."

"Her cat's disapproval of most people is legendary, so Momo must have really liked you," Rose said. "But come on, tell us about the ghost and the letter."

All eyes were on me as I repeated Momo's story about the Lovelorn Ghost. "So when I remembered I had seen daisies in the library, I rushed back and found the letter. I mean, I assume there's a letter. I didn't open the envelope."

"You have more patience than I do," Neal said. "I would have ripped it open on the spot."

"It wasn't easy, but it's more fun to share the discovery with Hotel Jeanne's owner," I said.

Beau kissed me on top of my head. "Thank you, darling. Now let's see what's inside!"

He gently opened the flap of the envelope. His hands shook slightly as he took out a yellowed, folded piece of paper. He gasped as he laid it on the table. "It's addressed to Daisy!"

I leaned over the paper and read out loud:

Dear Daisy,

My heart is overflowing now that I know you feel the same way I do. You're as beautiful as your name. Your smile lights up every place you go. When you share your heart and soul with me, I am whole. Thank you for taking a chance on me.

With love always,

Your Beloved

While the chattering and clinking of glasses surrounded us, our table was quiet. I closed my eyes, picturing a young woman in the 1920s reading this beautiful love note. The heavy creases on the paper must have meant Daisy read this letter over and over again. I wondered what letters she wrote back to her beloved.

"Sissy, are you crying?" Neal asked.

I opened my eyes and looked at Sissy, wiping a stray tear from her face with a napkin. I reached across the table and squeezed her hand. "Oh, Sissy."

"She gets engaged and now she's a big softie." Neal put his arm around Sissy. "Do your patients realize you're a soft touch now?"

"If that story and letter didn't get to you, you have no soul." Sissy playfully elbowed Neal. "But I saw you smiling at Rose when Sammy read the note, so don't you hassle me."

"You can't live in New Orleans without a sense of romance." Rose picked up Neal's empty beer bottle. She winked at Neal. "Some of us just need the right person to bring it out. And here's your right person, Sammy."

Rose stepped out of the way, and Connor was standing there. "I knew I'd find you here." He bent down to give me a kiss. "What's all this about romance?"

Connor sat in the empty chair next to me. I caught him up on the story of the Lovelorn Ghost and the letter.

"Wow, that is amazing, but I'm not surprised you found the letter as our resident detective," Connor said.

"Speaking of resident detectives, before Rob shows up, I wanted to tell y'all he's moving in with me." Sissy fished a cucumber out of her Pimm's Cup and nibbled on it. "He hasn't found a place to live, and they sold his rental."

"He'll be a welcome addition to Thibodeaux Mansion," Andrew said. "We're happy not to lose you just yet."

"Y'all are never going to lose me." Sissy smiled at me. "Even when Rob and I outgrow my apartment, we'll always be in the French Quarter."

"That's the best news I've heard all week." I returned Sissy's smile.

"Now we have to behave," Neal said. "Think we can do it, Connor?"

"We can try." Connor laughed. "Sissy, are you sure he's not moving in to keep an eye on a certain neighbor who likes to solve mysteries?"

"Hey!" I pretended to pout. "I resent that remark."

"No, honey, you resemble that remark." Beau grinned. "Look, here comes the law right now."

We all turned to stare at the door where Rob stood, scanning the room. A few patrons nodded at him as he made his way through the packed tables to the back. His navy blazer was in one hand while he used the other to loosen his red tie. Sissy grabbed an empty chair from the table behind us and put it between her and Andrew.

"I just told everyone you're becoming part of the Thibodeaux Mansion, officially," Sissy said.

"I'm thankful Libby and William don't mind me joining the family," Rob said.

"We're glad to have you," I said. "I hope Sissy is giving you more than one dresser drawer."

"I think I might get two, if she'll get rid of her vintage concert t-shirts." Rob laughed.

Sissy shook her head. "Never, not even for you, my love."

"Rob, what would you like?" Rose had returned with another round of drinks.

"I'll take a coke with bitters," Rob answered.

"Still working?" Andrew asked.

"Hopefully not, but you never know," Rob said.

"Sammy's here so she's not causing trouble," Neal said.

"Thanks, Neal." My face grew warm from embarrassment and from my drink.

"I'm kidding! To make up for my horrible joke, I'll even share my food." He went to the door where a deliveryman held a large grocery bag. "Frank has the night off, but thankfully his grandmother has a backup."

The scent of fresh fried chicken wafted under my nose when Neal opened the bag. Frankie didn't make it often, so it was a treat to get her chicken that she fried in a cast-iron skillet with bacon fat. Neal lucked out, ordering food on a night she was cooking it. And now I was lucky too. I hadn't realized how hungry I was until I bit into the juicy chicken leg. Forget caviar and truffles. Frankie's fried chicken was my guilty pleasure.

"So, Rob, how is the investigation going?" Beau asked. "I'm eager for any news at the hotel. And I imagine Sammy is too."

I had a mouthful of chicken, but I nodded. Rob sighed and took a gulp of his drink before he answered.

"Let's lay some ground rules. Right now I'm Rob, your friend." He smiled. "Detective Armstrong is taking the rest of the night off."

Beau opened his mouth, but closed it when Andrew put his hand on top of Beau's. Once Andrew removed his hand, though, Beau said, "Of course, I'm sorry. I called Christine earlier to ask her for an update but she hasn't returned my call."

"She's out of town, but I'm sure she'll call you back tomorrow." Rob took a handful of chips out of the bag Neal offered him. While he said he was off duty, I could see that not talking was hard. After finishing his chips, he drummed his fingers on the table. If Beau and I weren't involved, he might have told us more. But Beau wasn't giving up.

"Is she traveling for work?" Beau held his martini glass by the stem and swirled his drink.

"She's in Mississippi." Rob looked directly at me. "We're following up on some leads, but that's all I can say for now. OK, everyone?"

"Yes, of course," I agreed, as I wanted to give him a break. And Sissy would fill me in later. It was good to hear that the detectives were running down leads that didn't include me.

"Thanks. I would tell y'all if you needed to know anything." Rob put his arm around Sissy. "Family takes care of each other."

Again, we all nodded and then the conversation shifted to normal topics like the weather and what day we all wanted to go to Jazz Fest together. While I joined in, my mind was thinking about what Rob said about family. Had Scarlett been taking care of her family when she started her search for my brother? And had my brother taken care of his family by murdering her?

35

<hr>

The next morning, I wasn't too worried that my brother had taken care of Scarlett. Sissy called me as soon as Rob left for work to tell me that Christine had tracked Joey's movements from Huntley to Biloxi. While she couldn't be positive, a man matching his description was seen gambling at the casino the night Scarlett died. I relaxed at the news; as much as I didn't want to be a suspect, I didn't want Joey to have murdered anyone else. The detectives were also considering a burglary turned murder, and I was all for it. Scarlett's death would still be tragic, but it wouldn't involve me.

I was, however, involved in another search at Hotel Jeanne. Beau and I met in the afternoon to look for more secret panels in the library. Ambrose was having a staff meeting in the lounge, so we would have the main building to ourselves. Except for Daniel, who was manning the front desk. But I didn't expect him to bother us. Beau asked him to write up a marketing plan to attract business travelers, and Daniel was laser focused on the project.

Beau and I looked over the floor plans the original hotel

owner left. Besides the guest rooms, this part of the hotel had a library, a kitchen, an office, and a powder room. We had already searched the office, but didn't find any daisies.

"Are you ready?" I grabbed my backpack and put my hand on the doorknob to leave the room.

"I hope we don't get caught."

"Beau, it's your hotel! You can do what you want, remember?"

He pulled down the sleeves of his crisp white shirt and sighed. "Yes, technically I own it, but I still feel like an outsider. I've run bars and of course, I rent out the Marie Laveau house, but running a hotel is a whole other world."

"You an outsider? You fit in wherever you are, my friend."

"Normally I would agree with you, but somehow I am out of sorts here."

"Did you feel that way when you came here before you bought it?"

"No, I was at home when I walked through the door. The energy was so positive, so invigorating." He frowned. "Maybe I was just enamored with playing hotelier."

"Did the energy change immediately?" I sounded like Ruby. But Beau's firm belief in the spirits and their energy was important to him.

"It did." He perked up. "I know, I need to find out what the ghosts think about me." His mood shifted again. "Oh, no, but what if they don't want me here?"

"Everyone adores you," I insisted. "You just have a bad case of nerves. Running a boutique hotel is hard."

"It is a lot of work. Ambrose reminds me of that all the time."

"He is dedicated to this place."

"That he is. I should be thankful for his love of the hotel, but he acts as if I don't belong."

"You could fire him." I said.

"True, but he knows everything about the hotel."

"And he seems good at his job."

"Mostly. I've received a few complaints from the guests about his attitude."

"If the complaints are from my aunt, ignore them." I sighed. "I think she'd find something to complain about the Pope if she met him."

Beau's laughter brought out a smile on his face. "Of course she would. She'd complained the Pope didn't give her enough wine at communion."

"She has a thing for wine."

"Yes, for free wine. No offense, Sammy, but your aunt is a cheapskate."

"She calls herself frugal." I did air quotes when I said frugal.

"I'm just glad you're not like her, no offense — again."

"None taken. I'm happy to pay for my alcohol."

"Good, you're buying at The Gas Light after we explore."

"It's a deal. I'll even buy the ghosts a drink, too."

"That could get pricey."

I followed Beau out of the office. "It'll be worth it if we find out what your hotel ghosts are up to."

"If you were a heartbroken young woman, where would you hide your treasure before dying?" Beau stood at the top of the staircase with his hands on his hips.

"My treasures are my books, so I'd say the library, but we've already checked there."

"I guess all that's left is this floor then."

Beau and I had searched everywhere on the first floor. We inspected every closet, every cabinet, and every loose floorboard for treasure. All we had to show for it were dust bunnies, rusty nails, and utter disappointment. We didn't find any more daisies. The only daisy the carpenter apparently left was in the library.

"Remind me to call my interior designer tomorrow," Beau said as he unlocked the first guest room. The rooms on this floor were unoccupied, which made it easier for us to search. Although it wasn't good for the hotel to have this many vacancies. "The kitchen needs a total remodel. How disappointing that the cabinets were replicas and not built by our Lovelorn Ghost's carpenter."

"I'll check the bathroom, but my guess is we'll find nothing. I know they were remodeled two years ago." Beau left me in the bedroom, where my hopes were dashed quickly. The furniture in this room looked antique, but a tag on the back of the dresser gave the name of a modern manufacturer. Before I moved the dresser back in place, I noticed a mark along the baseboard. I crouched down on the floor and grinned as I recognized the daisy carved into the wood.

"Beau! I found something!" I sat in front of the image. I ran my hand over the daisy and closed my eyes. I imagined Daisy in the same position, looking at her lover's mark. The board jutted out just a hair more than the other, but no one would have spotted it unless they were sitting on the floor.

"You found a flower!" Beau moved the dresser over so he could sit down next to me. "Is it a hidden compartment?"

"Let's find out." I tried to slide the baseboard, but it didn't move. Next I ran my finger along the top of the board and discovered it was loose. I pulled the board toward me and it popped out.

Beau gripped my arm as I picked up the small envelope stuck to the wall. It was yellowed with age, with the name Daisy written in cursive script.

"Open it!" Beau looked like a kid waiting to unwrap his Christmas presents.

I handed it to him. "No, you should have the honors."

He carefully opened the envelope which wasn't sealed. He took out a folded piece of paper. His face changed from the earlier smile to a slight frown. I asked, "Beau, are you OK? What does it say?"

He put the letter and envelope in his lap and took out a handkerchief from his pocket. After he dabbed his eyes, he handed the items to me. "Sammy, it's so beautiful and sad. I can't imagine the heartbreak of these two young people."

I read the letter out loud:

My dearest Daisy,

I can't wait to see you tonight. Meet me at nine o'clock at the railway station. I put money for you where the daisy chain hides. Our new life will begin soon.

I love you and our baby.

Your Beloved

I gave the letter and envelope to him and rested my head on his shoulder. "So we know that part of the story is true — they did plan on leaving together."

"It's so tragic." Beau put the letter in the envelope. "It's a good reminder to cherish our relationships."

"Very true." Thinking of Connor and how Scarlett almost wrecked our budding relationship came to mind. Actually, I was really the one who almost gave up on our romance.

"You and Connor are going to be just fine," Beau said, as

if he was reading my mind. "You two are lucky to have each other."

"Thanks." I lifted my head off his shoulder. "Let's get off this floor and see what else we can find."

"You'll have to help me up. I haven't sat like this since kindergarten."

"I was going to say the same to you." I stood up and offered him my hand. "But as the younger one, I'll help you up."

"Now you're just being mean." Beau laughed. "Let's go find where the daisy chain hides."

36

"Do you have the key to the attic?" I asked Beau as he locked the last guest room.

"I do." He held up the keyring in his hand. "I was told no one has gone in there in years."

"Didn't you check it out when you were thinking of buying the hotel?" Not only did I assume he had inspected the attic as part of the buying process, but also to search for ghosts.

"I did briefly, but I wasn't seeking hidden daisies or treasure."

"Well, let's go. Hopefully, there won't be too much dust." Even though we had been crawling on floors, Beau's jeans and shirt were still pristine.

"Or spiders." Beau shivered. "But perhaps we'll find the infamous family fortune."

Was the treasure the money Daisy's beloved left for her? The legend says she didn't leave town with her lover, so she might have hidden it and other valuables. But for neither Beau nor me, the monetary value didn't mean as much as finding the truth about Daisy. Having Beau as a partner in crime, so to speak, in this search made it more rewarding for me.

If we discovered more letters, it would be a great story for the hotel. And Daisy must have wanted her tale told if she left these items to be found. But who was she leaving them to? Did she leave a letter for the baby they forced her to give away? Perhaps it was enough for her that the world would know her truth. But did she really believe someone would find her hiding places? Was I just lucky, or did the ghost of Daisy lead me to them?

My luck ran out temporarily. Raised voices and stomping feet came up the stairs before we could open the attic door.

"I told you, Gideon, we are not telling our guests not to photograph your home. If you don't want people to stare, take that tacky painting out of your window." Ambrose reached the landing first.

"I'm sure it's not just our guests stopping in front of your house, sir," Daniel was next in line with a flushed Gideon Pearce following him.

"First, the painting isn't tacky. Cherry did an amazing job portraying the angst of a vampire searching for love in the French Quarter." Gideon sputtered. "Everyone else passes by with a smile, but it's your guests at your urging, taking pictures and laughing at it. It breaks Cherry's heart."

Beau and I shrugged our shoulders at each other. Apparently, neither of us had noticed the disputed painting. The three men crowded around the top of the stairs, staring at Beau. I didn't envy him, as they all looked at him in frustration.

"Sorry, Mr. Boudreaux, it appears we've interrupted you

and Samantha," Ambrose said. "Is there a problem up here?"

"No, no, Sammy and I were just checking for books in the guest rooms." Beau said it with such conviction that I almost believed him.

Both Ambrose and Daniel eyed us suspiciously, but they said nothing.

Gideon reached out his hand to Beau. "I must speak to you, as your staff won't help me. We need to talk about your guests gawking at my home."

"Well, now, I've been so busy I haven't seen this, um, interesting painting." Beau gave him a warm smile. "Let's head out to the courtyard and have a drink to discuss this."

He pointed toward the staircase, and I saw the frustration on Ambrose's and Daniel's faces.

"I could use a drink," Gideon said. "We can also chat about the parking lot. Do you really need it? I would be happy to buy it from you."

"It's not for sale, Gideon." Beau said. "And neither is the hotel."

Beau gestured again for the men to go down the stairs. Ambrose led the way, followed by Daniel and then Gideon, who didn't make eye contact with Beau. I ran my hand down the railing as I walked down, wondering if the Lovelorn Ghost's beloved made the staircase. The elegant lines of the bannister and the spindles shined under the recent polishing of the housekeeping staff. The newel post was topped with a perfectly shaped oval. I traced the design on the base that held the oval, thinking at first it was just a ribbon motif. But my finger stopped at a small daisy woven into the pattern.

My reaction caught Daniel's attention. "Hey, Sammy, what's wrong?"

Beau rushed over to me and hugged me. "You did it! You've found another daisy!"

"What are you talking about?" Ambrose crossed his arms. "Is there something you'd like to share with the manager of the hotel?"

Beau crossed his arms, too. "Sammy and I have been gathering information about the origins of one of the ghost stories. Of course we'll explain it now."

"What story?" Daniel and Gideon said in unison.

"Sammy, why don't you tell them?" Beau said.

I recounted the story and explained how I discovered the letters. Watching the reactions of each man was interesting. Ambrose's eyes widened as I told Daisy's story, but narrowed when I explained I found the daisy marks around the hotel. Daniel tapped his foot at varying speeds, but stopped when Beau put his hand on his shoulder. Gideon let his eyes wander around the hallway as if he wasn't interested, but he stared at me when I mentioned more daisies could be inside the hotel.

"So you mean all this time there's been a treasure here?" Gideon asked. "Beau, is that why you bought the hotel? For the money?"

"No, I had no idea there were things hidden here," Beau insisted.

"Are a few letters really a treasure?" Daniel said.

"Sometimes you are so insipid." Ambrose pinched the bridge of his nose and then gave an exaggerated exhale. "Treasure comes in all shapes and sizes. It can be personal or have worldly value."

"While that's a noble thought, I'm with Daniel. Treasure isn't a bunch of weepy letters," Gideon said.

While they were chatting, I checked the newel post, searching for a hidden compartment. Nothing opened on the post, so I moved back to the design on the base holding the oval. I tried sliding the daisy design, but nothing happened. Moving my finger around the base, I found a slight notch on the side facing up the stairs. I lifted up and the entire base rose. The men stopped talking and rushed over to me.

"You did it!" Beau said. "What's in there?"

I peered into the post, expecting to find a letter underneath it. Instead, I found that it was hollow, with a shelf halfway down. "Beau, can you reach in there? My arms are too short."

He reached down and pulled out two envelopes and a small, shiny object. He handed me one envelope, and he opened the other. Written in elegant cursive *To Whomever Finds This* and inside was a note on faded yellow stationery with a daisy embossed on the top. I read out loud:

> *I pray this letter is in the hands of my daughter or of her descen-*
> *dant. I never wanted to give up my child, but returning with her*
> *to this home was not possible. I had no way to raise her on my*
> *own without her father or the support of my family. I have left*
> *my treasures throughout the house and hope they have been*
> *found. My love has no end.*
>
> *Marguerite Daisy Fuller*

"Is that part of the treasure?" Gideon said.

Beau held up the object. It was an oval-shaped diamond brooch with a basket design dotted with tiny emeralds as flowers. "It's a pretty piece. If we don't find her relatives, we can display it in the library along with her letters."

Gideon, Daniel, and Ambrose spoke at once. Their words were all jumbled together, so I couldn't understand any of them. Ambrose put his hands up, and the other two stopped talking.

"As I was saying," Ambrose said. "The Fuller family died out decades ago."

"What were you going to say, Gideon?" Beau said.

"I heard the same, too. But do you think there's more jewelry? Or other valuables?" Gideon said.

"Is that why you want to buy the hotel? For the treasure?" Beau said.

"No, I want, I mean, wanted to buy this place to make sure it stays true to the neighborhood." Gideon huffed. "A measly diamond pin is worth little to me."

Daniel took the pin from Beau and inspected it. "I know a bit about jewelry from my mother. This looks real."

"I think so, too, but even if it has no monetary value, the historic value is priceless." Beau put out his hand, and Daniel placed the pin in it.

"What was in your envelope?" I asked, and Beau handed it to me. "Oh, it must be the money for the train. She didn't even get to the station."

"How sad," Beau said. "Ambrose, let's place these items in the hotel safe until we decide how to display them."

"What about our talk about the painting and the parking lot?" Gideon trailed after Beau, Ambrose, and Daniel. "It's important, too."

"Later, I promise." Beau tried placating Gideon as they walked into the office. I started to join them when Jasper called out my name.

"Hi, Jasper!" I strolled over to him. He sat on the edge of a chair in the reception area. "What are you doing here?"

"Just waiting for Momma. A friend of hers is taking us to dinner," he said. "Sounds like y'all were having quite the conversation. What's going on?"

"You heard us?"

"I've been here a while." He raised up a grocery bag from Frankie's. "I ran to the store to get a bottle of wine to take with us. It took a little longer than I expected, but of course Momma is still running late."

I laughed. "Well, at least you had some entertainment while you were waiting."

"I heard a bit, so there's a secret treasure here?" Jasper asked.

"Don't you remember I told you that story?" The scent of citrus perfume hit me before I had time to turn around and say hello to Charlene. "That's why we picked this hotel."

"So, you knew about the ghosts?" I said.

"Oh, yes, Scarlett had a friend who cleaned house for the lady next door. What's her name, Birdie or something?" Charlene said.

"You mean Momo McBride?" I said.

"That could be it. Any-who, we gathered there were ghosts and maybe even a hidden treasure." Charlene dug into her purse for a tissue and dabbed her eye. "Scarlett loved a good ghost story, didn't she?"

Charlene hugged me, then headed to the front door. "I'll see you soon, darling. Come on, Jasper! Betty's double-parked outside."

"Scarlett didn't love ghost stories, she loved stories about money," Jasper said as he trailed after his mother.

That was an interesting tidbit I hadn't expected. Was Scarlett searching for the treasure when she was killed? Even if she was searching for it, a ghost didn't kill her. But which human did? I still didn't have the answers, but I knew two people who might.

37

But those two people didn't know who killed Scarlett, and they weren't giving up much else, either.

"Sammy, you're here for another t-shirt, aren't you? I could have brought one home to you." Rob met me at the police station reception area after I had stopped by my apartment.

"Actually, I'm here to return Christine's clothes." I held up the plastic bag that had Christine's pants she had lent me after I pulled Scarlett's body out of the pool. "I washed and pressed them."

"Thanks." Christine took the bag with an inquiring stare. "Is that all?"

"Since you asked, how's the investigation going?"

"Didn't Sissy tell you what I told her?" Rob said.

"She did, but I thought y'all might have more info this evening," I said. "Do you?"

"I wish we did, but nothing new to share." Rob put his arm around me and walked me to the front door. "We will let you know, I promise."

"Sure will," Christine called out before I stepped outside. "And be sure to tell us anything you find."

I waved and headed back to Thibodeaux Mansion. A quartet playing *When the Saints Go Marching In* buoyed my weariness. But I completely forgot about my exhaustion when Connor called. I fell into his arms when I met him at Napoleon House. My favorite cocktail, my favorite dinner of a muffuletta sandwich, and my favorite man made for a relaxing evening. As we walked home arm and arm, the thoughts of ghosts and murder disappeared. I enjoyed a sense of normality, of living in the real world without worrying about my family or ghosts. I crossed my fingers and toes that the next day would be the same.

Apparently, I hadn't wished hard enough.

"Miss Ruby, what are you doing here?"

I climbed down the ladder as she walked into the library. My morning at the shop had been uneventful, and I hoped for the same at the hotel in the afternoon, but my neighbor's arrival changed that. Dressed in her usual layers of lilac chiffon, she waved her ring-laden hands in the air. She wore multiple necklaces, each featuring a different colored crystal.

"I am here to communicate with the spirits. Beau engaged me to speak with those that are trapped in the hotel, seek answers, and help them toward the light."

Beau, clutching Daisy's letters, followed behind Ruby. Her presence explained why he hadn't answered my texts earlier. I was dying to explore the attic after yesterday's interruption. Apparently a visit from our local ghost whisperer took precedence.

"Are you going to do a seance?" I asked.

Ruby snickered. "Seances are a waste of time. You need participants who have faith in the great beyond and open minds." She looked me up and down. "I see no one who fits that description."

I bit my lip so I wouldn't laugh at Ruby's snarky manner. Her seriousness was hard to take as she clutched her crystals, closed her eyes, and chanted words in Latin. I should have been insulted, as I considered myself open-minded. But my belief in the afterlife was definitely not as strong as Ruby wanted.

"Oh, I assumed that's what we were doing tonight." Beau's face showed his disappointment. "What is your plan?"

"Papa, can you bring my tools in here for me?" Ruby asked.

To my surprise, Papa came through the door carrying a large, white leather duffel bag. He handed it to Ruby. I was glad I had climbed down from the ladder, because I would have fallen off in shock at the smile Ruby gave Papa.

Well, well, Miss Ruby and Papa were apparently keeping company.

"Hey, Sammy. Isn't this exciting? I can't wait to watch Ruby in her element." Papa gave me a peck on the cheek. "And I hope she'll reach your cousin for you."

"Thanks, Papa." Did I want her to communicate with Scarlett? I wasn't sure, but then again, I hadn't decided if I believed in the spirit world.

"You haven't seen Miss Ruby contact the spirits?" Beau shook Papa's hand. "I thought you two worked together."

"Oh, no. I'm a Voodoo man and Ruby is a spiritualist," Papa replied. "I respect her beliefs and practices, but I go about things differently."

"Well, if Ruby can't connect with the ghosts here, then I need to hire you," Beau said.

"I don't think so." Papa laughed. "If Ruby can't reach them, I'm not going to try."

Ruby smiled at Papa, then scowled at Beau. "Papa is gifted, but if the ghosts don't speak to me, they will not speak to anyone."

Papa nodded his head and followed Ruby to the other side of the room.

"She is sure of herself," I said.

"For what I'm paying her, she should be," Beau said. "But it'll be worth it to find out what is going on here. We had more complaints again last night about noises. And now that we have the letters, hopefully Ruby can speak with Daisy."

"If Ruby does contact Daisy, what are you going to ask her?"

"Well, first, if she's making the noises, could she please stop?" Beau grinned. "But also, about the treasure. Finding it would be a lovely end to her heartbreaking story."

"I agree." I lowered my voice. "But no matter what, we still need to search the attic."

Beau nodded, but he stared at Ruby, who lit a stick of incense. The overpowering scent of cedar filled the air.

"OK, tomorrow then?" I hated to wait, but I realized there was no way Beau would do anything other than what Ruby said. While we spoke, his eyes followed her as she wandered from each corner of the room, placing her hands on the walls and bookshelves and inhaling and exhaling deeply at each spot.

"Yes, that sounds good." Beau moved to Ruby's side. "Anything?"

"Not yet," she said. "May I see the letters and the brooch?"

Ruby took the pin first and held it to her heart. "Oh, yes, the owner is nearby. Yes, I feel a presence."

"What's going on?" Daniel startled me as he whispered in my ear. "Ambrose is beside himself."

Daniel and Ambrose had entered the room while Beau and I watched Ruby. Ambrose pursed his lips as he tapped his foot. After looking at the collection of candles and crystals Ruby and Papa had placed on the bookshelves and on the desk, he sighed.

"Can we make sure the candles don't drip onto the furniture?" Ambrose walked over to Ruby. "We wouldn't want the antiques to be scorched."

Ruby glared at Ambrose. "I am a professional, Mr. Fortner. Your mother says to show some respect or she'll twist your ear from here to Sunday."

Ambrose went pale and stuttered, "My apologies, Miss Virtue." He raced back to the doorway and stood there, staring at the floor. Beau moved over to him and they whispered for a few moments. Ambrose said, "Thank you, Mr. Boudreaux. I agree I will stay in the reception area in case I'm needed."

"What was that all about?" I asked Beau.

"Ambrose claimed that's what his mother said whenever he was sassy. He's in a bit of shock, so I told him he didn't need to be here if he was uncomfortable."

"Come on, that was a lucky guess," I said. "Doesn't Ambrose seem like the type of child whose mother pinched him on the ear?"

"Ye of little faith," Beau said. "Ambrose took it seriously, so you should, too. Be prepared in case your cousin or even your parents show up."

Beau gave me a quick squeeze and returned to Ruby. I hadn't imagined my family appearing. If both sets of my parents showed up, I'm not sure I'd know what to do. But then again, I wasn't a complete believer, according to Ruby. But I couldn't help but wonder what tonight would have in store for me.

38

"Love radiates from these envelopes." Ruby had exchanged the brooch for the letters.

"I thought the same!" Beau followed Ruby as she went to the bookshelf with the secret panel. He explained the hiding place to her. He had to steady the ladder for Ruby, who insisted upon looking at the hidden panel. She held onto the top rung with one hand while she twisted back and forth, her eyes darting around the room.

"So many spirits come and go through here." Ruby said.

"Well, it is a hotel." Daniel laughed, but stopped when Ruby and Beau shushed him. "Sorry, I thought it was funny."

Daniel sat in a chair and took out his phone, pretending to ignore Ruby, but he glanced at her from time to time.

Papa came over to me and pointed at Daniel. "That was amusing, but he's too brash. If he's going to work in the tourism industry, he's got a lot to learn. The first thing he needs to know is you don't disparage spiritualists."

"I guess it's too late for me." I grinned. "But I'm on good footing with some spiritualists."

"With me you are, and you are with Ruby, too." Papa laughed at my shocked face. "She does like you in her own way."

"I doubt that, but she likes you."

Papa turned from me and followed Ruby's descent down the ladder. Considering she was wearing countless layers of wispy chiffon, she nimbly climbed down the rungs.

"Anything you'd like to tell me?" I said. "You and Ruby are chummy these days."

"What?" Papa looked confused, but then he laughed. "You think we're going steady? No, no, we're just old friends."

"Hmm, very close old friends by the smile on Ruby's face when she looks at you."

"Now, now, Sammy, really, we're two people who reconnected. And we have much in common so we like to spend time together."

"OK, whatever you say." I winked at him. "Are you here to help with the trapped spirits?"

"I'm here to carry her supplies." He lifted Ruby's bag. "And I'm curious to see how Ruby works."

"Me and you both."

On cue, Ruby came over, giving me a sour look and then smiling at Papa. "Thank you for helping, Papa. Your positive energy calms the spirits, which will help me engage with them."

"Is there a Ouija board in there? Sage? A bottle of the tears of a unicorn?" After I asked that, I remembered Ruby had no sense of humor. Thankfully Papa did, as he grinned quickly before putting on a serious face.

"If that was an attempt at humor, you failed, Samantha. Ouija boards are for slumber parties. I use sage to cleanse spaces, not call forth the spirits. And I have yet to find a crying unicorn." Ruby picked up the bag. "I only know happy ones."

She took Papa's arm and led him over to a bookshelf, where they set up more crystals and candles from her bag.

"I didn't think she had a sense of humor," Beau said. "Or was she serious about the unicorn?"

"Apparently Ruby has a sense of humor. Unless she has a unicorn hiding in her apartment."

"I wouldn't put it past her." Beau laughed. "I just hope she can contact the spirits."

"For your sake, I hope this works. But don't be upset if it doesn't," I said. "You can always try again if nothing happens tonight."

"I don't need your negativity," Ruby snapped as she spun to face me and Beau.

I protested, but I realized she was pointing to someone over my shoulder. Gideon Pearce had arrived. He opened his arms as he walked through the doorway. "Am I too late for the show?"

"Beau, you are not selling tickets for this evening, are you?" The ice in Ruby's voice was undeniable.

"Of course not!" Beau insisted. "Gideon, what are you doing here?"

Gideon walked around the room, eyeing Ruby's candles and crystals before he answered, "I heard a seance was going on tonight and I just had to come over."

"Why?" Ruby grabbed Gideon's hand before he picked up a pink crystal on the desk. "You don't strike me as a believer."

"Oh, but I am, Miss Virtue." Gideon kissed Ruby's hand

and held it before she withdrew it roughly. "I have heard of your abilities, and I wanted to see them in person. Also, I own the home next door and I thought my spirits might come over here tonight."

"The only spirits you know about are the drinking kind." Papa snorted.

"Oh, Papa Gede, you're here, too. Beau has pulled out all the stops." Gideon put out his hand, but Papa just crossed his arms. "I realize I'm not an invited guest, but I would be honored if I could stay. Think of it as a neighborly gesture."

Beau looked at Ruby. She sighed, but then nodded her head at Beau. "Fine, Gideon, but you must be calm. Miss Ruby needs us to follow her instructions or you will have to leave."

"Wonderful!" Gideon clapped his hands. "What can I do? Light more candles? Chant some archaic spells?"

"You can sit and be quiet." Ruby pointed to the empty chair next to Daniel, who barely contained his laughter. "And, Mr. Lane, you need to clear your heart, along with Mr. Pearce. I will banish you both if you keep distracting me."

It was nice to see other people on the receiving end of Ruby's ire. Daniel and Gideon didn't appear phased by the admonishment. They sat silently like two boys in detention who communicated with eye rolls. That was until Ruby glared at them as if she had eyes in the back of her head.

Beau and I waited as Ruby performed her ritual. She lit the candles, moved her crystals in random patterns, and then said, "Spirits, we welcome you to communicate with us. You are among friends."

She glided around the library, chanting louder with each movement. Her hand movements became more frantic as she moved until she stopped in front of the desk. She slapped her hands on the desk and snapped, "Out! All of you out! I cannot work with all this conflicting energy in the room."

"Miss Ruby, what is happening?" Beau's eyes were wide as he stepped in front of Ruby. "Are the spirits communicating with you?"

"Nothing right now," Ruby said. "Beau, please take everybody out into the courtyard and I will join you as soon as possible."

"Everyone, this way, please," Beau gestured toward the hallway. "We'll wait by the fountain for you, Miss Ruby."

"Thank you," Ruby said in a much gentler voice. "No, not you, Samantha. You stay."

I stopped in the doorway and turned to face Ruby. "Me?"

"You want Sammy to stay?" Beau looked heartbroken. "I can help you."

"I need a woman's energy right now, so all the men need to leave." Ruby smiled kindly at Beau. "Now please."

Papa picked up Ruby's bag and then ushered everyone out, and their voices were loud until the courtyard door squeaked shut. Ruby sat at the desk with her hands cupping a flickering purple candle. Not sure what to do, I moved closer to her and waited for her to speak. My stomach flip-flopped as I watched the wax drip slowly down the candle. The star-shaped candleholder collected the melted wax like a rain barrel collecting a slow drizzle.

"Samantha, I lied to get the others to leave."

I made eye contact with Ruby. She blew out the candle and stood up from the desk. She reached her hand to me and for a moment I wasn't sure if I was supposed to hold it. Were we going to do a seance? I hoped not, as I wasn't ready for this kind of intimacy with her. But if I had to, I would. I reached out to take her hand, but she dropped it.

"We're not holding hands!" She smiled ever so slightly and then said, "I need what you've taken from Daisy."

39

"I didn't take anything from her," I protested.

"Daisy insists you did." Ruby pointed past my shoulder "She's behind you saying you have a book."

I turned around, but no one was there. Not that I expected to see Daisy. But my backpack sat in the corner, and it had a book in it.

"You mean this belonged to her?"

I handed Ruby *The Mysterious Affair at Styles*. She took the fragile cover off and then opened the book. She closed her eyes and put her finger on the inside of the book cover. "Her name is right here. Didn't you see it?"

Sure enough, written in elegant but small cursive handwriting was *Daisy Fuller*. It wasn't visible with the paper cover on the book. I stared at her name as if it appeared by magic. "She and I have the same taste in books."

"Yes, Daisy agrees."

Once again, I turned around as if Daisy stood behind me. There was a slight chill in the air, which I knew to be a supposed sign of a spirit. It was probably my imagination, but it put me on edge. "What else did she say? Did she hide other things in the house? Should we keep looking?"

"She just nodded. Daisy? Where are you?" Ruby waved her hands and quickly relit the candle. "Oh, she's gone."

"She left?" My heart sank; there was more I wanted to learn from Daisy. Did I really believe Ruby was speaking to a ghost? As crazy as it was, I decided to give Ruby the benefit of the doubt. I could use any help I could get about the Lovelorn Ghost.

Ruby's disappointment was palpable as she clutched at her crystal necklaces and called out, "Daisy, come back, my dear!"

While she did that, I went through the book, hoping Daisy had left another letter or some kind of clue. Nothing but Agatha Christie's words filled the pages.

Ruby blew out her candle and grabbed her bag from the corner of the room. "We're done here. Daisy must need space or she's told us all she can or wants to."

"You seem disappointed, Ruby."

She sighed and brushed past me toward the courtyard door. "I would have liked to speak with her more and ask if she's the one making the noises. And I would have asked if she needed help to transition to the next world. But Daisy seems very determined to stay here at the hotel."

"What now?" I said.

"We'll go outside and discover if anyone else would like to talk. Are you ready?" Ruby took her hand off the door-knob and stared at me.

I followed Ruby out the door and into the courtyard. At least I thought I was ready, but now I wasn't so sure. If my cousin spoke to Ruby, who knew what she would say. But at least she couldn't push me into the pool this time. Or could she?

Beau, Daniel, Gideon, and Papa were all sitting at one of the courtyard tables. Gideon appeared to be holding court, or at least trying to. Either he didn't see or care about the bored faces of the other men.

"Ladies, you are a sight for sore eyes. These fellows are no fun." Gideon stood up. "I take it your female energy provoked the right response."

Ruby gave him a withering stare and walked past him to the Joan of Arc water fountain. Daniel was the first to follow her and stood by Ruby. "Ma'am, what did you learn inside?"

"Are you interested personally or professionally, young man?" Ruby asked.

"I guess both," Daniel answered. "I'm the night manager here, but I haven't seen any ghosts. But I get to listen to all the noise complaints from the guests."

"Hmm." Ruby placed her hand over Daniel's heart. By his wide eyes and twitching mouth, I bet he was wondering what in the world she was doing. She took her hand away and said, "You have energy surging through you and around you. If you channel it, the spirits will speak to you. Open your soul."

"OK, thanks," Daniel stammered.

Now Daniel had a personal reading from Ruby, along with Ambrose. Poor Beau looked crestfallen; Ruby had said nothing about Beau's spiritual abilities this evening. And he was the true believer of this ragtag group.

"You're welcome, Daniel." Ruby turned her attention back to the fountain. She dipped a finger into the water and swirled it around.

"Do you get anything from that thing?" Gideon snorted.

"Besides rust, I mean. Beau, you really should do some maintenance on this place."

"Gideon, if I had any nerves left, you would be on my last one," Beau snapped. "Remember, you're a guest here."

"Sorry, I didn't know you were so sensitive," Gideon said. "But honestly, Miss Virtue, what are you doing?"

"I'm listening for anyone that wants to speak to me, and I don't mean you," Ruby said. "Water can be a conduit for the spirits connected to the environment."

"Are you speaking to the first owners of the building?" Gideon asked. "Is the fountain covering up the treasure that's supposed to be here? What do you see?"

"Considering there's a spirit who is dancing while wearing a leisure suit, I suspect he isn't the first owner," Ruby said. "This fountain isn't original to the courtyard."

"You're correct." Ambrose joined us. His face wasn't as pale, but his eyes showed a wariness that I hadn't seen before. "That must be Mr. Grady. He owned the hotel in the 1970s and put in the fountain after the Joan of Arc statue was dedicated to the city."

"So, he's not staying alive?" Daniel said. "That was that old disco song, right?"

"Disco wasn't that long ago," Beau barked.

I placed my hand on Beau's arm, and he took in a deep breath. "Sorry, I'm just on edge. I hope we can connect to the ghosts who are disturbing our guests."

"Yeah, but no one is complaining about anyone dancing to old music." Daniel grinned.

Beau and Ambrose said in unison, "It's not old music!"

They stared at each in surprise and then laughed. Ambrose's low, deep laugh was charming. But more so was the smile that he gave Beau. Could the freeze be over between Ambrose and Beau? I hoped so, for both of their sakes.

"If we're done reminiscing, let's move on to the pool." Ruby took the arm Papa offered her. "Several spirits are pulling me toward them."

We followed Papa and Ruby to the pool. Beau raced in front of them and removed the "Closed for Maintenance" sign so we could go into the pool area. A chill ran through me as I stepped past the sign. The setting sun still lit up the courtyard, but the air was cooling. I doubted it was the temperature that was causing my chills — I couldn't look at the pool and not think of Scarlett's lifeless body. Beau put his arm around me and pulled me close to him. His actions were enough to warm my body and my heart until Charlene's voice rang out from the other end of the courtyard.

"Stop! Don't start without us!" Charlene stomped her way over, with Jasper following close behind. "We should have been consulted about this if you're going to talk to my baby."

Beau strode over to them and tried to put Charlene at ease. "Mrs. St. Martin, I'm sorry I didn't invite you. I wasn't sure if you were interested in the spiritual world."

"I'm interested in anything that has to do with my Scarlett." She put her hands on her hips. "If there's a chance we can find out the truth I'll take it."

She stared at me, and I nodded in agreement. Charlene raised her eyebrows as if she was surprised I wanted to learn what happened to Scarlett. I guess she still had doubts about me. Jasper didn't seem to as he walked over to me. "Hey, Sammy. You doing OK?"

"Yes, thanks. How did you hear about Ruby's visit here?" I said.

"We were heading out to dinner when the woman at the reception desk asked if we had spoken to the psychic." He sighed. "There was no stopping Momma when she heard that."

"I'm sorry. I guess y'all should have been invited. I found out about it at the last minute," I said.

Ruby stood by the deep end of the pool, with Papa to her right and Beau to her left. The rest of us huddled together by the other side, facing the brick wall. She took her bag from Papa and removed five white round candles. With a lighter from his pocket, Papa lit the candles and Ruby then placed them in the water where they bobbed up and down. Ruby took a handful of multi-colored crystals from the bag and placed them on the edge of the pool. Beau watched Ruby intently, following her every move. I hoped Ruby would let him help her at some point. But all she did was hand him her bag to hold.

"I need silence. Powerful vibrations are coming through." She clutched the crystals in her hand. "I need to listen to each voice."

She swayed back and forth and turned away from us so I couldn't watch her face. As tempted as I was to move so I could watch her from the front, I knew better than to disturb her. Would Scarlett's spirit speak to Ruby? If she did, I hoped she would reveal who killed her. What if Scarlett didn't see her attacker? Would she accuse me of the murder out of spite? A shiver ran down my spine as I watched Ruby kneel at the edge of the pool.

"Stop it! One at a time, ladies!" Ruby demanded. "I will bear witness to your stories, but you must behave."

Apparently the ghosts listened to Ruby since she stayed where she was. The group glanced around at each other, but no one spoke. After a few minutes, she stood back up and turned to face us, brushing her hands on her caftan.

"Miss Ruby, what did you hear?" Beau pleaded.

"There were two women speaking," Ruby answered. "The first was Anna, who is quite chatty. She asked if they convicted her sister for killing her."

"What did you tell her?" I said. Did Ruby read up about the ghosts? If so, she knew the answer was no.

"I told her I didn't know, but it didn't matter. She needed to move on because living in this purgatory is not good for her. The light is where she needs to go. Staying here hoping to exact revenge on her killer won't help her."

"So her sister, Alice, isn't there with her?" Beau asked. "She's alone?"

Ruby studied Beau's anxious face and answered, "No, she is with the other spirits. There is a young man here who obviously loves her."

"Oh, that's good," Beau said.

"Is she the one disturbing our guests?" Ambrose said.

So much for Ambrose not believing in ghosts. Ruby's early message from his mother must have changed his mind.

"She claims not to be," Ruby said.

She seemed to put Ambrose at ease with her answer, and he stepped back. Gideon whispered in his ear, and Ambrose shook his head and refused to make eye contact with him. What in the world did Gideon say?

"Is Scarlett St. Martin here?" Daniel asked. "Can you ask if it's all right if we open the pool again?"

Beau and Ambrose both whipped their heads around to frown at Daniel. Even Gideon looked surprised by Daniel's bluntness.

"What? Am I the only one being practical here? The guests want a pool." Daniel shrugged his shoulders. "I don't mean any disrespect."

"Forget the pool!" Charlene demanded. "Tell her I need her to come talk to me. I am her mother!"

Ruby squinted her eyes and breathed in deeply. Charlene took a step back, evidently feeling her anger.

"First, this is not a seance. Second, I cannot demand that a spirit speak to you. The spirits do what they want." Ruby's stern face softened. "I can sympathize with the loss of your daughter, but I cannot make her do anything against her will."

"So Scarlett won't have changed in the afterlife, then?" Jasper whispered to me. We smiled at each other, but quickly looked away. It wasn't the time to joke, but I was glad that Jasper was comfortable with me.

Charlene pushed herself in between us and clutched Jasper's arm. "That woman is just plain rude. All I want to do is speak to Scarlett. I have questions. So many questions..."

"Yes, we all want to know who killed her, Momma," Jasper said. "I think the police might have better luck than a psychic."

"What? Oh, yes, I wanted to ask her about her murderer," Charlene stammered.

By her awkward response and the distracted look in her eyes, she appeared to have more questions for Scarlett than who murdered her. What did Charlene want from her daughter? She'd already discovered her husband's extortion money wasn't in the tomb.

Papa came over to me and placed a hand on my shoulder. "Are you OK, Sammy? You're pale."

"I'm fine," I said. "This is my first time at an event like this."

"The spirit world can overwhelm you, especially when

it's your first time," Papa said. "And if your cousin is here, it's going to be an interesting night."

"That's what I'm afraid of."

"Anna and her suitor will consider moving on," Ruby proclaimed after five minutes of chanting while walking around the pool. "Her sister, Alice, refuses to, but she promises to leave her sister alone."

"That's a wonderful start," Beau said. "Were you able to find Scarlett?"

Ruby walked past Beau and stood in front of Charlene. "I'm sorry, but your daughter's spirit isn't here."

"Is that bad?" Tears streamed down Charlene's face. "Where is my baby?"

"Not all spirits stay where they've died." Ruby took the handkerchief Papa handed her and gave it to Charlene. "She may have crossed over or she could be somewhere else that had meaning to her in her life on this earth."

"She's probably with Daddy." Jasper put his arm around his mother. "He'll take care of her. And I'll take care of you. We're still a family."

Charlene sobbed, and Jasper guided his mother out of the area. His gentle manner with his mother warmed my heart and when he turned back to say, "It's all OK," I almost cried, too. It was like Jasper was including me in his talk about family. My desire to connect to my birth family couldn't be denied any longer.

The rest of us stayed around the pool as Ruby closed her eyes and chanted once again. Shelby opened the house-keeping door and stopped cold. She had a stack of folded towels in her arms and almost dropped them. We must have looked like an odd group. Beau, with his anxious face, hoping to see or hear the spirits. Ambrose looking exhausted. Daniel appearing blasé, but watching Ruby intently. Gideon was acting as if he'd lost interest in Ruby, but he hadn't left. There was Papa, keeping close to Ruby and grasping her elbow so she wouldn't fall in the pool. And there was me, confused by the deep sadness that filled me.

"I'm sorry. I didn't mean to intrude," Shelby said. "Is this a seance or something?"

"It is a spiritual exploration, Shelby. Nothing to worry about," Beau said.

"Oh, I beg to differ, negative energy forces are at work here," Ruby snapped her eyes open and scanned the courtyard. "Everyone should take heed and protect themselves."

"OK, that's my cue to leave," Gideon said. "Thanks for a fascinating production."

No one acknowledged Gideon, and by his firm stance, he appeared to be expecting someone to say something. He frowned and said, "Well, good night everyone, including the ghosts."

"If you're waiting for the spirits to wish you a good evening, you'll be here all night," Ruby said. "They have shown no interest in you, Gideon Pearce."

Beau, Papa, and Daniel laughed loudly, while Ambrose covered his mouth, barely stifling his giggles. I broke into a grin as Gideon turned quickly and stomped away. I couldn't wait to tell Sissy that Ruby put the infamous Gideon in his place.

"Um, Miss Virtue, are you only talking to the hotel ghosts?" Shelby timidly moved closer to our group.

"That's all that's here tonight," Ruby said. "Have we met? You look familiar."

"My nana brought me with her when she had you read

her tarot cards," Shelby said. "I was only thirteen, but I haven't forgotten it."

Ruby stared at her and pursed her lips. "Come back and see me now that you're of age. In the meantime, keep your heart open. The spirits are drawn to you. We'll talk more later."

"Yes, ma'am." Shelby's smile lit up her face, and she trotted over to the lounge. She turned before she entered the room. "Thanks. I hope the night goes well for everyone."

"She's a charming young lady," Papa said. "Full of positive energy and curiosity. Just like another young lady I know." He winked at me. "Now, Miss Ruby, are we done here?"

"We are."

Ambrose thanked Ruby for an enlightening evening, while Daniel nodded and followed Ambrose back into the hotel. Ruby and Papa picked up the crystals on the ground while Beau fished the candles out of the pool with a net. Ruby put everything back in her bag, and then she took Papa's arm.

They returned to the library. Beau and I accompanied them silently; he looked as exhausted as I felt. We helped Ruby collect her other crystals and candles and I put *The Mysterious Affair at Styles* back on its shelf.

"Daisy is happy that her book is in its proper place," Ruby said to me as I climbed back down the ladder. "She is interested in you, Samantha. Keep looking for her treasures."

"I will." And I meant it. While I didn't have Ruby's psychic skills, my intuition told me there was more to Daisy's story.

"Good." Ruby reached in her bag and took out a small

envelope and handed it to Beau. "Here is my invoice. Prompt payment is appreciated."

"Thank you for all your work tonight, Miss Ruby," Beau said. "I hope you'll come back again."

"And by the way, all the spirits say they are not making the noises. They insist those disruptions are caused by the living, not the dead."

And with that, Ruby took Papa's arm and left the hotel.

40

"Nubi, it's too early! Stop walking on my head," I pleaded.

"Meow." Nubi disagreed, so I stumbled out of bed and followed my perky cat to the kitchen. After spilling coffee grounds on the counter and pouring cereal for Nubi instead of cat food, I took a moment to center myself. Beau and I returned to Thibodeaux Mansion last night and shared a bottle of wine. Beau didn't want to talk about the evening in front of his employees.

"Sammy, the ghosts said they aren't causing the noises, so that means it's someone working at the hotel." Beau had moaned after finishing his first glass. "I need to question the entire staff to figure out what's going on."

"So you believe Ruby?" I had asked. "Or rather, do you believe the ghosts?"

"Yes, I do," Beau had said. "Do you suspect there are more of Daisy's treasures?"

I had said yes, so we made plans to search the hotel again, but the date and time were up in the air. Beau had meetings lined up, and he wasn't sure when he could break away to investigate with me. I wanted to look on my own, but I could tell Beau felt he needed to be there. His disappointment at not being able to see the ghosts lingered as the night wore on.

At least I'd keep busy with my library work. When I walked into Hotel Jeanne at nine, Ambrose was helping guests, but he gave me a wide smile. Did last night's experience soften Ambrose's manner? Or could it have been the spirit of his mother threatening to tweak his ear if he didn't behave?

Whatever the case, the atmosphere in the hotel felt lighter. I might have been imagining it, but I'm sure Ruby would say the spirits were responsible for this calming environment. I set up my laptop on the desk and opened my inventory file. There was still one more bookcase to catalog, but I also planned to search each shelf again for any daisy-marked hidden compartments. But before I did that, I checked the entire room again. Beau and I had searched thoroughly, but Ruby's declaration from Daisy that there was more to find motivated me to get down on my hands and knees and inspect each baseboard.

Nothing.

The desk was my last hope in the library, so I crawled underneath it. There wasn't much room, and I quickly discovered a tag from Sears. The desk wasn't an antique. Just as I tried to extract myself from the tight space, I heard Ambrose.

"No, I will not change my mind. You shouldn't have been at the seance," Ambrose said.

I waited for a response, but there wasn't one. He must be on the phone. As he continued to talk, his voice grew louder, along with his footsteps. "It's not working, and I have decided to make the best of the situation. Yes, I am serious."

His footsteps stopped, and I held my breath, waiting for him to enter the room. I planned to crawl out from under the desk, but his next words stopped me.

"Do not threaten me."

Ambrose was up to something, as Beau had suspected, but with whom? I hoped he would say the name of the person he was berating, but no such luck.

"Fine. We can talk tonight."

I finally exhaled when the courtyard door slammed shut. Who was Ambrose going to meet with that evening? Maybe I could follow him after he got off of work. Beau would kill me if I did. Well, if I went without him. He promised to come by Lagniappe Books after his meetings, so I'd share this bit of information with him then.

After I crawled out from under the desk, I brushed off the dust and checked my phone for the time. I agreed to bring lunch back to the shop so Andrew and I could go over the inventory list and other business. It was almost eleven, and I still had to catalog that last bookcase.

I grabbed my clipboard and moved the library ladder to the last bookcase. Needing both hands to climb the ladder, I placed the clipboard on a shelf. Between my exhaustion from yesterday and the nervous excitement of my renewed daisy search, I needed to be careful so I wouldn't slip. Or worse, damage the shelves or ladder. Or even worse, damage the books.

I gripped the rungs and planted my feet as I climbed up the ladder. When I was halfway up the ladder, the rungs were spongy under my hands. I grabbed them tighter as I continued, thinking I must just be exhausted. But when the top rung broke as I grasped it, and then the one underneath did too, I knew I wasn't that tired.

Yelling as I fell down, I caught my balance a bit, so I

didn't fall flat on my face or on my back. For once, I appreciated the extra padding on my backside as I landed firmly on the ground. I was stunned and looked up at the ladder, which was now missing two rungs.

"Sammy, are you OK?" Jasper and Ambrose rushed into the room.

"Samantha, what in the world happened?" Ambrose offered a hand, and I let him pull me off the ground. "Did you slip down the ladder?"

"She might have slipped, but it wasn't her fault." Jasper held a broken rung. "It's been cut through. This was no accident."

41

"What are you talking about?" Ambrose crossed his arms. "Mr. Boudreaux was worried about the ladder, but it seemed perfectly stable when Samantha used it last."

"Look at the ends of the rungs. They're smooth. They would be uneven if they had just broken off," Jasper said. "See for yourselves."

He handed each of us a rung and sure enough the edges were smooth, not fractured as I expected. I had assumed the ladder had weakened with my continual use this week. My stomach churned at the implication — this was no accident. But I didn't want to make a big deal about it until I talked to Beau.

"Really, I'm fine." I lied.

"Mr. Fortner, you need to call the police about this. Someone is trying to hurt my cousin."

While I appreciated Jasper was worried, it wasn't the time to talk to the police. That's the last thing the hotel or Beau needed. "Let's not jump to conclusions, although I appreciate your concern. Ambrose should talk to Beau first."

"I agree." Ambrose took the rungs out of our hands. "I will take these and discuss this with Mr. Boudreaux and Daniel. We need to inspect the ladder to check if it was normal wear and tear or an act of vandalism."

"But..." Jasper started to say, but I cut him off.

"Yes, Ambrose, that sounds like a great idea. Can you have someone take this ladder away? I can use a regular ladder to complete my inventory."

Ambrose's face relaxed. "Of course, I'll have our maintenance man remove it immediately. Will you need a ladder now?"

"No, I'm done for today. I need to get back to Lagniappe Books." I smiled through the increasing pain in my backside. "Thanks."

"Very well. I am sorry this happened to you." Ambrose left the room.

"Sammy, are you OK? Really?" Jasper asked.

"Yes, I guess I've been eating too many beignets." Trying to act like I wasn't in pain or concerned, I laughed a bit too loudly.

"I doubt that."

"You haven't seen me at Cafe du Monde on an empty stomach."

"Sammy, you're doing a good job masking your pain, but I see the fear in your face," Jasper said. "You can tell me the truth."

I stared into Jasper's pleading eyes, wanting to confide in him, but I stopped. Memories of my brother acting the same way after I discovered the body in the shotgun cottage flooded my head. That day I believed he was a concerned friend, not the murderer he turned out to be. Jasper had the same kind face as my brother. I didn't want to compare the two of them, but at times like these, it was hard not to.

"I'm fine, but I will be more careful around here. So what are you up to today?"

"Oh God, I forgot." Jasper smacked his hand on his head. "Momma wanted me to pick up more heartburn medicine at the drugstore. She'll be ranting and raving when I get back late."

"You better go." I smiled. "You can blame me for keeping you."

"I wouldn't throw you under the bus," Jasper said. "But I'm not going to tell her about the ladder. I don't want her worrying about you."

"That's a good idea." But really, would Charlene be that concerned about me?

Jasper waved and headed out. Thinking I was by myself, I rubbed my sore butt and sighed. I opened my backpack, hoping there was a stray aspirin at the bottom of my bag, but no such luck.

Shelby entered the room. "Ambrose had me bring you this pack of aspirin and an ice pack."

"He must be a mind reader." I took the ice pack and put it on my tailbone. I had no shame at this point. "And you're a saint. You even brought water."

I swallowed the aspirin with a gulp of the bottled water Shelby handed me. "Thanks."

"You're welcome. So what exactly happened? You fell down the ladder?" Shelby went over and looked at the missing rungs. "I mean this ladder is old and all, but I'm surprised it broke."

"You and me both."

"I don't think the ghosts did it, and not just because Miss Ruby said they weren't causing problems."

"You heard her say that, huh?" I hadn't realized Shelby

was around when Ruby made her declaration at the end of the night. "I didn't see you after Ruby spoke to you."

"I didn't plan to eavesdrop, but her voice carries." Shelby blushed. "I guess I blend into the scenery."

"Oh, I didn't mean that," I insisted as I sensed I hurt her feelings. "I was so distracted by Ruby's theatrics."

"Don't worry. People overlook me sometimes, especially in uniform." She smoothed down her apron. "It's not just guests who act like housekeepers are invisible. Other employees do the same sometimes."

"I think you stand out for your brains and beauty. You can't hide even in a gray housekeeper outfit."

"Thanks." Shelby blushed again. "But I figure it's good practice for when I'm a detective. You know, watching people when they don't realize it."

"Is there anything you've noticed lately that you'd like to share?" I asked. Shelby might be young, but she was observant and apparently using her job at the hotel as part of her education in criminal justice.

"Not just yet, I'm still investigating." She grinned.

"Shelby, you need to be careful. I'm speaking from experience." And with today's fall off the ladder, I was even more concerned about what was going on at the hotel. After the revelation about the found treasures and the potential for more, it appeared I wasn't the only one interested in finding more of Daisy's belongings.

"I'll be careful, I promise," Shelby said it as if she had said it a thousand times. I had used that tone with my own parents. "And I promise to let you know if I find anything."

I opened my backpack and took out a business card for the bookshop and wrote my cell phone number on the back. "Good. Here's my number. Call or text me any time. And don't get into any trouble."

"Thanks!" She put the card in her pocket. "See you later, Sammy!"

She bounced out of the room, and I couldn't help but smile. Shelby was an enthusiastic young woman, but I hoped she wasn't up to anything that would get her into trouble.

Or hurt like me. I returned the ice pack back to the refrigerator in the hotel kitchen and left with less pain, but with more worries that more trouble was to come at Hotel Jeanne.

42

"What a surprise. What brings you to Lagniappe Books?" I looked up from a box of books and saw Daniel walking through the door.

"I'd like to say it was you and the books, but Mr. Boudreaux brought me." Daniel stepped inside the shop, and Beau followed him in.

"Call me Beau, please. We're all part of the Hotel Jeanne family," Beau said. "Daniel and I met for coffee and when I said I was coming to the shop, he joined me."

"Welcome," Andrew said to Daniel. "We haven't met yet. I'm Andrew Ballard."

"Nice to meet you. So you're Sammy's boss?" Daniel picked up a book from the box I was unpacking.

"She's actually my business partner," Andrew said. "And you're the night manager at the hotel, correct?"

"I am. It's great now that Beau owns the place," Daniel said.

"You still think that after I said no to the business

center?" Beau laughed. "Sorry, I couldn't help myself. But I do like some of your other ideas."

"I'm glad you're willing to listen at least." Daniel handed the book he didn't even look at back to me. "So, Sammy, how's the library these days? Besides the ladder breaking."

"You heard about that?" I stared at Daniel. If he had been with Beau, how did he hear about the ladder? Before I could grill him, Beau intervened.

"Ambrose called me while we were meeting." Beau came over and hugged me. "He said you were fine, but you seem a bit shook up still. Are you sure you're OK?"

"Yes, just my pride hurts." I laughed it off in front of Daniel, since I wanted to chat with Beau alone. I wondered how much Ambrose had told him.

"We'll get a new ladder if you're still willing to finish the project," Beau said.

"Nothing would keep me from it," I said.

"Glad to hear it." Daniel smiled and winked at me. "I'll see you there soon, I hope."

I returned Daniel's smile, but not his wink. Although I didn't want to be rude, I didn't want to encourage him.

"Thanks again for meeting with me during your off-hours, Daniel." Beau walked with him to the front door. "We'll meet with Ambrose this week and go over the plans for the hotel."

"Sounds good. I better go get ready for my shift tonight." Daniel took a step out the door, but turned around to say, "I'm hoping the ghosts will be quieter after last night's seance."

"Fingers crossed." Beau called out and then shut the door. "Now, Sammy, I can see by your face Ambrose didn't tell me the entire story. What happened?"

"Someone sabotaged the ladder, that's what happened." Andrew's voice was full of anger and frustration. "I can't believe he glossed over the fact that someone tried to hurt Samantha."

Although I had been back at the store for hours, Andrew was still fuming about the incident at the hotel. While I appreciated his concern for me, I didn't want him to take it out on Beau. He was the one person at the hotel who wouldn't do that to me.

"Andrew, we don't know if the damaged ladder was meant for me," I said.

"No, Andrew is right, you're the only person who uses that ladder." Beau flopped on the loveseat in the sitting area. "Someone is trying to hurt the hotel and by extension, me."

"Well, I have a couple of ideas." I told them about the conversation I overheard Ambrose having with an unidentified person. "He might have been talking to Gideon. Both men wanted to buy the hotel, so what if they're working together?"

"It's possible." Beau sat up straight and pulled me down to sit next to him on the loveseat. "But I don't want you looking into this. I couldn't bear you getting hurt."

"Exactly." Andrew took the seat across from us. "Beau needs to have a heart-to-heart with Ambrose."

I tried to keep my frustration in check, but I couldn't stay silent. "Yes, he should talk to Ambrose, but wouldn't it be better if he had more information going into that conversation? If you know it's Gideon he's meeting tonight, you'll be able to confront him with the evidence."

Beau and Andrew exchanged glances; I was going to be outvoted. But Beau seemed to waver when he tapped his foot lightly and broke eye contact with Andrew. I pounced.

"Wouldn't it be good to discover if they're the ones making the noise?" I pleaded. "We just need to follow

Ambrose when he gets off of work tonight. It's that simple."

"I beg to differ," Andrew said. "It's not right for Beau to follow his employee like some two-bit gumshoe."

While Andrew smiled, I didn't believe he was joking. And now he and Beau were back on the same side.

"Sammy, I appreciate your help. Really, I do. But I would never forgive myself if something happened to you." Beau held my hand. "Again. We need to sort out this ladder business."

"Fine." I sighed. This was a losing battle, and I needed to move on. "But please don't tell me we're giving up on finding more of Daisy's treasures."

"No, but you and I should do it together," Beau said.

"That's an excellent idea." Andrew's body relaxed, and I felt guilty that I had made him worry.

"Good!" Beau clapped his hands. "We'll meet tomorrow morning and search the attic. Andrew, do you want to join us?"

"As much as I would love to rummage through a dusty attic, I have an appointment with Catherine here at ten."

"I would pick the attic over Catherine Chapman any day." I laughed, and Beau joined me.

Andrew smiled slightly, but then defended his publisher's publicist. "She's grating, but she means well. She wants to discuss the marketing of my book's paperback version before she works on the publicity this time."

That was a relief. Catherine's social media campaign for the release of Andrew's hardback book horrified him. But she didn't turn out to be a murderer, so that was a relief, too. "Well, just be sure to have black coffee and no gluten, dairy, or nut-filled pastries for her."

This made us all laugh. As much as I wanted to see what

Ambrose was up to, I needed to respect Beau's wishes. Andrew only had my well-being in mind, especially when Connor came through the door.

"Hello, gorgeous." Connor strode across the store with a grin on his handsome face. He wore jeans and a blue Preservation Hall t-shirt that matched his eyes.

"Hello to you, too." Beau laughed and got up from the couch. "Oh, you meant Sammy, didn't you?"

"You're gorgeous, too. And Andrew, of course." Connor sat down next to me and put his arm around me. "But I'm Sammy's."

"Story of my life. Thank goodness Andrew likes me though." Beau and Andrew smiled at each other.

"I do, especially if you'll help me close up the shop."

"But I can help you," I said. "Connor can wait until I'm done, right?"

"I'm sure he would, but we didn't plan it that way," Andrew said.

"What?" I asked.

"Andrew texted me earlier and said you needed a night away from ghosts and secret treasures," Connor said.

"Wait, you texted someone?" I gasped theatrically. "Are you feeling all right, Andrew?"

"I am inching my way into the world of texting." Andrew stood up and went to the office door. "And I wanted Connor to surprise you."

Andrew brought out my backpack out of the office. "You need a night with the living, not the dead."

"So it's settled, you're coming with me." Connor grabbed my bag from Andrew. "No ifs, ands, or buts. Well, just your cute butt."

"Aren't you funny?" I swatted at his arm. "Where do you plan to take me?"

"Yes, do tell," Beau said. "Or is it a surprise?"

"It's a surprise," Connor said. "Sammy doesn't need all the answers just yet."

"I agree." Andrew smiled. "Go out with your young man. Us old men can handle the shop."

"Who are you calling old?" Beau puffed out his chest. "I look young from my head to my toes."

"Your hair is as gray as mine, I bet." Andrew ran a hand over his salt and pepper hair. "I know your stylist and she's famous for making her clients look young."

"Sounds like Marie Laveau is your hairdresser." Connor laughed and put up a hand. "Don't yell at me. I understand our Voodoo Queen wasn't a hairdresser. And yes, I know she's dead."

"You two are just plain cruel." Beau pouted. "I should get a Voodoo doll for both of you. Sammy, let's go see Papa."

"He wouldn't make them." I kissed Beau on the cheek and then gave Andrew a hug. "At least not one of Andrew."

"Hey..." Connor protested, but a grin spread across his face.

"I promise not to let Papa make one of you." I took my bag from Connor and pushed him to the door. "Unless this is a bad surprise."

"Oh, I doubt it is." Beau walked over to Andrew and put his arm around him. "We'll close up the shop so you two kids can have fun."

"Have a great time." Andrew smiled. "Remember, wait for Beau tomorrow before you go searching, Sammy."

"Scout's honor." I held up my fingers in what I believed was the Girl Scout pledge.

"Make sure she's not crossing the fingers on her other hand," Beau called out as I followed Connor.

"I promise," Connor said before closing the door behind

us. "Now let's head out somewhere we won't get into any trouble."

"That doesn't sound like fun." I giggled.

"Well, I'll just have to prove to you I can show a woman a good time." Connor put his arm around me.

I wrapped my arm around his waist, hooked my finger in one loop on his jeans, and pulled him closer to me. Breathing in the faint scent of his sandalwood aftershave and feeling the warmth of his body close to mine, I relaxed. "You're off to a good start," I said. "Let's see what you have in mind for tonight."

43

―――――――

"**I** should have guessed where we're going from your t-shirt." Connor and I turned onto St. Peter Street. The world-famous Preservation Hall stood in the middle of the block, although the line for the next show was almost to the corner.

"I was worried that your sleuthing skills were slipping when you didn't guess where we were heading."

"I thought I wasn't supposed to wear my detective hat tonight."

"You're right," Connor said. "But you can use it one more time to figure out who we're going to sit with this evening."

I scanned the area as we walked down the block toward the entrance. Although the next show didn't start for over an hour, tourists and locals alike waited since they didn't sell tickets in advance. It was first come, first serve. Fortunately, our friends stood at the front of the line.

"There they are!" Sissy waved at us. "I almost drank your Hurricane."

"Glad we got here in time." I took my drink from Sissy. The popular Pat O'Briens bar was next door to Preservation

237

Hall and their iconic cocktail, the Hurricane, made the wait easier. Neal, Rose, and Sissy each had their own cup. But another person stood behind Neal.

"Jasper, you're here!" I gave him a quick hug. "What a wonderful surprise."

"Connor invited me," he said. "I've never been here before."

"Me, neither. This will be fun." I hugged Connor, whispering in his ear, "That was sweet of you to include him."

"I thought it'd be good for him and you." Connor kissed me and then raised his cup. "Now that we're all here, I want to make a toast. To friends, old and new!"

"Yes!" Neal shouted as we all raised our cups. "And to a night of awesome music and no worries."

"I'll drink to that," I agreed.

We were waiting for the six o'clock show, so we had time to chat and drink outside the building. Preservation Hall, with its distressed facade and unassuming signage, was easy to miss if you didn't know about this historic place. Since the 1960s, the venue hosted concerts featuring all types of music, but it was the jazz bands that drew locals and tourists.

My excitement grew as the gates opened and we walked through the courtyard entrance and then into a large room. Connor had explained what to expect, but I was still in awe as we found seats on a bench on the side of the room. This wasn't a fancy concert hall. From the well-trodden wooden floors to the crumbling plaster walls lined with art and signs, a sense of history filled the air. Quickly the benches were taken, as well as the floor seating.

In front of the room, chairs that looked like someone had pulled them from a dining room table set made up one row. Behind them was a drum set and a piano. The band came in and took their seats to the cheers of the crowd. As much as I loved listening to musicians on the street corners, this was an exceptional experience.

Our entire group clapped and sang along with the band, especially Connor. After our favorite song, *What a Wonderful World*, ended, I squeezed his hand gently. "One day you'll play here," I said in his ear.

Connor kissed me and whispered back, "From your sweet lips to God's ears."

Neal caught us kissing and grinned. "OK, you two love-birds, it's time to get clapping again." He pointed to the sign on the wall that said, "Traditional Requests $5, Others $10, The Saints $20." Neal took out his wallet and gave twenty dollars to the bandleader. They played *When the Saints Go Marching In* next. I'd heard it a thousand times, but cheering and singing along to it in this historic venue with some of my favorite people made it feel brand new.

Scarlett's murder and the ghosts slipped out of my mind for the forty-five minute concert, and in its place a sense of contentment and hope took over. While I didn't know if it would last, I would take it for now.

"Oh, when the saints..." Neal sang as we walked back to Thibodeaux Mansion.

"Don't drop the pizzas!" Sissy said. "I'm starving and you don't want to see me hangry."

"I've got them," Neal insisted, but Rose took them out of his hands and we all let out a sigh of relief. The music had kept our minds off of food, but once we walked out onto the crowded street, the smell of freshly baked pizzas overcame us. Connor led our group over to a pizza shop on the other side of the street and ordered two large pizzas and two six packs of Abita Beer.

"Hey, no cell phones tonight," Connor said. I had taken my phone out to check for messages. "Let's concentrate on actual people, not online folks."

"Good idea." But before I put my cell phone away, I read a text from Shelby, *Hi, it's Shelby. Just wanted you to have my number. I'm looking into some stuff tonight and I'll call you if I find anything.* She had sent it at five o'clock. I didn't see any voicemail notifications, so she hadn't called. She must not have found anything, and I was relieved because I didn't want her to get into any trouble.

I opened the courtyard gate, and we walked to the table where Libby and William were eating cake and drinking red wine.

"Well hello there," Libby said. "If I knew y'all were coming back, I would have brought home the entire cake from the cafe."

"I'm not sharing." William pulled his plate closer to him and smiled.

"Not even for a piece of andouille sausage pizza?" Connor opened the first box of pizza that Rose had placed on the table. "It's your favorite."

"You're an hour too late," William said. "Your mother brought home chocolate praline cake, and I am stuffed."

"More for me then." Neal took a seat and waved Jasper over. "Come on over, buddy. You must be hungry."

"Thanks." Jasper walked over and sat in-between Neal and Libby. He'd been so relaxed at Preservation Hall that it surprised me to see him act so timidly. Was he nervous to be around Libby and William? He hadn't seen them since he and his family showed up out of the blue a few days ago.

"Jasper, I am sorry about your sister." Libby patted his

hand. "I'm so glad you're spending time with Sammy and her New Orleans family. I hope it's a comfort."

"Yes, ma'am, it's helped to be with Sammy and y'all." Jasper's face relaxed a bit. "And I'm sorry my momma and I haven't thanked you for the flowers and pastries you sent to the hotel for us."

"Oh, that was nothing," Libby said. "I find food helps in almost every situation. And those are Sammy's favorite scones, so I thought you might like them, too."

I sat down across from Libby and smiled. She must have sent over sweet potato scones.

"My momma and I both loved them, Mrs. Tyler," Jasper said.

"Call me Libby, honey. Now Jasper, tell me all about you." She turned her chair to face him directly, and the two of them chatted away.

"Hey, Connor. I think it's your turn to play music," Rose said.

"I don't know. I'm not like the musicians we heard tonight." While he protested with his words, he immediately headed toward his apartment. "But I can try."

He came back with his trumpet and played a few songs. Even though the sun had already set, the air was still warm. But it wasn't just the weather that made the courtyard feel comfortable. Connor's soulful tunes bounced off the brick walls. Neal and Rose were slow dancing by the fountain while Sissy swayed to the music from her seat. Jasper tapped his toes, and I noticed he hadn't rubbed his crescent moon scar all night. The evening wasn't only good for me, but also for Jasper, it appeared.

"Everyone's having a great time, aren't they?" Libby moved her chair over to mine. "It's wonderful to be together, isn't it?"

"It is." I squeezed Libby's hand. "I'm so thankful for this evening."

"I'd say your cousin is, too." Libby said. "He fits right in."

"He does, doesn't he?" I said.

Sissy grabbed Jasper's hand, and they joined Neal and Rose to dance to Connor's version of *When the Saints Go Marching In*. "I know y'all just met this week, but you two are more alike than you realize."

"You mean we both like sweet potato scones?" I laughed, hoping Libby wouldn't drag me into a psychoanalyzing session. She always meant well, but I didn't want to ruin the lighthearted mood with a study about my family relationships. Either Libby recognized my resistance, or she had never planned to act as my therapist.

"Yes, but who doesn't love them?" She giggled. "What I mean is that you've both looked for a family connection and here it is."

Jasper wanted to connect? Libby noticed something that I didn't. As I focused on Connor's latest tune, I thought about Libby's observation. Jasper and I were getting along well, all things considered. Perhaps I needed to put more effort into our relationship. I couldn't keep comparing him to my brother; it wasn't fair to him or to me.

"And speaking of relationships." Libby's words interrupted my musings. "I'm glad you and Connor are back on track. He was so worried. He really cares for you."

"I care about him, too."

"That makes me so happy." Libby's eyes teared up. "He's finally settling into himself and you're a big reason for that."

"Don't pressure her, Libby," William had walked over and stood behind Libby's chair. "But it's true. You brought all of us together."

I nodded, as I couldn't get any words out. My heart was

overflowing with emotions. How lucky was I that I had found a community here in New Orleans, a romantic partner, and now a cousin from my birth family? The music washed away the worries of the past few days, and love surrounded me in the courtyard. I hoped these good feelings would last more than just one night.

44

———

Around nine-thirty, I walked into Hotel Jeanne to find Ambrose and Beau at the reception desk. "Shelby didn't come home last night, and she hasn't shown up here," Beau whispered to me.

"Mrs. Jones, Shelby is on the schedule this morning, but no one has seen her. Yes, I'm sure." Ambrose was on the phone with an exasperated expression on his face, but his voice was full of patience. "She worked yesterday, but her timecard shows she clocked out at 8:02 p.m."

I clutched the edge of the desk as my knees buckled. When I finally checked my cell phone this morning, I discovered Shelby had left a voicemail at 8:30 p.m. Her voice was a pitch higher than usual when she said, "Hey, Sammy. I'm on to something. I'll meet you in the library when I get to work tomorrow. Bye!"

Expecting Shelby to tell me her theories and potential evidence about the noises, I'd brought an extra scone for her. She sounded so excited that I assumed she would find me right away. I couldn't believe she wasn't here. The hairs on the back of my neck bristled as I listened to Ambrose.

"Yes, I will double-check for you. Can you hold a minute, please?" Ambrose put the call on hold and turned to me. "Samantha, you look pale. Do you know something about Shelby?"

"She left me a voicemail last night," I said.

"Here, talk with Mrs. Jones." Ambrose handed me the phone and took the call off of hold.

"Hello? Mr. Fortner?" a woman pleaded.

"Mrs. Jones, I'm Samantha Richardson…"

"I know who you are. Shelby talks about you." I heard a bit of relief in her voice. "She's taking her education more seriously because of you."

"Shelby's a smart woman and she'll do well in school," I said. "So tell me, what's going on?"

"She didn't come home last night. I know girls her age stay out sometimes, but not my Shelby."

"Could her cell phone be dead? Maybe she stayed with a friend and hasn't called?" I prayed that Mrs. Jones would agree and Shelby would walk through the door, either at home or here.

"No, her phone goes to voicemail. She answers my calls unless she's working." Her voice cracked. "Shelby always checks in with me. Something's wrong. I can feel it. Can you help, please?"

Ambrose whispered, "Shelby isn't answering my calls, either." He put the receiver down on the other desk phone.

"Mrs. Jones, does Shelby have a laptop at home? Or an iPad?" I asked.

"She has an iPad. Should I get it?"

"Yes, please."

I heard Mrs. Jones drop the phone, and heavy footsteps followed. I turned to an anxious Beau and Ambrose and told them about Shelby's text and voicemail. Beau's face paled, and his eyes darted between me and Ambrose. He whispered, "Do you think Shelby found something?"

"If she did, and if it was of value, I am sure she would have told me." Ambrose paused. "Or Daniel, since he was working last night."

"Call Daniel and ask him if he saw Shelby last night?" Beau said. Ambrose nodded and went back to the other phone.

"I'm back, Samantha. What do you want me to do with it?"

"Open the 'Find My' app. If her phone is still on, we can locate it and I bet we'll find her with it."

"I'm opening the app now." Mrs. Jones sighed loudly, and then there was silence.

"Just let me know when it finds her phone," I said, after waiting for the longest minute of my life.

"It found her." Her voice sounded confused.

"Where is she?"

"It says she's at the hotel."

45

____

"Are you sure?"

Beau and Ambrose stared at me as the phone shook in my hand. I gripped the handset and asked again, "Are you sure, Mrs. Jones? Could it be at the coffee shop a few doors down?"

"No, it shows at the hotel. It's not the main building but the one that has the housekeeping room."

"Well, then she must be in there and turned her ringer off." I tried to sound perky, but it sounded fake even to me. "We'll go there right now and I'll make sure she calls you immediately."

"Should I come down there? What if she's hurt?" Mrs. Jones pleaded.

"I promise we'll call you if we don't find her. And call us if she comes home or calls you," I said.

We hung up, and I looked at Beau. "We need to search for Shelby."

Just then a couple came to check-out, so we left Ambrose at the reception desk. He chatted with the guests, but his voice had an undertone of anxiety. I hadn't expected him to be so worried about Shelby.

Beau and I rushed to the housekeeping room first. "Here, let me." I took the master key from Beau's shaking hands. I flung open the door and call, "Shelby? Are you here?"

Not a word.

I searched the room, including the industrial size washers and dryers. Beau's face turned green when I did that, and it didn't change when we locked the door behind us.

"Where to now?" Beau looked around the courtyard. "Should we check the pool?"

I didn't answer him, but continued to the back and held my breath as I scanned the bottom of the pool. There was nothing but a few stray flowers from the jasmine vines floating on the surface. "It's empty, Beau. Are the guest rooms next to Housekeeping occupied?"

"No. Let's go through them." Beau reached into his pocket. "Oh, do you still have the key?"

"Yes, come on." I had already opened the door to the first room. A blast of icy air hit me. "Shelby? Are you here?"

Beau followed me and shivered. "I can't believe someone left the air conditioner like this, especially in May. Let me go turn it off."

He went to the other end of the room and turned down the thermostat. "The room looks fine."

I agreed with him. A white duvet covering the queen-size bed was in place, as well as the matching pillows by the headboard. The nightstands, entertainment center, and dresser looked pristine. The bathroom door was open, so I stepped in to check the shower. "All clear in here."

"Sammy, come look." Beau stood in front of the closet door.

I joined him and saw the door was ajar. I reached out to pull the door aside, but I jumped back when I heard a cell phone ringing. It wasn't my phone and by Beau's face I knew it wasn't his. After saying a prayer, I grasped the handle and slid it back.

The cell phone stopped ringing as I stared at Shelby curled up in the closet.

"Is she sleeping?" Beau whispered.

"No." I swallowed the sob that I wanted to let out. "She's dead."

"How can you be sure, Sammy?"

I wished I had a different answer, but dried blood coated one of Shelby's multi-pierced ears. Besides the head wound, the belt from the hotel-supplied bathrobe was knotted around her neck. I peered at her fingernails and didn't see any flecks of blood. She must not have touched her wound or fought when she was strangled. That would be one saving grace if Shelby hadn't suffered.

Beau crouched down and stared at Shelby. "Oh, sweet girl, what happened to you?"

"Did you find her?" Ambrose stepped into the room, and his face paled as he stepped toward us and looked into the closet. "She's dead, isn't she? Oh, no."

Ambrose slumped, and I put my hand on his back so he wouldn't fall. Fortunately, he straightened himself almost at once. "I'm fine, thank you."

At least one of us was. Beau hadn't moved away from Shelby. I wrapped my arms around myself in hopes I would stop shaking. My body was racked with sorrow, but also guilt. I should have checked my phone last night. If I had called her back, could I have saved her? Taking in a few deep breaths, I calmed myself. I would mourn Shelby later. Now I needed to find her killer.

46

"The victim called you last night? Can you play the voicemail for us, please?"

Rob gestured for me to sit on a chair in the pool lounge. After we pulled ourselves together, I had locked the room while Beau phoned the police. Ambrose called Daniel to come in and then he gathered the staff to explain there had been an accident. They milled around the courtyard for a bit, but Ambrose got them to go to the kitchen. But not before they all looked at me suspiciously. Apparently, my presence made them wary. And with good reason. Here I was finding another dead body at the hotel, and it was one of their own.

I played Shelby's voicemail for Rob and Christine. My hands shook, and I clutched my phone tighter as I recounted my conversation with Shelby, explaining she said she was investigating the noises. "She told me guests and employees didn't always notice housekeepers, so she saw and overheard things."

"You think she discovered what or who was causing

them." Rob put his hand on top of my mine. "Do you know who she suspected?"

I shook my head. "She wouldn't tell me. I told her to be careful and call me if she found anything." I wiped my eyes with a napkin on the table.

"You didn't come back to meet her?" Christine asked. "You must admit Sammy, you've been known to do research on your own." The hint of sarcasm in Christine's voice when she said research set me off.

"No, not this time," I snapped. "But maybe if I had, Shelby would be alive." I covered my mouth to hold back a sob. The reality that she was dead and that I might have prevented it shattered me.

"Or you might have been killed, too," Christine said with a soft voice I'd only heard a few times. "We don't have the time of death yet, so she might have been killed this morning when she arrived for her shift."

While I appreciated Christine's attempt at lessening my feelings of guilt, it didn't work. "My gut says her message had something to do with her death. The noises are disrupting the hotel and along with the search for the treasure, there's a lot going on here."

I then explained about Daisy's letters and the implication there was a hidden treasure in the hotel. Both detectives raised their eyebrows when I told them about Ruby's declaration that the ghosts weren't causing the noises. "Well, that's a first," Rob said. "Usually mediums claim everything is related to the spirits."

"Please wait here, we'll be right back," Christine said.

They headed toward the door and I heard Christine say to Rob, "I wish the hotel had an electronic keycard system instead of actual keys." I had to agree with her. After this second murder, I bet Beau would change the metal keys out for plastic cards.

As soon as they left, Beau sat down next to me. He had been with another detective explaining his version of events while Ambrose was at the reception desk.

"You think it's the same person who killed your cousin?" Beau asked.

"Two murders in a week is suspicious to say the least."

"You're right and they both were young women." Beau gasped. "Do we have a serial killer at the hotel?"

"I don't know, but we need to be careful."

By careful, I didn't mean to wait for the police to solve the case. Shelby and Scarlett both deserved justice, and I would make sure they got it.

47

Ambrose joined us in the pool lounge with coffee. "I thought you both might need this."

"Thank you," Beau said. "How is everyone?"

"The staff is understandably distraught about Shelby. They are unaware of the details and I insisted they keep the news to themselves." Ambrose sipped his coffee. "By the amount of police here though, they are suspicious."

"Has anyone told Shelby's mother?" I put my coffee down with my trembling hand. "Her phone was still ringing when we left the room."

Rob and Christine walked back into the lounge and stood over our table. "We sent two detectives over to her mother's house already," Rob answered. "We'll go see her in a bit, but we have a few more questions."

"First, I need everyone's whereabouts between 8 p.m. and midnight last night," Christine asked. "Let's start with you, Sammy."

"That's when she died?" Beau said, before I answered. "You can tell even with that air conditioning turned up full blast?"

"You noticed that, too?" Rob said.

"Yes, and I checked with our head of housekeeping, Mrs. Wright. She cleaned the room yesterday and said she set the thermostat at seventy degrees," Ambrose said.

So the murderer turned the air conditioner up, possibly trying to hide the time of death. It reminded me of the pool heater that was off when I found Scarlett. That couldn't be a coincidence.

"We need to be the ones to ask the questions." Christine stared at Ambrose, who nodded, but didn't say a word.

"Let's get back to everyone's whereabouts last night. Sammy?" Rob played good cop to Christine's bad cop.

"I went to Preservation Hall and then home for the rest of the evening," I said. "Sissy can vouch for me along with Jasper, Neal, Rose, and Connor. And Libby and William stayed with us until the party broke up."

"What time was that?"

I had to bite my lip not to say that he had the answer. He came into the courtyard while we were cleaning up and left with Sissy to her, now their, apartment. "Around eleven."

"Can anyone vouch for you after that?" Christine asked.

"Yes, Connor." My face grew warm, which was ridiculous. We were adults.

"OK, then. Ambrose, how about you?" Rob asked after giving me a quick smile.

"I left the hotel at approximately 7 p.m. and then I returned home," Ambrose said. "I'm afraid no one can confirm my whereabouts."

Beau and I gave each other a knowing glance. Did Ambrose cancel his meeting with the person he talked to yesterday? I couldn't tell if he was lying, since his face was completely blank.

"I spent the evening with Andrew and was home by 11:30

p.m. My neighbor, Mrs. Landry, stopped me outside my house, and I spoke with her until well after midnight. She is a chatty woman," Beau said.

"Thank you all," Christine said. "We'll be in touch."

"May I tell the guests now? Or rather, may Mr. Boudreaux talk to them?" Ambrose turned to Beau. "I assume you'd prefer to explain the situation to them."

"We can do it together, if the detectives agree?" Beau said.

"Yes, and please inform them we'll need to speak to each of them. You can go ahead. We just have a question or two for Sammy," Christine said.

Beau gave my shoulder a quick squeeze and left the lounge with Ambrose.

"All right, Sammy, you must have some theories about Miss Jones' murder, so let's hear them," Christine said. She and Rob sat in the vacated chairs. I took a sip of my now tepid coffee and gathered my thoughts.

"The hotel is supposed to be haunted, but the noises have increased since Beau bought it," I said. "The guests are complaining more and more. It isn't good for Beau's investment."

"Who do you think is behind the disturbances?" Christine asked.

"Do you know Gideon Pearce?" Rob's pen flew over his notepad as I explained Gideon's obsession with the hotel and his interactions with Ambrose. Then there was Daniel, who worked last night and was also a bit too friendly with Shelby, according to her.

"Thank you for your insights, Sammy," Christine said. "Did your cousin Scarlett know any of those gentlemen?"

"She must have met both Ambrose and Daniel, but I'm not sure about Gideon." I took another sip of my coffee and wished I hadn't since it tasted bitter. "If he saw Scarlett I bet he would have approached her."

"Sissy told me about your run-in with him the other night," Rob said. "He's known for being overbearing, but would he kill for the hotel?"

I shrugged my shoulders. "I've seen Ambrose and Gideon talking, and I can't help but wonder if it's about the hotel. Both wanted to buy it. The hotel seems to be the only thing the two have in common."

"Thanks for all the information. Now I need to ask this." Christine looked me straight in the eye and I braced myself for her question. "You and Shelby talked a lot. Did she try to blackmail you about your cousin's murder? Did you delete any other voicemails from her?"

"What?" I yelped and stood up, but I sat back down as my knees shook. "First, Shelby was not the kind of woman to blackmail people. Second, I had nothing to do with Scarlett's death, so there is nothing to blackmail me about. And no, I didn't erase any messages. Take it." I pushed my phone across the table to Christine.

She scrolled through my voicemail and texts, and then carefully put the cell phone in front of me. "Thank you."

"Don't be upset, Sammy. We can't have anyone think we didn't investigate you properly," Rob said. "It's awkward for all of us, but you know we need to rule everyone out so we can look for the killer."

"I understand." My breathing had returned to normal. I understood they had to ask me, but I worried other people would think I had something to do with Shelby's murder, along with Scarlett's.

"That's all for now." Christine stood up. "Are you OK to walk home? An officer can escort you."

"I'll be fine, thanks." I'd had enough of the police for

today, although I appreciated Christine's gesture. Both she and Rob were just doing their jobs and while they always took each case seriously, the worry in their eyes seemed deeper this morning. Two deaths at a hotel in one week wasn't good for the city. Tourism was the bread and butter for New Orleans, especially the French Quarter. But I knew Rob and Christine were concerned more about the victims and their families.

I left the lounge and headed into the main building. A group of guests had surrounded Beau and Ambrose, demanding an explanation for the police presence. The occupancy of the hotel was already low from Scarlett's murder and I imagined more people would check out. Charlene and Jasper were part of the group, so I tried to sneak by, but Charlene saw me.

"Sarah Jane! What are you doing here?" Charlene trotted over, holding her white purse to her chest. The police commotion must have caught her during her morning beauty routine. She had curlers in her hair and her pink lip liner was on, but no lipstick.

"Sammy, are you OK? You look like you've seen a ghost." Jasper put his arm around me. "What happened?"

"Follow me." I turned around and headed to the library. I didn't want to speak in front of the other guests. When we passed the kitchen, the quiet sobs from the hotel staff made my stomach turn. From the devastation on their faces, they hadn't just lost a co-worker, but a member of their work family.

Once we were in the library, I explained to my relatives what happened to Shelby. "That poor child." Charlene sat in one of the wing chairs and pulled a tissue out of her bag. "And her momma is going to be devastated."

Jasper stared at me. "She's dead? I can't believe it."

"Did you know her?" I asked.

"I saw her around the hotel, but I didn't meet her until she cleaned our room after the police searched it," Jasper said. "God, she was just a kid."

"This hotel is cursed." Charlene blew her nose. "I know your friend owns this place, but something is not right here. That psychic didn't get rid of any ghosts."

I agreed that something wasn't right at the hotel, but I believed it was someone, not something, that was wrong. Ghosts didn't kill two women; a human being did.

And most likely it was someone connected to the hotel. From what I gathered, all the staff had access to the room keys. Even I knew where they were behind the reception desk. Beau had grabbed the master key from the office, so anyone could have found it and used it. With the familiarity Gideon showed around the hotel, I bet he could find them.

Why was Shelby in the room? There had been no noise complaints in that part of the hotel and Daisy hadn't lived in that section, so there wouldn't be any of her treasure there. Was Shelby lured into that room? What did she learn that was worth killing her over?

"Sammy, will you be OK?" Jasper put his hand on my shoulder. "You're pale."

"I'm fine," I lied. "I'm going home."

"Jasper can walk you there if you need someone, honey," Charlene said. "We have a meeting with the funeral home, but if he comes right back, it'll be fine."

"Thanks, but I'm OK on my own." I smiled at Charlene, whose eyes watered. I'd been so concerned with my emotions that I hadn't considered how the news about Shelby would effect her and Jasper. "Let's talk later."

"Yes, we should keep in touch." Jasper offered his arm to his mother. "Be careful."

They left, and I looked around the library, wishing I had taken up Charlene's offer. I took a deep breath and braced myself to go outside the hotel. Hopefully, I'd make it home quickly so I could mourn Shelby privately. And come up with a game plan on how to find the murderer.

48

———————

Just before I got to the door, Daniel stopped me. He rushed out of the reception room and grabbed my arm. "Hey, Sammy. Don't go out that way, it's a zoo."

He led me over to a window and pulled back the curtain. Sure enough, the police had taped off the front of the hotel, but journalists stood up against the barrier. I only spotted one TV crew, but there were other reporters with tape recorders in their hands and looks of desperation. By the crossed arms and expressionless faces of the officers guarding the entrance, the media weren't getting much information. Anyone walking out the door would be fair game to them.

"Thanks, Daniel. Any suggestions on how to get out of here?"

"I'd recommend going through the parking lot." He headed down the hall, so I followed him. "You'll have a fighting chance at least."

We stepped into the courtyard where the crime scene investigators were coming in and out of the hotel room where Shelby was killed. I averted my eyes as we went past, but Daniel craned his neck to look. Of course he would be curious, but when he started talking, I doubted his sincerity in walking me out.

"So you found Shelby? I bet it was horrible." He took out his keys to open the back gate that led to the parking lot. "Two bodies in one week must be a record."

Actually, it wasn't, but I wasn't in the mood to share that information with him. "Did you hear anything last night? When did you see Shelby?"

"Whoa, you sound like the cops." Daniel smiled as if he wasn't offended. "I told them I saw her around seven-thirty. It was a quiet evening, so I got caught up on all the reports Ambrose insists I do."

"You didn't notice any strangers?"

"Nope, sorry."

"Hey! What are you two doing?" A police officer rushed over to us as Daniel unlocked the gate.

"I work here, sir. I'm just letting this young lady out through the parking lot so she can avoid the reporters," Daniel explained.

"You should have asked first before you opened it." The officer waved over a woman in a CSI jacket. "What if they hadn't fingerprinted the gate?"

"My prints are all over it." Daniel said.

"That doesn't matter," the officer grunted. "I'll walk Miss Richardson through the lot. Give your fingerprints if you haven't."

I mouthed, "Thanks" to Daniel as he followed the crime scene investigator.

"How did you know my name?" I asked as we walked through the parking lot.

"I'm Benny Stevens. I saw you when you and Rob's girl-friend came to Armstrong Park."

Oh, now I remembered. Sissy kept the police distracted so I could check out a crime scene. Although Sissy did an excellent job chatting the officers up, Christine found me trying to get inside. I hoped Officer Stevens didn't have any hard feelings.

"Of course!" I smiled. "And here you are again at another crime scene."

"I could say the same to you." He said flatly, but there was a gleam in his eye. "But this time I hear you didn't sneak in. Are you OK after seeing the victim?"

"She was such a sweet girl, so it was hard." I shivered, thinking of Shelby.

"Well, stay safe. And don't take this the wrong way, but I hope I don't run into you again anytime soon." He tipped his hat and left me alone at the gate to the sidewalk. I hoped the same. I'd had enough crime scenes for a week, if not my lifetime.

"There you are!" Andrew pulled me into his arms after I walked out the parking lot exit. "I've been worried sick about you."

I relaxed into his embrace, but tried to keep myself from crying on his pristine white shirt. "I'm so glad you're here."

"Beau called me, so I came right over." Andrew put his arm around me. "He's frantic, but he wanted to make sure you weren't alone."

"He's a good man," I said. "And so are you."

Before we could take a step toward home, a flushed Gideon rushed up to us.

"Andrew! Samantha! What in the world is going on now?" Gideon demanded. "By the amount of police surrounding the place, I'd say it was another murder. Spill the beans!"

"Gideon, don't you harass Sammy." Momo stood behind Gideon, who jumped at the sound of Momo's stern voice. "I heard there was a murder. By the look on Sammy's face, she must have known the victim."

I nodded, knowing I shouldn't say anymore, but I was dying to ask Gideon if he knew anything. Momo did it for me.

"So, Gideon, what did you see last night?" Momo jutted her face at him. "Speak up!"

"I saw nothing. I stayed home all night," he stammered. Finally, here was a woman Gideon couldn't smooth-talk.

"No, you weren't! Lady Clementine and I watched you walking about eight o'clock." Momo flicked the ashes from her cigarette, barely missing Gideon's blue loafers.

"Lady Clementine must be mistaken." Gideon laughed, but his eyes didn't. "Too much catnip for her? Or too much bourbon for you?" He chuckled again and headed down the road, but not toward his home. I wondered if the police had interviewed him about Scarlett's murder.

"That man is rude, but also a liar," Momo said. "The street was empty except for him. I'm going to tell the cops. He may not be a murderer, but he is obsessed with the hotel."

Momo stomped off and grabbed the cop standing behind the yellow tape and insisted she speak to the person in charge. The policewoman patiently listened to her, but put her hand up when Momo tried to go under the tape. "Now, ma'am, why don't you tell me first what you know?" the officer said.

Momo berated the policewoman, so Andrew and I left before she got us involved. Hopefully Christine and Rob were ready for the wrath of Momo. But more importantly, I hoped her observation would help track down a killer.

49

Momo distracted the media, so Andrew and I walked away from the area unnoticed. He listened as I explained what happened that morning. His grip around my shoulders tightened as I described finding Shelby.

"Oh, Samantha, you and Beau had such a horrible experience."

"Yes, but Beau also has to keep running the hotel. The police are going to be there a while, and I'm sure guests will check out."

"Maybe so, but he'll also have people wanting to stay at the scene of the murder," he said. "Sorry, now two murders. Speaking of which, did you see your aunt or cousin?"

"I did. They're going to the funeral home this morning."

"You've had quite the week, my dear." Andrew opened the apartment building gate. As we entered the courtyard, we found Connor, Neal, Ruby, and Papa talking.

"Sammy!" Connor came over and hugged me. "I can't believe there was another murder."

"Who died?" Neal asked.

"Shelby Jones," I whispered.

"Shelby is dead?" Ruby's voice cracked.

"Yes." I stepped out of Connor's embrace and kept my expression blank, even though I was shocked by Ruby's reaction. Her hands shook slightly. Papa grasped them, although Ruby didn't seem to register his affection.

"Such a young girl. I wish she had come to see me." Ruby's voice returned to normal. "The spirits foretold trouble, but no one mentioned a murder."

I wanted to snap at Ruby that a human killed her, not a spirit, but then Ruby said, "Shelby's poor mother. Everyone, especially you Samantha, needs to be careful at that hotel."

Ruby looked at me with a level of concern I hadn't seen from her before. Was she getting soft? It didn't last long.

"Keep that crystal I gave you with you at all times." Ruby dropped Papa's hands and walked to her front door. "You need to repel negative spirits, not welcome them."

There was the Ruby I knew, and it actually made me feel better: she acted as she normally did toward me. I just wanted life to go back to the way it was before Scarlett's murder, and that included my relationship with Ruby.

Papa came over to me and put his hand on my shoulder "Sammy, please come see me at my shop tomorrow morning."

"I'll be there." Papa had helped me before, and I sensed he wanted to do so again.

Once Ruby and Papa left, Neal shared he was at Frankie's picking up lunch when he heard the news about the murder. When he didn't find me at the shop, he came here and met with Connor, Ruby, and Papa. All they knew was that someone at the hotel was killed.

"Frankie hadn't heard who it was, so I better run back

and tell her," Neal said. "She was worried you or Beau were involved."

"Unfortunately, we both were." I explained how Beau and I found Shelby, but only shared a few details. I wanted to keep my promise to the police not to talk about the murder, but I also didn't want to relive finding Shelby.

"Sammy, that's awful." Neal kissed me on my cheek. "I'll light a candle for her on my cathedral tour today. Andrew, are you heading out, too?"

"Yes, I need to get back to the store. Connor, will you stay with Sammy?" Andrew asked.

"Definitely," Connor said. "I'll make sure she eats and gets some rest."

I could have been offended that they talked about me like I wasn't there, but I was too exhausted to protest. I didn't want to deal with anything or anyone. At least for a while.

Connor and I went inside my apartment, and that's when I fell into his arms and cried for Shelby and her mother. I couldn't imagine her pain.

If only I had talked to Shelby last night. I didn't believe she was killed for no reason. It must have been the same person who killed Scarlett. Both women deserved justice.

A bowl of cereal and a long nap made the afternoon a bit more bearable than I had expected. Connor stayed with me even as I napped. I woke up to find him sitting at my kitchen counter, bent over a notebook.

"Hey, sleepyhead. How are you feeling?"

"My headache is finally gone." I moved a sleeping Nubi off my stomach and onto the loveseat and got up. Nubi gave me the evil eye before trotting off to the kitchen. He sat in front of the cabinet where his treats were stored.

"Let me get them for you, Nubi." Connor slid off the stool and grabbed Nubi's snacks. "I promised I would give him a treat if he let you sleep."

"He's got you wrapped around his paw." I laughed and took his seat. "Are you writing music? That's great."

Connor looked over my shoulder. "It's a start. Everyone in the group brings something they've written, and it's my turn tonight."

Nubi meowed and jumped on top of Connor's sheets of music. "Nubi, don't be rude," I said.

"My first critic, and it's a cat." Connor grinned, but then his face grew serious. "I don't need to go tonight if you'd like me to stay."

"I won't be alone." I showed Connor my cell phone. "Sissy will be here any minute with her mother's gumbo and a bottle of wine."

"The cure-all for everything." Connor's face now relaxed. "If you're sure…"

I kissed him as my answer. As much as I would have loved to curl up on the couch with him and listen to music, he needed to meet with the band. He had waited so long to become a full-time musician, and I didn't want him to miss this opportunity to present his original song.

"That's not helping me leave," Connor said after we kissed. "But that knock on the door must be a sign that I should go."

"Hey, Connor, take this. Sammy, come here!" Sissy shoved the grocery bag at Connor and rushed around him to grab my hands and give them a quick squeeze. "Let me look at you. You're pale, but no fever."

I took her hand off my forehead and held it. "Nothing physical is wrong. My heart is just broken."

"Honey, I'm so sorry about your friend." Sissy pulled me over to the loveseat and we sat down. "Rob gave me the barebones, but I can only imagine how horrible it was for you and Beau."

"I'll leave now that you're in good hands." Connor leaned down and kissed me. He then kissed Sissy on the cheek. "Thanks for staying with Sammy. Call me if you need anything. Promise?"

I nodded, and Sissy walked over to the door with Connor. She locked the door behind him. "Time to open that bottle of wine, my friend. You need to fill me in on what's really going on at Hotel Jeanne."

Sissy grabbed two wineglasses from the cabinet. "And you can share your plans to solve these murders."

50

———

"Don't get into any trouble today." I called out to Nubi as he trotted toward the back of the courtyard, where Cleopatra and Nefertiti waited. The sun shone on them as they lay on the slate tiles. They watched a lone bird that had landed on a table. They meowed a greeting to Nubi, or maybe it was a reply that I shouldn't get into any trouble either. Whatever the case, the three black cats jumped onto the top of the wall and escaped to their daytime haunts. Fortunately, they left before I had to lie to them; I had too much to do today, and trouble would most likely follow.

Last night Sissy and I drank wine and ate her mother's comforting gumbo and went over the events of the past week. We concluded the murders at Hotel Jeanne must be connected. Sissy said Rob wasn't giving her any information, no matter how hard she tried. "He's so wrapped up in these cases that he didn't notice I threw out his holey socks and moldy bread," she had said.

I believed both murders were related to the treasure Daisy had alluded to in her letters. Someone must want it, and now she or he had murdered two women to get it. Sissy believed my brother was involved. While I preferred to brush off that idea, after getting my mail this morning, I couldn't.

Waiting for me with my bills and the latest copy of People magazine was an envelope from my brother. It was postmarked in Algiers Point, a city across the Mississippi River. I took a deep breath, but the warm, humid air didn't help my nerves as I opened the envelope. Joey had sent another photograph.

I ran my fingers over the picture, staring at my birth parents for the first time — at least as an adult. Charlene was right; I looked like my mother. We had the same smile and nose, and she must have also liked comfortable shoes as she wore tennis shoes with her jeans and paint-splattered t-shirt. My father and I shared the same red hair and freckles. My brother and I had matching yellow t-shirts covered in paint. The four of us appeared to be laughing as the picture was taken in front of the same New Orleans cottage from another photo Joey had sent me. My shaking hands flipped the photograph over to find the words *We were a happy family.*

The photo showed a happy family, but what made my brother finally send this picture of us? The postmark suggested he was close by.

Did Christine and Rob consider him a suspect in Scarlett's murder still, or even Shelby's? Even if they did, I didn't. Of course, I had been wrong about him before, but there was no reason for him to kill Shelby. My gut kept telling me this was all about the hotel and that Scarlett's and Shelby's murders resulted from them getting in the murderer's way.

I wiped away a single tear that fell onto the photo before I put it back in the envelope. Rob and Christine would want to know about it, but I imagined it would be way down on their list of items to review. And I had a list of my own; first was a stop at Cafe du Monde. I didn't want to show up at Papa's without beignets and cafe au lait. He liked the doughy sweet treats just as much as I did. And I suspected Papa had a bit to tell me after I ran into him and Ruby yesterday. Whether it was about the murders or my spiritual needs, a visit with my friend would do me good.

With two bags of piping hot beignets, a cafe au lait, and a cup of cold milk, I opened the door to Papa's Spirits & Charms. Before I announced my presence, my feet stopped just inside the entry. If I hadn't seen the sign outside, I would have thought I was in a different store.

Before I met him, the only time I tried to visit Papa's voodoo shop, I turned right around. It reminded me of an abandoned warehouse. Half-filled jars of unknown substances lined the cold metal shelves, while overhead florescent lights barely lit the store. There was not only the look and smell of decay, but the feeling that the place was dying. The shop and its owner had appeared to have lost their soul.

Now with its clean shelves, well-stocked and labeled merchandise, and a happier owner, it was like a flower shoot rising through the dirt. While the shop wasn't sparkling, it had a warmth to it that hadn't been there before.

And I could say the same about the owner. Gone were Papa's threadbare tuxedo jacket and fake smile. He still kept his top hat, but now it was on a head that had a face of joy.

"Sammy! I'm so glad you came to see me this morning." Papa greeted me after walking out from behind a sales counter at the back of the shop. "And you even brought breakfast. You know my weakness."

"I'd like to think our love of beignets is a strength, not a weakness." I grinned as I put the food down on an empty wooden table with two mismatched chairs that were to the right of the sales counter. "Can we eat here?"

"Sure can." He walked over, using his cane. "My bones are just creaky in the morning, don't you worry."

"Papa, I owe you a new walking cane." It had only been a little over a week since I'd used Papa's cane as a weapon — in self defense. The brass snake head was intact, but there was a chip in the shaft. At least it wasn't stained with blood, but after what Papa did for me, he deserved a pristine cane.

"No, no, no." He rubbed a finger along the chipped section. "I don't mind the blemishes. They remind me that Marie Laveau is looking out for me. And she's going to take care of you, too."

"While I need all the help I can get, I don't practice Voodoo. Don't I have to be a believer for her to help me?"

"Oh, I think you're a believer, Sammy." Papa winked. "You have an open heart and mind. Miss Laveau sees that, I'm sure."

I wasn't sure if New Orleans's famous Voodoo queen knew anything about me. But whatever religion someone offered to pray for me in, I would accept.

Papa and I gossiped about the weather, the new artwork at Libby's cafe, and the possibility of Mr. Hugo working for Neal. After we finished our last beignets, Papa said, "We've chit-chatted about everything else but what happened at the hotel yesterday. Are you ready to really talk?"

"Papa, I don't know what to say." I hung my head. "I feel responsible for Shelby's death."

"Of course you do. You take everything to heart." Papa patted my hand. "But I also know you don't let things go, so you're working on solving this yourself."

"You've been known to do the same." I lifted my head to

smile at my friend and pointed at his cane. He was on to the murderer at the same time as I was, but he got to the crime scene first. "We made a good team."

"While I appreciate your kindness, that was all you." He pushed up from the table with his cane. "Since you're going to go detecting, I need to give you a tool for protection."

"Like your cane?"

"No, you need spiritual protection. Come on back to my altar."

I followed Papa around his sales counter to the room behind it and whipped my head around to try to take everything in. "Wow, Papa, this is incredible!"

The burgundy back wall showcased Papa's collection of alligator skulls. Even with all my years of living in Florida, I had never seen that many alligator skulls and definitely not one almost two feet long.

Surrounding the large skull were ones in varying sizes, spread out in a circular pattern. The rest of the room followed suit, with more alligator skulls hanging on the walls. To my left was a door that said, "Private." On the other side of the room was a table fashioned together with worn wood with specks of moss on a few of the edges. But it was the items on top that made me gasp a little.

"Papa, is this your altar?"

"It is. I do all of my work here." He placed his cane to the side of the table and lit a candle with a picture of Marie Laveau on it. "I have one at home, too."

Besides the candle, there was also a framed drawing of Marie Laveau. "Is your altar dedicated to her?"

Papa smiled. "Yes, she's been my guide in life, along with my ancestors. All of them are going to help with your gris-gris bag."

"You're going to make one for me?" While I'd been to a

few of the Voodoo shops in the French Quarter, I only bought books, not anything else. Gris-gris charms were usually sachets that held a particular combination of herbs, oils, and stones for all kinds of needs, like love, money, and luck. They also had other uses like revenge and intimidation. Papa had a special one in mind.

"I'm worried about those spirits, and the humans, at that hotel, so I'm making you a gris-gris for protection."

I couldn't argue with that, and while I was still carrying Ruby's crystal, it seemed I could use more help. Since this was my first personal gris-gris, I scanned the table to see what was needed. There was an empty leather drawstring bag, three inches by three inches, in the center of what appeared to be a circle of items needed for the ritual. On the top of the circle was a stick of incense, which had a pleasant scent of cinnamon. To the right was a black candle in a simple brass candleholder. At the bottom of the circle was a bowl of dirt, and to the left of it was a bowl of clear liquid.

"Is that graveyard dirt?" I pointed to the small white china bowl heaping with dirt. "And if it is, do I want to know how you got it?"

"The answers are yes and no." He laughed and pinched a bit of the dirt and let it drop back into the bowl. "I'm just kidding. Yes, it's graveyard dirt, but I came by it legitimately."

"What are the other items and do they have a specific meaning?"

"Yes, these four things represent the four elements of nature. The dirt is the earth." Papa pointed to each item as he spoke. "I filled this small bowl with holy water from St. Louis Cathedral. It's the water while the incense is the air and the candle is fire."

"Should I worry the candle is black? Does it have a dark meaning?"

"Don't you worry. I picked black because it takes away evil. Although it's also used to hurt others, that's not me."

There were other items on the table, including a statue of the Virgin Mary, which would surprise those not familiar with Voodoo. Catholicism and Voodoo were intertwined in New Orleans, and many people followed both religions. There was a small alligator skull, but that wasn't the only remains I saw.

"How about these?" I tapped my fingers next to a pile of tiny, delicate bones. "Did you order these from a catalog?"

"Those are fresh from last night's dinner. Cajun fried frog legs just like my momma used to make." He rubbed his belly. "I'll cook them for you sometime."

"Let's just stick to beignets for now." I wrinkled my nose at the thought of a frog leg dinner. I didn't believe it tasted like chicken.

"Speaking of beignets, bring me that bag from Cafe du Monde."

I brought it over to him. "It's empty. Did you want me to get more?"

"Maybe later, but all I need is a bit of this." He scooped some of the powdered sugar from the bottom of the sack. "Can you open that leather bag for me?"

Pulling open the drawstrings on the bag, I held it open and Papa put the powdered sugar in it.

"A bit of the sweetness that we share." Papa nodded at the sugar, and I couldn't help but smile. He wiped his hands with a handkerchief from his pocket. "Now we've got to put the rest of the ingredients inside."

He took a frog leg bone and a pinch of the graveyard dirt and placed it in the bag. Next Papa opened a worn cigar box and picked up a bit of shedded snake skin, a blue and white bead, and a dried mushroom.

"I recognize the snakeskin and the mushroom, but what's the bead?" I asked.

"It's the evil eye to ward off those who wish you harm." Next, he took out a plain white envelope from his pocket. "And feline power."

"Is that cat hair?" He dropped a quarter-sized clump of black fur. "Is it from my cat?"

"Yes, it's from Nubi, excuse me, Anubis." He laughed. "Ruby insisted I use his correct name when I blessed this gris-gris."

"Of course she did." Ruby had in fact named Anubis, and it irritated her to no end when I called him Nubi. While he acted like an Egyptian God with his regal poses and demanding nature, he was also a sweetheart and deserved a nickname.

"Ruby included Cleopatra and Nefertiti's fur, too."

"She did?" I couldn't believe Ruby was actually trying to help me. Had I misread her all these months?

"Yes, ma'am. She said you needed all the help you can get..."

"That's the Ruby I know..." I interrupted Papa, but then he cut me off.

"Now, Sammy, she cares about you." He brushed off a bit of cat hair from his hand. "I know she comes across harsh, but she cares in her own way. There's a lot of heartache under all her scarves."

The softness in his eyes and the gentleness of his voice conveyed his affection for my neighbor. Oh, no, had he seen what was underneath her scarves — literally or figuratively? I didn't need that image in my mind. I nodded, and Papa continued with his work.

"Now, I have seven things in here — it's got to be an odd number and no more than thirteen items in the bag."

"Why's that?"

"Honestly, I don't know." Papa grinned. "But that's how my momma taught me, and she never steered me wrong. "

"Well, let's not break the tradition." I laughed. "What comes next?"

Papa pulled the drawstrings tightly and placed the bag back in the center of the circle. He dipped his fingers in the holy water and flicked it onto the gris-gris. Then he picked it up and held it close to his mouth and said, "Ancestors of mine and of Samantha's, please protect her now and always." Papa blew onto the bag and then handed it to me.

"Here you are. Carry this in your left-hand pocket. Keep it with Ruby's crystal and you'll have all the protection we can offer you."

I slipped the gris-gris into my jeans pocket, where Ruby's obsidian crystal was waiting. My pocket now bulged with spiritual protection, and instead of feeling silly, Ruby and Papa's offerings comforted me.

"Thank you, Papa." I kissed him on the cheek. "I'm lucky to have you watching out for me."

"I'm just one of many, darling." He picked his cane back up, and I followed him back to the table. Taking his handkerchief out once more, he wiped the small dots of perspiration off his brow. He sighed as he sat down, looking as if he had walked a mile in the blistering sun.

"Can I get you a glass of water?" I took the seat across from him and grasped his hand. "You look tired."

"No, I'm fine. Gris-gris making always takes a bit of my energy from me. But don't you worry." He squeezed my hand. "I'm going to take a little rest and keep checking in with my ancestors. It wouldn't hurt for you to do the same."

"Will do," I said, although I wasn't sure how I was supposed to go about that. Hopefully chatting with them in my head as I walked to work would suffice. "Thanks again, Papa. And thank Ruby for me."

"Anything for you, Sammy. Now you be careful, though. You've got some protection, but it doesn't mean you can jump into a dangerous situation without repercussions."

"You're one to talk," I teased. "I recall you beat me to the last dangerous situation I was in."

"Now don't talk ill of your elders." Papa's twinkling eyes confirmed he enjoyed my teasing. "I'll walk you out, but really I need you to be careful."

We walked to the front door, and before he opened it, he said. "There's a lot of unrest at Hotel Jeanne, so watch out for those spirits."

I nodded and left the shop. While the ghosts may be restless, it was the humans I was worried about. But that wouldn't stop me from investigating at the hotel. I now had protection from a spiritualist and a Voodoo man. What else could I need to keep me safe?

51

Apparently, I needed to stay away from Hotel Jeanne to keep safe. At least that's what Andrew thought.

"Well, there you are," he said as I walked into Lagniappe Books. "I was about to call you to make sure you weren't at the hotel."

"But if you were, did you find the treasure?" Beau was sitting next to Andrew in the seating area. Andrew glared at him, and Beau toned down the excitement in his voice. "Sorry, that was inconsiderate of me. You shouldn't be there by yourself."

"Or looking for supposed treasure," Andrew said.

"But if we find it, we can use it for Shelby's scholarship," Beau said.

"Scholarship?" I sat across from them.

"I spoke with Shelby's mother last night and she told me all about Shelby's dream to go to college." Beau picked up his coffee mug and took a sip. "I asked her what we could do for her, and she said nothing, but we must honor that bright girl."

"So Beau and I are going to visit Mrs. Jones this evening. We're going to tell her that the hotel and Lagniappe Books will set up a scholarship in Shelby's name."

"That's wonderful." Beau and Andrew's kindness caused tears to stream down my face. I grabbed a tissue from the box on the table. "Let me know what I can do to help."

While Beau and Andrew talked about the details, I came up with my own plan to help fund the scholarship —Daisy's treasure. I needed to get back into the hotel and start looking for more daisies.

"Sammy, did you hear me?" Andrew asked. "Do you want coffee? Although you must have had a cup already, along with beignets." He pointed to the speckles of powdered sugar on my jeans.

"I'll take more coffee, but yes, I had beignets with Papa already."

Andrew picked up Beau's now empty mug and went to the office.

"How are you holding up, Beau?" While he looked as handsome as always, with his hair brushed back and his immaculately pressed clothes, there were dark bags under his eyes. His normally manicured nails were misshapen, as if he had bitten them.

"Exhausted. I was at the hotel most of the evening." Beau sighed. "The staff is holding up as well as expected."

Andrew put down our coffee. "You're handling it well, too. Hopefully, the police will have more information soon."

"No news?" I asked.

"Not much, I'm afraid. They believe Shelby was killed in the room, which narrows down the scene of the crime," Beau said.

"And the list of suspects," Andrew said, looking directly at me. "So anyone connected or staying at the hotel last evening is being questioned. It isn't a place to be alone in right now."

I sipped my coffee to take a moment before I spoke. Andrew didn't want me back at the library or exploring the hotel by myself. But I didn't feel I could wait to look for Daisy's treasure. If the murderer found it, he or she would most likely disappear, and there would be no justice for Shelby and Scarlett.

"I assume that means you don't want me to finish up at the library today." There was disappointment in Beau's eyes, but he kept quiet. "I can wait, but I have plans to visit my aunt and cousin there later today."

An earlier text from Jasper asked me to meet him at the hotel, so I really had a reason to be there. If I looked around and found any hidden daisies, wouldn't that be a lovely surprise? And burning a hole in my backpack was Beau's master key to the hotel. When I took it from his shaky hands yesterday to open the hotel door, I put it in my pocket. Yes, I should have offered the key back, but since I didn't, I might just need to use it. Actually, that was no might — I planned to use the key today.

Not that I said any of this to Beau and Andrew.

"Of course, you'll want to see your family. Your aunt was distraught last night when the police questioned her and Jasper. I overheard a bit and I have to say Christine and Rob were gentle with her." Beau put his mug down and reached for my hand. "But they were rough on your cousin."

"Oh?" Jasper hadn't mentioned that in his text. Is that why he wanted to meet me?

"Well, he and Shelby were seen talking together the night before she died. But then again, so many other people were seen with her, too." Beau squeezed my hand. "I'm sure it was nothing. Christine and Rob really want to solve Shelby's murder."

"And Scarlett's too," Andrew added. "So there is no need for you to worry."

By worry, he meant interfere.

"I'll try not to," I lied.

"Why don't we search the rest of the hotel tomorrow?" Beau said. "The police should be done by then."

"That sounds good." I stood up. "You two must have a lot to do for Shelby's scholarship, so let me handle the store today."

"Aren't you going to see Jasper?" Andrew asked.

"Not until this evening. He and his mother are visiting a friend out in the Garden District. They're supposed to leave tomorrow for Mississippi."

"I'm sorry this wasn't the family reunion they envisioned," Beau said. "Or the one you wanted."

"Perhaps they'll come back later and you can try again." Andrew nudged Beau off the loveseat. "In the meantime, I will take you up on taking care of the shop this afternoon. We haven't eaten, so let's grab lunch and then work on the scholarship proposal."

"I guess I should eat. You'll be all right by yourself, Sammy?" Beau hugged me. "You had a shock yesterday, too."

"The store will keep me busy until I go see Jasper," I said. "But thank you for thinking of me. When are you going to meet with Shelby's mom?"

"At six," Beau replied. "Did you want to come?"

"That's OK, three people might overwhelm Mrs. Jones," I said.

Andrew gave me that "I don't believe you" stare that I knew all too well.

"That's a good point. And you're seeing your cousin

tonight." Beau hugged me again and whispered in my ear. "Don't get into trouble, but let me know if you come across anything from our Lovelorn Ghost."

Beau and I smiled at each other. Andrew looked at us both suspiciously, but must have decided it wasn't worth the battle.

"Fine, but be careful. Did Papa make you a protection gris-gris this morning?" Andrew asked as he joined me at the sales table.

"He did." I pulled it out of my pocket, along with the obsidian stone. "And I'm carrying Ruby's crystal, so I'm doubly covered."

"Just because you have their protection doesn't mean you shouldn't be diligent," Andrew said.

"Ruby and Papa should return to the hotel when the police are through." Beau picked up his leather messenger bag from the floor and put it across his body. "But in the meantime, we'll hope the Lovelorn Ghost and the other spirits will keep an eye on the humans."

Andrew followed Beau to the door, but turned to face me. "You can reach me by phone anytime this afternoon or tonight. Call me if you need anything. And I mean anything."

"I promise to call, but I'm sure everything will be just fine today."

At least that's what I hoped. I was protected, wasn't I?

52

I didn't have time to think about anything, as the shop kept me busy from the minute Andrew and Beau left. Restocking shelves, helping customers find the perfect book, and coming up with fresh material for the shop's website was the ideal way to keep my mind off Hotel Jeanne's troubles.

Going into a corner store, I picked up a Diet Coke and a Snickers to eat as I walked to the hotel. Normally I would have gone to Frankie's, but I didn't have the time or the energy to chat with my favorite grocer. I was tempted, though, as Frankie collected all the neighborhood gossip. But I'd save that for another day.

I wolfed down my candy bar as I looked through the wrought-iron gate of a building like Thibodeaux Mansion. While I loved peering into courtyards, this one was a mess. Stacks of bricks and piles of lumber filled the area. They must be renovating the house. With the peeling paint and missing shutters on the facade, it needed help.

The mild evening weather had brought out locals and tourists to the French Quarter. Musicians dotted the corners while artists showed their wares along the fence at St. Louis Cathedral. The hypnotic rhythm of a group of drummers caused me to slow down, but I didn't stop. Jasper and I planned to meet at seven, and I wanted to check out the attic first. I'd have less than an hour, but I hoped it would be easy to find a hidden daisy. Or maybe the ghosts would lead me to it. I squeezed the gris-gris bag and crystal in my pocket, hoping they'd work for finding things, not just protection.

Luckily, I didn't need my charms to help me avoid Gideon. Momo did the job for me. As I walked up to the hotel's entrance, they were talking by Gideon's doorway. Or rather, Momo was chastising her neighbor.

"I know what I saw! Don't you tell me I'm wrong, Gideon." She poked his chest with her crooked finger. "I may be old, but I'd recognize your ridiculous swagger from ten miles away."

"I wasn't out, and I had nothing to do with that murder." Gideon stepped back from Momo. "Or any other murder. I realize you think poorly of me, but really, calling me a killer is outrageous."

"I didn't call you a killer, but if you are one, you won't be able to hide under your fake tan and fake confidence."

Gideon paled underneath his fake tan and opened his mouth, but quickly shut it. Apparently Momo's words made him speechless. He took a step toward her, but then he noticed me.

"Sammy, darling! How are you, my dear?" He sidestepped around Momo, but she put her hand on his arm, so he stopped. "Do you have any information about the murder?"

"I could ask you the same thing," I said. "Since you live next door, I assumed you had all the news."

"Ha! No one's going to tell him anything important."

Momo winked at me. "No one on the block knows anything yet."

"Sammy, perhaps you'd like a drink? It is cocktail hour," Gideon said, but once again, Momo kept him in line.

"You leave her alone. We're not finished yet." Momo pulled her neighbor toward his door. Gideon gave me another pleading look, but I had no desire to save him from Momo's lecture. I glanced back before I entered the hotel to see them arguing.

Entering the foyer, the stillness in the air worried me. Perhaps the guests were out, but where was the staff? The reception room was empty, so I knocked on the office door. No answer there. I considered ringing the bell at the front desk, but decided against it. I could sneak upstairs without being seen, but I wanted to know where everyone was hiding.

The kitchen was empty, as well as the library. I opened the door to the courtyard and saw Ambrose and Daniel talking by the Joan of Arc water fountain. By Ambrose's pointed finger at the police tape across the room where Shelby died, I guessed they were discussing the murder. While I would have loved to know what they were talking about, I needed to go to the attic.

When Ambrose turned toward the door, I was sure I'd lost my chance. He nodded, but he didn't call out to me. I got a smile from Daniel, but it turned to a frown as Ambrose kept talking to him. After a quick wave, I rushed back into the hotel, dropped off the bag of books, and went directly upstairs before they finished their conversation.

When I got to the attic door on the second floor, I held my breath, waiting for someone to spot me. There weren't any noises from the guest rooms, so I took out the key and put it in the lock. At first I thought I had the wrong key, as it didn't budge. Finally, it turned, and I heard a click and the door was open. Time to find Daisy's treasure before the murderer did.

53

The attic door creaked as I swung it open. Humid, musty air hit me when I placed my foot on the first step. If it was already this uncomfortable on the stairs, the attic would be worse. For a moment I considered coming back in the morning when the temperature dropped, but no, I needed to explore it now. After stepping completely inside, I locked the door behind me, flipped on the light switch, and climbed the steps to the top.

From the fine layer of dust on the floor, I suspected Beau's first visit to the hotel was the last time anyone came up here. That boded well for me; most likely no one had searched this area. The low ceiling height might have kept them away. Although I was petite, I would have to crouch in parts of the attic, especially at both ends of the room where the roof sloped down.

The walls were brick and the wood roof trusses were visible. The dormer windows let in a sliver of soon-to-be fading sunlight on each end of the long room. Two bare bulbs lit the room, although both flickered erratically, so I worried I would lose the light. My flashlight app on my phone would only help a little, so I needed to work fast.

Dusty white sheets covered different shaped items in the back of the attic, so I headed that way. Stacks of sagging boxes marked "old files" intermingled with steamer trunks with rusted locks and disintegrating handles. When I got to the far side of the room, I tried to open a window, but it was painted shut. Instead, I cleaned off a patch of a pane with my sleeve and saw Momo walking by herself toward her home. Gideon must be off the hook for now.

My phone dinged with a message from Jasper saying he was running late. I replied he should text me when he arrived and I'd meet him in the library. The extra time would be helpful. I turned off my phone ringer, and I started with the five objects covered with sheets.

The first piece I uncovered turned out to be a disco ball inside a wooden crate. "Well, Mr. Grady, I believe this belonged to you," I said into the air. The spirit of the former hotel owner didn't reply, so I moved on to the next sheet-covered object.

A side table with a deep scratch on the top didn't yield any daisies. The tallest item in the room was an armoire. My heart skipped a beat, thinking this could be the one. A stale odor hit me when I opened the stiff doors. The back panel of the wardrobe had peeled off, so I knew right away it wasn't an antique. But I checked for daisies, just in case. I found two shriveled mouse carcasses and three rusty bobby pins.

"All right, Daisy, can you give me a clue?" I placed the sheet back over a lopsided night stand that definitely did not come from the 1920s. "This has to be it, right?"

I pulled the sheet off the last object and answered my question.

The six foot long desk with the same flourishes as the library shelves must have been the work of Daisy's carpenter. It was a commanding piece of furniture with four drawers with brass handles on each side of the desk. One wide drawer was in the center. The kneehole was wide enough that a large chair would fit in the space. The bottom of the desk had the same beveled edges as the library shelves.

It was a shame the desk was hidden in the attic. Someone must have decided its size and worn condition made it unusable. But with a bit of polish, it would look perfect in the library.

First, I opened each drawer, but they were empty except for faded hotel stationery in the center drawer. No daisies. I ran my hand around every outside surface and got a splinter for my effort. The last place was the kneehole. I dropped to my knees and stuck my head into the space. Using my flashlight app on my phone, I searched for daisies.

I stopped at the right side of the base of the desk. I gasped when I recognized a mark in the back corner. A carved daisy was on the edge. It matched the other ones I had found in the hotel. There was a lump in my throat as my shaking hand touched the daisy. The Lovelorn Ghost, in her human form, must have been in this same position, waiting to open the secret compartment. Would I discover more letters? Perhaps it would be more jewelry or cash, but there might be nothing in it at all.

Before I could try to find a hiding place behind the daisy, I heard the squeaky attic door open. I'd locked the door behind me, so someone with a key had opened it. I waited to see who came up the stairs, assuming they would call out to me.

Silence.

The click of the lock and the firm footsteps on the creaking stairs made my stomach drop. Beau would have guessed I was up here and said my name. It had to be someone else with a key to the attic. Was it Ambrose or Daniel? Gideon must know where the keys are. Even a guest like Jasper could sneak into the office and take a key.

My throat suddenly went dry, and I suppressed the urge to cough. The footsteps continued into the attic, and then halted. I should have announced my presence, but my gut said something was wrong.

My gut was right.

"Come on out, Sammy, and hand over the treasure. I don't want to have to kill you, too."

I slid out from underneath the desk and raised my head to see Shelby's and Scarlett's murderer pointing a knife at me.

"Surprised to see me?"

Daniel held a chef's knife toward me. Sweat dripped down his neck onto the collar of his white dress shirt. His beige suit hung off his body, making him look like a child wearing a hand-me-down suit. He gave me his usual warm smile, but his eyes were cold.

"How did you know I was up here?" I tried to focus on his face and not on the knife.

"After I escaped Ambrose's daily rant, I looked for you in the library. I guessed you were up here looking for the next daisy."

"Lucky guess." I braced my hands on the desk. "But I doubt anything is up here."

"I don't believe you." Daniel grinned and took a step forward, but stopped when I moved backward. "You've had too much luck finding all the other hiding spots. If you haven't found it yet, you will."

"Why would I find it for you?"

"Isn't this enough?" He raised the knife. "I meant it when I said I didn't want to kill you."

"But you wanted to kill Scarlett and Shelby?" I stepped toward him, wanting to get in his face to confront him, but I didn't. With no weapon, I couldn't defend myself against his knife. I needed to keep him talking while I came up with a plan. Fortunately, Daniel needed to chat.

"Oh, come on, Sammy. No one, including you, mourned Scarlett's death." Daniel laughed, and the knife wavered in his hand.

While I didn't like Scarlett, I didn't want her dead. She was family, after all. "No one deserves to die. Especially since I can't think of what she did to justify killing her."

"She was rude and just plain mean, isn't that enough?" He grinned, but I heard the doubt in his voice.

"No, it's not. What happened?"

The doubt in his voice now showed on his face.

"Come on, Daniel, tell me what happened. It was an accident, right?"

"It was her fault," he stammered. His face grew red, but he regained his composure and started ranting. "I was in the lounge on the floor, looking for a hiding place. I had my momma on speakerphone when your cousin came by and overheard me talking about the treasure."

"And she wanted part of the treasure?"

"Yes! I acted like it was a joke, but she didn't believe me."

One greedy liar had recognized another one. But she shouldn't have died for it.

"Why didn't you just agree to give her some money?" I asked and watched Daniel bow his head in what appeared to be shame. "You haven't found anything, have you?"

"You've found more than me," he said. "But there has to be other stuff in the house."

"Honestly, there's nothing up here," I lied. "Why don't we go downstairs and talk this through? Are you doing this for money or do you and your mother want your family heirlooms?"

Daniel launched into an explanation about his connection to Daisy. His great-grandmother was the baby Daisy gave up. She had left a letter telling her baby who she was and that she was from New Orleans. They passed the letter down from generation-to-generation, but no one else in his family besides him and his mother believed the story. But Daniel researched the legend over the years and discovered the letter was authentic and that the Fuller house had become Hotel Jeanne.

"After college, I came to New Orleans and waited until a position opened up here. The night shift was perfect because I got to search the hotel without too much interruption."

"You're the one making the noises."

"I guess, but according to that crazy psychic lady, ghosts are here." He laughed, and I saw his grip loosen on the knife. Maybe if I kept him talking, he'd finally drop it and I'd have my chance to escape. He would attack if I started yelling, so I needed to outrun him down the stairs. While he continued with his story, I casually scanned the attic for a weapon.

"If Daisy is here, I'd wish she would just tell me where to find the treasure." Daniel sighed. "But you found all the daisies instead. Why does Daisy like you? Maybe we're related."

I hoped not; being related to one murderer was quite enough. I ignored his remark and took a chance on asking him about Shelby. Wrong move.

"Daniel, why did you kill Shelby? She wouldn't have tried to blackmail you. She was a kind person."

"Yeah, she was a good kid." Daniel gripped the knife so

hard his knuckles turned white. "But like you, she figured things out."

"What happened?"

"She caught me checking out the lounge again and announced she knew I was the one making the noises," Daniel replied. "Shelby said she saw me sneaking into the guest rooms. I never even noticed her."

Her observation that she went unnoticed in the hotel was true. I wished she hadn't confronted him with that information.

"So why kill her? I'm sure you could come up with an excuse for your nighttime checks."

"I tried, but she figured out I was lying. And when she brought up Scarlett, I knew she was on to me." Daniel pointed the knife at me. "And she followed you around like a puppy dog, so she'd tell you eventually that she suspected me."

Nausea crept up my throat. He was right; Shelby's voice-mail message said she had something to tell me. "Why didn't you just leave the hotel?" I insisted. "Shelby had no proof, did she?"

"I couldn't take that chance. And I needed the treasure before I left. My mother is counting on me."

"Have you told her you killed two people for the treasure?"

Daniel nodded his head. So any hope of using his mother as leverage to talk him out of killing me disappeared. Keeping him talking until someone noticed we were missing, or I found a weapon against him, seemed to be the only solution.

"Were you the one who texted me from Scarlett's phone?" I asked. "Why did you do that?"

"Sorry, but I needed the police to look at other suspects.

After your fight with Scarlett, you were the perfect patsy. Nothing personal."

"Framing someone for murder is the very definition of personal."

He shrugged his shoulders. "If you say so. But let's get back to finding the next daisy."

We both jumped at the sound of a cell phone ringing. I had turned my ringer off. It was his.

"Momma, I'm busy!" Daniel snapped into the phone he had taken out of his jacket pocket. "Sorry, I didn't mean to yell, but I'm trying to find the treasure so I can leave."

Daniel turned around and kept talking. I prayed he'd move away from the path to the stairs, but he didn't. He paced back and forth, alternating between berating, defending, apologizing to his mother, and then listening to her.

Even with his phone up to his ear, Daniel had a firm grip on the knife. I was tempted to push him down and rush down the stairs, but I'd still have to unlock the door. Unless I put him out of commission, he would get to me first. I couldn't risk that. If a guest or a hotel employee heard me, I might be stabbed already. Or dead.

He had a knife, and he blocked the only way out of the attic.

55

I wasn't ready to be a ghost like Daisy, so I needed a plan.

While Daniel's phone call distracted him, I tiptoed to the corner of the attic. If he came back here, I would be trapped. But there had to be some kind of weapon around. Next to the armoire stood a faded yellow parasol with daisies embroidered around the edges. I grabbed it and relaxed a bit when I realized the wooden handle was firm. Wielding a vintage umbrella against a knife was a long shot, but nothing else in my reach looked like a weapon.

With the umbrella in my hand, I took out my phone and texted *911* to a group chat that included Connor, Sissy, Neal, Libby, and Andrew. One of them would get it, certainly. Daniel's voice made me drop my phone.

"Sammy! It's time to get the treasure."

Apparently, his conversation with his mother gave him the second wind he needed to continue threatening me. I kept quiet, listening for which direction he was coming.

"Come out, come out, wherever you are!" Daniel's feet creaked on the floorboards. "Let's make this easy."

I bit my lip so not to answer him. I wouldn't make this easy on him. He stomped across the attic, heading toward the window. With my pseudo-weapon, I crept along the wall in the opposite direction. If I reached the other side of the attic, I could rush to the stairs and hopefully out the door. He wouldn't stab me if I was at the door, would he?

Yes, he would.

"I'm done fooling around with you. If you're not going to help me, you'll just be another dead woman at Hotel Jeanne."

It was now or never. I raced down the wall, pushing boxes out of my way. Dust plumes filled the air as I ran on the creaky floorboards. Daniel appeared confused at first as towers of boxes tumbled onto the floor. He rushed toward me and grabbed my ponytail just before I reached the staircase.

"Not so fast!" He yanked me backwards so hard that I fell on top of him and the knife fell out of his hands and skittered under the side table. My umbrella dropped and rolled away from me.

Daniel seemed stunned by the fall, so I rolled over and tried to stand up. With the knife out of reach, I planned to run down the stairs. Reaching into my pocket for the key, I realized I'd put it in my backpack. All I had was the crystal from Ruby and the gris-gris bag from Papa. The leather tie was loose around the bag, but it wasn't long enough to restrain Daniel. Not that I had the chance.

"We're not done, yet." Daniel grabbed my ponytail again and yanked me backwards. Once on the floor, I reached into my pocket and untied the gris-gris completely. His face loomed over me, and his hands reached for my neck. Knowing this was my only chance against him, I threw the contents of the gris-gris bag at Daniel's eyes. I turned my head so I wouldn't inhale the graveyard dirt, powdered sugar, and all the other ingredients.

A strangled cry came out of his dirty face, and I rolled away from him. I still needed the key, but I couldn't risk running back for my bag. I stumbled toward the staircase, screaming, as my trembling hand reached for the railing. My cries were so loud that I didn't hear the door being unlocked and swung open.

"Sammy, oh, thank God, the ghosts didn't get you!" Beau stood in the doorway with a panicked look on his face.

"The ghosts aren't after her, a human is." Rob pushed Beau out of the way and bounded up the stairs with his gun drawn and his partner right behind him. "Drop it!"

Beau and I followed the detectives. Daniel held the knife in one shaking hand as the other wiped the contents of the gris-gris bag off his face.

"Don't be stupid, it's over. Let go of the weapon," Rob said firmly, but there was a gentleness in his voice. "Daniel, your family doesn't want to lose you."

"But I didn't get the treasure for my mother." The knife fell to the floor as Daniel's body shuddered with sobs. "And she won't have it or have any family now."

Christine handcuffed Daniel and sat him down on a stack of boxes. "Yes, she will because you're still alive."

Would Daniel's mother care about him, even though he failed her? I had little sympathy for a man who had killed two innocent women, but a bit of my heart hoped they would still have each other.

Beau wrapped his arm around me just as I noticed Jasper was at the top of the stairs.

"Jasper, how did you know I was here?" My heart was still pounding, but Beau's firm grip on me and Jasper's kind eyes calmed me.

"I saw your bookshop bag in the library when I got back, but I couldn't find you," Jasper said.

"When I returned to the hotel, Jasper told me he didn't know where you were and Daniel was missing, too. When you didn't answer, I thought you might be in the attic." Beau frowned. "Even though you promised you wouldn't."

"Sorry." I mumbled, although I knew that wasn't enough of an apology. But Beau didn't hold it against me.

"I wouldn't have waited either," Beau said. "Rob and Christine arrived just as I was calling your cell phone for the millionth time."

"Why are y'all here?" I asked the detectives.

"We came to ask Daniel about the discrepancies in his statements. And we heard from a variety of people that his actions were suspicious," Christine said.

"I am one of those sources." Ambrose entered the attic. "Daniel, I should have trusted my instincts earlier that you were up to no good."

"Don't lecture me! I've seen you sneaking around, talking to Gideon Pearce," Daniel barked at Ambrose.

"Yes, I must admit I spoke with Gideon numerous times about buying the hotel together." Ambrose bowed his head. "We thought Mr. Boudreaux might change his mind on owning the hotel if he found the employees... difficult."

"Ha! I knew it. You're a fake like me." Daniel cackled but Christine's stern look made him stop.

Ambrose stiffly turned to Beau. "I am sorry for my actions. My desire to own the hotel clouded my judgement, but I assure you I am dedicated to being the best manager I can be for Hotel Jeanne."

"I understand." Beau smiled at him. "We'll work together from now on."

"Thank you." Ambrose's body relaxed. "Daniel, I may

have acted poorly, but I am nothing like you. Everything I did was to better the hotel."

"You're an old man with old ideas for a hotel you could never own." Daniel shook his head. "This hotel should be mine. My great-grandmother should have inherited this place and anything that her mother left for her."

"So you did all this for some stupid inheritance? You killed my sister and that kid for what? A bunch of letters. Was that worth it?" Jasper's voice grew louder with each sentence, and both Ambrose and Beau put a hand on each shoulder. He didn't shake them off, but he said, "You ruined two families for your own. And you got nothing."

"But there has to be something," Daniel pleaded, his tears making streams through the dirt caked on his face. "Sammy, you found it, didn't you?"

I breathed in deeply and brushed the dirt off my hands onto my jeans. My legs wobbled as I took my first step, but I regained my strength at the thought of finding Daisy's treasure. I walked over to the desk and crawled underneath it once again. Feeling for the daisy, I pushed it, but nothing happened. Then I tried sliding it, and with a bit of work, the panel slid backward to reveal a compartment. Reaching into the dark space, my hand touched a hard object. I pulled it out and found a white bag with a large daisy stitched on the front. From the rectangular shape, I guessed there was a book or a box inside.

I turned to the group. "Here is Daisy's treasure."

56

———

"What is it? It's mine!" Daniel screeched and lunged toward me. Christine put one hand on his shoulder to pull him backward.

"Try that again, and you won't find out what Sammy discovered," Christine said. "Understood?"

Daniel grunted but kept quiet. I loosened the drawstring around the bag and looked inside. The only item in there was a black book. I wiped the dust off the cover, expecting to find a mystery novel, but found a Bible.

"Sammy, what is it?" While Christine stayed next to Daniel, the rest of the group surrounded me at the desk.

An envelope was in between the first two pages. I opened it and read out loud:

My name is Marguerite Daisy Fuller and this is my Bible. I had little to leave my daughter or her children. Hopefully, my other letters have been found throughout the house. It is not much, but I was never one for monetary gifts. What I can give you is knowledge.

I fell in love with a clever young man. He was a carpenter, but really he was an artist. I was honored that he loved me, too, although my parents did not feel that way. We hid our love until my pregnancy was obvious.

My parents fired my beloved from his job, and my father ruined any chances he had of finding another position in New Orleans. We made plans to leave, but he died before we left. Some say he took his own life, but he would never do that to me and our child. As much as I tried, I never discovered the truth.

Soon I will join him in the afterlife as disease and heartbreak ravage my body. I hid letters throughout the house in the hiding places my love made for us. And in here I leave the greatest gift I own. Inside my Bible, you'll find our family tree. While I couldn't raise my child with her father, I can at least share her birth family. If you're reading this Edmee, I hope it will bring comfort to know where you came from and that your parents loved you.

With my eternal love,
Marguerite Daisy Fuller

"That's it?" Daniel sputtered. "The treasure is an old Bible?"

"Yes, and your family history," I said. "Daisy's child was named Edmee."

"I knew that already. My great-grandmother's adopted family kept the name Daisy gave her. The story goes that was her only request. Besides the letter she left for the child," Daniel answered.

"Did Daisy's letter mention treasure?" Beau asked. "Did she say there was money or jewelry?"

"No." Daniel dropped his head against his chest. "I just assumed."

"And you killed two women for a supposed monetary windfall. You are heartless." Ambrose glared at Daniel with an intensity that surprised me. And apparently Beau, too, by the look he gave Ambrose.

"I agree." Beau put his hand on Ambrose's arm. "We will do right by these women, I promise."

"Thank you... Beau." Ambrose smiled at Beau. "Samantha, what does the family tree say? Who is Daisy's beloved?"

"Edward Highsmith." I traced his name with my finger and suddenly shivered, as if a cool breeze had blown through the attic. The windows were still closed, though. Perhaps Daisy was in the room with us.

I showed the inside cover to the group. Daisy wrote a family tree for her and Edward that went back four generations. Even though her family banished her lover and forced her to give up her child, she needed to share this information. However tenuous her relationship was with her family, she wanted her child and their children to know where they came from.

All the adrenaline that rushed through my veins earlier dissipated. I closed my eyes to gather myself, and when I opened them, I found Jasper standing in front of me. Had he realized I was thinking about my birth family, my origin story? Even if that wasn't the case, he hugged me back when I put my arms around him.

When we parted, I saw Beau and Ambrose beaming at us.

"Family does matter, doesn't it?" Ambrose said.

"Yes, families of all kinds matter." Beau grabbed my hand. "And the luckiest of us have many families."

"I couldn't agree more," I said.

57

"I'm going to bury Scarlett next to her daddy back in Huntley," Charlene said. "New Orleans wasn't her home. That tomb has caused more trouble than it's worth."

I stood outside of Hotel Jeanne with Charlene and her pile of suitcases while Jasper retrieved their car from the parking lot. Her eyes were red-rimmed from an evening of crying after we explained how Daniel had killed Scarlett when she caught him searching for the treasure. We didn't tell her Scarlett tried to blackmail him. Some things were better left unsaid.

"I understand," I replied.

New Orleans would never be a happy place for her, especially with Jasper's announcement. He had returned to Thibodeaux Mansion with me and we stayed up most of the night talking about our past and our future. After I encouraged him, as well as Connor, Neal, and Sissy, he had decided to move to New Orleans. He even had a place to live; Neal offered him the extra bedroom in his apartment. Jasper would return to Mississippi with his mother to get her settled and come back as soon as he could.

"If you change your mind, let me know," I said. Jasper drove up and got out of his mother's car. It had to be hers with its bright yellow seat covers and orange-shaped air freshener hanging from the rearview mirror.

"I won't," she answered brusquely, but she then plastered a smile on her face. "It's kind of you to offer, though. I'll bring my girl home while my boy will stay here. Hopefully, this city won't kill him, too."

Jasper shook his head at his mother's words. From his look of frustration, I bet they had an intense discussion about his moving to New Orleans. But it appeared he hadn't given in to Charlene's demands.

"We'll take care of him," I said to Charlene, but I looked at Jasper. "He's got an entire group of people that are ready to make him part of our family here in the French Quarter and at Thibodeaux Mansion."

Those weren't the words Charlene wanted to hear.

"Family? His family is in Mississippi," she barked. "I realize you didn't grow up with your family so you don't understand that blood is thicker than water."

"I grew up with family," I snapped back, but then I regretted my tone. She would never accept my feelings, so why should I bother trying. I put a smile on my face and replied calmly, "We have a different definition of family, and that's OK. I wanted you to know that Jasper will be part of our community. He won't be alone."

"We'll have to agree to disagree, I guess." Charlene sighed. "You're not really a Southerner so you don't understand blood relationships."

"Momma, that's enough. If you want her to stay family,

you need to stop picking at her." Jasper grabbed their suit-cases. "Let's not lose anyone else."

Charlene's eyes widened in apparent shock at her son's firm tone. "Fine. You're right, we have to stick together. It's just us three."

Actually, there were four of us, since Joey was still out there. I didn't say that to Charlene, as that would open up a whole other can of worms. The photo I received yesterday flashed before my eyes. The family in that picture had changed since the hurricane killed my parents. It took me away and destroyed my brother's life forever. But looking at Jasper, who, even through his agitation and frustration with his mother, loved her. Did I care about my brother? I cared about him as Joey. His true self, Samuel, wasn't who I loved. But could I separate the two, or did I have to love both sides of him?

Jasper kissed his mother on the cheek and then gently nudged her toward the car. He could put aside his mother's behavior and still love her. But being a murderer differed from being an overbearing person. I guess Charlene was right; it was just the three St. Martins left.

But Jasper would become part of the Thibodeaux Mansion family when he returned. I hugged him before he joined Charlene in the car. "I can't wait for you to come back."

"Me, too," he said. "My new life will begin here."

"Come on, Jasper!" Charlene stuck her head through the window. "Now, Sarah Jane, sorry Sammy, I'll always have a place for you."

I leaned down and kissed her on the cheek. "Thank you, Aunt Charlene."

Tears welled up as she reached out and put her soft hand on my face. "That's the first time you called me aunt."

"Well, we are family, aren't we? And you can call me Sarah Jane if you like."

I looked over at Jasper, who mouthed, "Thank you." I hoped this would make the car ride easier for him. And as long as he was part of my life, so was she. Charlene smiled and waved as Jasper eased the car into traffic. My eyes watered as I watched them leave. I was going to have to take the good with the bad. I guess that's what family was all about.

After their car was out of sight, I turned to go home. Connor was waiting for me by a horse-head hitching post. I rushed over to him and threw my arms around him.

"Hey, I'm happy to see you, too." Connor pulled me into a tight embrace. "Everything OK with your family? Jasper's coming back right?"

"Yes, everything's fine. In fact, everything is great." I kissed him. By the whistles of the passerby, it was a good kiss. And by Connor's grin when we drew apart, he apparently agreed.

"Well then, let's grab a drink and celebrate." He put his arm around me. "I think a Pimm's Cup is in order."

"What are we celebrating?"

"Your new family, your New Orleans family, another successful mystery solved, and us." He stopped to kiss me. "We're in the French Quarter, so anything is cause to celebrate!"

I grinned. "Yes, we can celebrate all of that and more. There's no one I'd rather do that with than you."

"As much as I'd like to have you to myself, you need to check-in with our friends. They're waiting in the courtyard for you."

"We'll have to celebrate on our own later."

"Yes, ma'am." Connor held my hand. "But your New Orleans family needs you first."

And I needed them. While there was a resolution to the murders and the ghosts, the haunting wasn't over. Whether Hotel Jeanne's spirits roamed through the halls and courtyard was up for debate, my personal ghosts were definitely still around. Embracing Jasper and Charlene along with my Thibodeaux Mansion family was the right thing to do. But what about my brother?

I couldn't put that ghost to rest just yet. Most likely, my brother would reappear in my life. He could come back to try to kill me again or to apologize; I wasn't sure. I would deal with him when I had to. For now, my past wouldn't haunt me; my future was waiting for me right here at home.

THE END

Sammy's New Orleans adventures will continue in *Bury the Past*

ACKNOWLEDGMENTS

Once again, my ever-supportive husband stood by me as I wrote another book. Dave, thank you for believing in me and understanding my coffee, mystery, and New Orleans obsessions. I love you even though you won't stay at a haunted hotel.

And to my children, Jack and Jill, who also put up with my obsessions and throw out ideas for my books. I love you and you'll always be my babies.

Dad and Wanda, you're still the best cheerleaders and proofreaders a writer could have. Thank you for your help and your love through the years and the miles. Love y'all.

Two years and counting, my BARN critique group keeps pushing me to be a better writer. Thank you Amanda, Amelia, and Doug for your feedback and your friendship.

Once again, Jenna, you agreed to be a beta-reader and once again, you're a tremendous help. Your insights are always spot on and I appreciate your support and encouragement. Thank you for continuing with me on this journey and for your friendship.

Katy, thank you for keeping me sane during the pandemic. Your friendship means the world. And a huge thank you for being a beta-reader and supporting my work as an author.

You stepped into the role as beta-reader just as easily as you became my first PNW friend, Leann. Thank you for your feedback and your friendship. And for your baked goods.

And another big thank you to my friends, family, and readers. Your support and encouragement of my books helps more than you know.

ALSO BY JEN PITTS

The French Quarter Mystery Series:

Coffee, a Scone, and a Place to Call Home - a Short Story Prequel

The Key to Murder

The Gates to the Afterlife

A Deadly Check-In

Bury the Past

The Dead End Tour

A Corpse in the Cafe

Happy Homicide

The Witches of the French Quarter Series:

Mardi Gras and Magic

Red Beans and Rituals

ABOUT THE AUTHOR

Jen Pitts is a lifelong mystery reader who turned her obsession into writing cozy mysteries of her own. When she isn't plotting fictional murder and mayhem, she's chugging coffee, traveling, reading, and enjoying life with her children and husband in the Pacific Northwest.

Keep updated on Jen's books and more through her newsletter. A free short story prequel, *Coffee, a Scone, and a Place to call Home,* is available for all newsletter members. To sign up, visit www.jenpittsauthor.com

You can also find Jen on the following social media sites:

facebook.com/jenpittsmysteryauthor

instagram.com/jenpittsmysterywriter

goodreads.com/jenpitts

amazon.com/author/jenpitts

bookbub.com/authors/jen-pitts

www.ingramcontent.com/pod-product-compliance
Lightning Source LLC
Chambersburg PA
CBHW020122180726
47992CB00020B/1501